The First Journey to America

Death of an American Family;

Joseph S Hinshaw

The Hinshaw Saga
Four Generations Series Book Two

TotalRecall Publications, Inc.
1103 Middlecreek
Friendswood, Texas 77546
281-992-3131 TEL
www.totalrecallpress.com

Copyright © 2021: Joseph S Hinshaw
Four Generations Series Book Two
All rights reserved
ISBN: 978-1-64883-0501
UPC: 6-43977-40501-2
Library of Congress Control Number: 2020942593
Printed in the United States of America with simultaneous printings in Australia, Canada, and United Kingdom.

FIRST EDITION
1   2   3   4   5   6   7   8   9   10

To My Father, William Lorraine Hinshaw, my mother Catherine Jean (Stewart) Hinshaw, my Son Brent Edward Adam Hinshaw and my Daughter Taryn Hillary Dawne Hinshaw, Hauser Bradley Heyward Houser II, Barrett Brahm Hauser, Jocelyn Rae Hinshaw and Becky Clark Haag.

To all of my brave and honest Ancestors who make the framework for these stories so enjoyable and real.

I thank my immediate family for providing the time, opportunity and the understanding to let an old man pursue his dreams and to support him in his efforts while forgiving him for all of shortcomings.

AUTHOR JOE HINSHAW

 Joe Hinshaw grew up in Indianapolis Indiana. Being born during the civil rights period of our nation and living through the turbulent 60s has put its mark on his thoughts and the way that he sees humanity. He was introduced slowly to his family history. His earliest memory of it goes back to a family reunion in his prepubescent years in a City Park in Lebanon Indiana. The memories of this event are very cloudy. The vision of a large hand drawn tree on a big piece of white cardboard is the clear surviving memory. He remembers tracing through its limbs until he could find his own name and see just what a large family it truly was. He remembers playing with family members who were mostly strange to him. Other than this one event he has vague memories of going to his great Grandparents house one time while they were alive but at such a young age that he could not know now if it was real. He remembers meeting a great Aunt in Hendricks County Indiana that was purported to be over 100 years at that time. She had a small home in the country outside of North Salem Indiana. She spent their time together watching professional wrestling and yelling "Get Him" for this entire visit. In his teens his father received a letter offering a coat of arms and a book on the family. His father ordered one and about one month later it was received. The Arms were cheap plastic but correct in its form. The book was not professional but had a supply of information in it. Out of boredom he picked it up and started to read it and follow the family tree once more. This began

To My Father, William Lorraine Hinshaw, my mother Catherine Jean (Stewart) Hinshaw, my Son Brent Edward Adam Hinshaw and my Daughter Taryn Hillary Dawne Hinshaw, Hauser Bradley Heyward Houser II, Barrett Brahm Hauser, Jocelyn Rae Hinshaw and Becky Clark Haag.

To all of my brave and honest Ancestors who make the framework for these stories so enjoyable and real.

I thank my immediate family for providing the time, opportunity and the understanding to let an old man pursue his dreams and to support him in his efforts while forgiving him for all of shortcomings.

AUTHOR JOE HINSHAW

Joe Hinshaw grew up in Indianapolis Indiana. Being born during the civil rights period of our nation and living through the turbulent 60s has put its mark on his thoughts and the way that he sees humanity. He was introduced slowly to his family history. His earliest memory of it goes back to a family reunion in his prepubescent years in a City Park in Lebanon Indiana. The memories of this event are very cloudy. The vision of a large hand drawn tree on a big piece of white cardboard is the clear surviving memory. He remembers tracing through its limbs until he could find his own name and see just what a large family it truly was. He remembers playing with family members who were mostly strange to him. Other than this one event he has vague memories of going to his great Grandparents house one time while they were alive but at such a young age that he could not know now if it was real. He remembers meeting a great Aunt in Hendricks County Indiana that was purported to be over 100 years at that time. She had a small home in the country outside of North Salem Indiana. She spent their time together watching professional wrestling and yelling "Get Him" for this entire visit. In his teens his father received a letter offering a coat of arms and a book on the family. His father ordered one and about one month later it was received. The Arms were cheap plastic but correct in its form. The book was not professional but had a supply of information in it. Out of boredom he picked it up and started to read it and follow the family tree once more. This began his interest and he decided then that he wanted to do this project writing a historical fiction series based on the real stories of the family genealogy. His own family had been such a disappointment to him that he knew there would be some redeeming value to this process. His parents had been good people. There were dark areas with his siblings and some of the family that he would know. Through this he found that the characters repeated themselves in each generation of his family. There were those that interacted from the fringes with the family that he would find in his own life from each generation. The stories are told with as much detail to history that research could find available to him. He would stay true to the stories themselves and choose his own path where multiple and differing possibilities would appear. The stories then have a fictional base to them to try to explain the possibilities of the events or reasons for some of these behaviors or migrations. Another element of the stories includes pure fiction. This fiction was added to make the stories cohesive and interesting. Even the fiction is based on possible scenarios that could be deduced or fabricated from the facts of the story or the history of the time it occurred. Either way, the reader should keep in mind that some of the stories are historically correct, some are from logical conclusions and some are pure fiction.

ACKNOWLEDGEMENT

I would like to acknowledge my parents, children and those that wrote down the history of the family from generations ago that gave me the basis and impetus to put these words and ideas to paper

Table of Contents

THE GENEALOGY OF WILLIAM HENSHAW

William Henshaw was born on or about 1608. He was christened Mar 3 1608, Walton on the Hill, Lancashire, England. His name was spelled "Henshall" in the christening record but "Henshawe" in the marriage record. Walton on the Hill today is a northern suburb of Liverpool. William was from Toxter (or Toxteth) Park, "aforesaid" (near Liverpool). He married Katherine Houghton, (Pronounced Hocton) Oct 12 1630, Walton on the Hill, Lancashire England.

> *Marriage license issued Sep 27 1630: "William Henshaw and Katherine Houghton, Parish of Walton, Lanc. Bondsman, Thomas Henshaw, father of said William. Licence to Revds. Neveil Key, Roger Tovey, and Hierom (Jerome) Orme, Clerks".*

Katherine Houghton, daughter of Evan Houghton and Ellen Parker, was born in 1615, Wavertree Hall, Liverpool, Lancashire, England. Katherine Houghton was the only child and heir of Evan Houghton & Ellen (Parker) Ratcliff of Wartre Hall, Lancashire. Joshua Henshaw's pedigree, her son, also says she was from "Wartre Hall, in the County of Lancaster".

William Henshawe died Jun 20 1644.1 William was killed in battle with his father-in-law, Evan Houghton, in the Storming of Liverpool, by Prince Rupert while fighting against King Charles I.[1]

> *William was "killed at the taking of Liverpool during the civil wars 1644". William's father-in-law Evan Houghton was also "killed at the taking of Liverpool in Lancashire by Prince Rupert, during the civil war in 1644, where he was in prison in 1638."*

Katherine Houghton died 1651. In that year a plague killed 200 persons in the Liverpool area, most being buried in Sickman's lane (now Addison Street); it seems likely that Katherine was probably a victim of this plague.

William's children, Joshua & Daniel, were deported to New England in 1652 by the executor of their father's estate, Peter Ambrose, claiming that he had sent them off to school in London where they both died of the plague. This was presumably in order to steal their inheritance.

http://www.rawbw.com/~hinshaw/cgi-bin/id?186

Some records show a son and some a daughter in addition to Joshua and Daniel to William and Katherine. This is not likely or they died in birth or miscarriage. For the Ambrose/Mather plot to succeed there could have been no other children and this plot is proven by history to have indeed achieved its nefarious goals.

The Crossing from England and the Betrayal by Peter Ambrose

The ship would spend another night at the mercy of gale force wind. They had barely left port when the wind blew up and the rains began. The boys were not acclimated to the sea. They were now eight and ten years old. They had made the crossing to Ireland a few times when they were younger with their mother but it was not in the recent past. The boys were seasick which added to their misery. Joshua was angry. The boys had lost their father and their grandfather fighting for their country against the Royalists in the siege of Liverpool. Last year their mother and grandmother had left them ten months apart. Their mother was the last. She died of the plague in 1651. This left the boys orphaned and in the charge of Peter Ambrose. He was deemed their closest relative through the Stanley family by marriage to one of their distant relatives. Their Uncle John, who was the only surviving brother to William, had immigrated to Ireland and was unaware of the boy's fates. He died prior to 1701 but the exact date has not been established. At his death he believed the boys had died of the plague in London while attending school there. He was unaware that they had never seen London or pursued their education there. This was the plot's goal and followed the intricate plan of Peter Ambrose and Richard Mather. He had one son who died in Ireland in 1699 and was unmarried. It is unclear where the boy's aunt Ellen and John Harrison, her husband, were during this abduction. In the years after William's death there is little on the couple to be found. It is possible that they immigrated or died during the wars or plagues. This ended this family line. The records of the Houghton holdings are listed below. This did not include the Henshaw family holdings that would be in addition to these lands and wealth. The two little boys, then seven and nine years of age, were left orphans, without near relatives, and with an immense inheritance. It ceded control of the estate to a family that had a financial interest in their holdings through a clause in the Will of the relative that put the lands in the hands of Evan Houghton and his only heir; daughter Katherine. In essence, if the boys died or disappeared from view, the entire estate returned to the hands of the Stanley family. This included into the hands of their appointed steward: Peter Ambrose. Here is an inventory of the real estate which they inherited from the Houghton's, not counting the property of their father. It comes from the Herald's College:

- Wavertree Hall,
- Lands in Liverpool,
- Penketh Hall,
- Lands in Ellell,
- Lands in Penyngton,
- Lands in Carltou,
- Lands in Worsely,
- Lands in Sowerby,
- Newton in Mackinfield,
- Lands in Warton,

- Lands in Knowlsley,
- Houses in Lancaster.

From the book "Our Family: A Little Account of it for my descendants" by Sarah Edwards Henshaw

The boy's parents had always tried to help poor Peter. He was fat and disgusting but the boy's parents had a long history with him rooted back into their own childhoods. Peter's mother and father had been less than stellar. When Peter was left orphaned; Joshua and Daniel's father and grandfather stepped in to take care of him and see him into manhood. They educated him and supported his business making him profitable. They could do nothing about his negativity and hate for them and their families. Peter grew up in an environment of hate. Most of this was directed at William Henshaw and his family. The cause of this hatred was the desire of Peter's mother to match him with Katherine Houghton. It was a lost cause from the beginning. The match of Katherine with William and been made almost at birth and was much desired by not only the families but the betrothed themselves. Eventually this failure would drive Peter's mother to insanity and his father to the life as an outlaw. In the end Peter had to kill his own father when he suddenly reappeared to him years later. Peter stayed quiet throughout these trials. He married to gain an heir to his ill-gotten gains but this marriage failed. He found a wonderful wife but his hatred and viciousness was unleashed on her causing him many problems in his circle of customers, acquaintances and community officials. He ruined his business and himself with his uncontrolled temper and his sense of entitlement. With the death of Katherine Henshaw it was surprising that Peter Ambrose was named as the steward of the Henshaw Estate. It was accomplished through a carefully executed fraud that he had seeded over many years. It was made possible by a clause in the Will of Evan Houghton's own mother stating that in the absence of an heir the lands would return to the Stanley family. It is unclear if the Stanley's supported or participated in Peter's plot but it is clear that they stood to gain immensely from it. More so Peter himself stood to gain both monetarily and in seeking vengeance on the boy's family. Peter's discovery that the Ambrose estate had been sold to Evan Houghton and was now part of the Henshaw holdings came as a complete surprise to him. Even though it was sold to care for Peter's needs after losing his parents and to keep it from the King's courts it pushed him over the edge. He cared little for anyone but himself and plotted to not only regain the Ambrose holdings but to deprive the Henshaw heirs of their own. With Katherine's death it was an ideal time to spring his trap and take the boys inheritance for his own. He wasted no time in taking advantage of the situation. His mother had wanted to destroy the Henshaw family but could never get this done before her death. Now he would dismantle the estate in a short period of time and no one was standing in his way to stop it.

Peter made the acquaintance of one Richard Mather. Richard was a minister. Mather's children were also in the church. The Mather boys had preceded him to the Massachusetts Bay colony. This unholy combination of Peter Ambrose and Richard Mather could only bring evil into the world. A deal was struck between the two. Peter Ambrose with his conspirators would abduct Joshua and Daniel Henshaw and take them across the sea to the new world and specifically the Massachusetts Bay Colony under the eye of Richard Mather. After their departure Peter Ambrose would announce at some opportune time that the boys had been sent to London for schooling. This would explain away several years of their absence. When the plague hit London during those years, he took the opportunity to pronounce their deaths in this time of the plague. The deaths went unverified and Ambrose's word was accepted as the only proof of the events. In this way he had stolen the extensive land holdings and wealth that were the rightful inheritance of Joshua and Daniel. The boys were still young and could do nothing in their own defense.

On board the ship Joshua was scared but he could not let it show in Daniel's presence. He was all that was left of his family and he was the oldest. It was his duty to be the leader. His parents had told him that he was the oldest son and would wear the mantel of the family one day. That day had come much too soon and with it came many responsibilities. They had started to groom him for his future but death took them too soon. He had heard some stories of the new world. It did not sound like a hospitable place and he had no desire to leave his old life and community. The family had many land and business holdings and it would be left to him to run them when he was old enough. He felt a responsibility to the family's heritage. He did not know what was happening or what would happen to his family's holdings after his abduction. He swore on his life that he would return to his home and set things straight. It was his duty now to protect his brother and see that he was in good standing. He knew the truth. He knew that Peter Ambrose had acted in a criminal way. He knew that Richard Mather was his accomplice. There was no one to tell now that would listen to him or assist him against Ambrose and Mather. Those they were surrounded with and those that they would be surrounded with in the future would steadfastly support Richard Mather in whatever enterprise he was involved. He was known as one of the founding fathers of the Massachusetts Bay Colony. His standing alone made any hope disappear for the foreseeable future. For now in this time Joshua did not know their status or their futures. He was sure that nobody would take the word of a child over the likes of Mather or Ambrose until he could grow and appoint himself to the task in a credible way. He could only reassure Daniel that everything would work itself out as time passed. These would be obstacles that had to be overcome before he could return home.

Peter Ambrose was a bitter man. He was indoctrinated in his entitlements. His parents were always on the path to rise to higher stations in society in his community. Historically he is insignificant. The only significance was the adversity he brought to the Henshaw and Houghton families and their heritage and futures and his ties to the Stanley family by distant blood. He did little in his life but grow his purse at the expense of others. He took advantage of the weak or indisposed. He bred these same traits into his offspring and taught his sole heir his hatred of the Henshaw family in hopes that he would carry his deeds forward if any challenge was made to his plot in the future.

Richard Mather: The Accomplice

Richard Mather

His accomplice in abducting Joshua and Daniel was Richard Mather. Mather was born in Lowden, Lancashire England in 1596. He was Oxford educated. He joined the ministry in Toxteth Park (Liverpool). He was twice suspended from his position by the Bishop of York for failing to conform to the Anglican Church. He then joined the Puritan movement and made the crossing to the new world and the Massachusetts Bay Colony in 1635. The Pilgrims who we celebrate on Thanksgiving were a part of the Puritan movement. Actually, the term Puritan was a derogatory name for those involved in the movement by their detractors. The Puritans themselves preferred to use the term "the Godly". Puritanism was not a religious sect. They were truly a collection of loosely grouped religious beliefs. What allied these groups was the belief that all institutions, including government, schools, families, communities, and the Church of England should be "purified". This would mean purifying by removing all individual cultural practices that they deemed "ungodly". More specifically purification meant cleansing the Church of England from all influence of Catholicism. The Pilgrims of this Puritan movement did not emigrate directly from England. They had fled England and settled in Holland to avoid the persecution of these tumultuous times.

Richard Mather led the First Church of Dorchester upon his landing in the new world until his death in 1669. Because of his religious pedigree he was referred to as a divine or "the excellent divine". He fathered six children. Four of his six sons—Samuel (1626-71), Nathaniel (1630-97), Eleazar (1637-69), and Increase (1639-1723)—followed their father into the ministry. These boys were boarded and educated at Harvard and lived in Boston. Increase Mather's son was Cotton Mather who was instrumental in the Salem Witch Trials later in the century. The family inhabited pulpits in England, Ireland, and in the Massachusetts Bay area. Mather is painted in history as a man of the church and somewhat of a statesman in the colonies. He published many writings on church policy and direction. Some of his writings crossed over to the Puritan governance of the Massachusetts Bay Colony. Along with John Cotton of Boston, Thomas Hooker of Hartford, Thomas Shepard of Cambridge, and John Davenport of New Haven he tailored what history considered "The New England Way". Mather was a man of position and power in the church that spilled over into the governance and law-making bodies of Massachusetts and later the whole of New England. As history played out, he never admitted to his complicity in this dastardly plot against the boys that unlawfully separated them from their rightful legacy. It is clear that his position at Toxteth Park gave him intimate knowledge of the Ambrose, Henshaw and Houghton families during his administration at the church. All of these families fought on the Parliamentary side of the

English Civil War except Ambrose who loosely supported the cause but did not go into battle against the King. Ambrose stood on the fence about the issues. He positioned himself so he could cater to the eventual winner to his own benefit. The war was driven by the religious issues brought to the Anglican Church in the three Kingdoms by Charles I and Archbishop Laud. The Parliamentary side of this issue was joined by the Scottish Covenanters in their alliance against the Royalist forces. This would put these families in the same frame of mind as Richard Mather. His refusal to conform to the churches will was the cause of his suspensions from the church in Toxteth Park. It was in the end the cause for his relocation to New England. Mather departed England in 1635 and landed in New England. This preceded the death of Katherine Houghton Henshaw by sixteen years. The binding of Ambrose and Mather in this plot is not hard to imagine. They stayed in close communication through those years. Mather received payment from Ambrose for the boy's care and education. Ambrose sent these funds after his announcement and publication of the boy's death in London shortly after 1651. Additionally, there were funds sent with them in the hands of the ship's Captain at the time of their abduction as a lump sum payment for their needs. It is unsure if these funds also included payment to Mather for his part in this unseemly plot although it was highly likely. It is a certainty that if Mather would have come forward with his story of the boy's fate, they would surely have been able to regain their legacy and return to their homes. He chose, over his life, to remain silent and accept the hush money from Ambrose. If he was true to his own faith, he certainly would have brought out the truth of this plot and made penance for his misdeeds. The religious history of this time was inundated with the need of the church for great riches, power and lavish surroundings. These men would want for nothing while their flock lived in squalor, hunger and disease. His history will be forever fouled by his participation, fraud, and the damages he inflicted on these innocent young boys at his hand. It seems a sure thing that when his judgment time came he would be left wanting at the gates to heaven

The Crossing Continued

The boy's voyage would take sixty to seventy days depending on the weather and other factors. They were sailing now to Richard Mather's home in Dorchester Massachusetts. They had been able to determine their destination from some of the officers on board the ship. None of those that would talk to them could tell them much beyond their destination. It was clear that their removal was under dark circumstances. Neither of the brothers knew what conditions or circumstances lay ahead for them. Of course, they had heard talk of the colonies and the new world. Their father had believed that there was a future to be had in trading across the sea before his death. They knew from the discussions they could remember from the adults in their lives that it was a wild and dangerous place. With the religious and political upheavals in England many had sought it out to find religious freedoms, escape the civil wars and to find a better life than the ones they lived in England, Ireland and Scotland. Indeed the King himself used colonization to relocate those that were vagrants, criminals or undesirables along with those hopeful souls that came of their own will. Here they could gain land ownership which was nearly impossible in England at the time. Immigration seemed like the proverbial "promised land" that they studied in their own ways in the common bible. In practice it would be much different.

The Colonies and the Conditions of the Time

It was not just those from England who came to these shores during this time. The French, Spanish, Dutch, Germans, Irish, Scandinavians and others had immigrated to this new land that held so much promise and danger. The Spanish colonized at

Santa Fe in 1610. The French settled at Quebec in 1608. There is evidence of the Vikings much earlier. The Native population had been there since the beginning of time as far as anyone could place them in that time.

The colonies were an inhospitable place at best. The first English attempt at colonization came on the coast of Newfoundland in the 1580s. It failed when its promoter Sir Humphrey Gilbert died in 1583. The migration began in the late 1500s in what is now considered the United States. Sir Francis Drake founded a colony in Roanoke Virginia in 1585. Drake was the half -brother of Gilbert. Once he established the colony he left for his business at home. When he returned it had simply disappeared. There was no sign of its settlers.

Spain was having a much brighter experience with their colonies. The English were slower to colonize due to Henry VIII reign and the Reformation. The purging of Catholicism in England took precedence over colonization. With the rise of Queen Elizabeth in 1558 protestant England was at war. Irish Catholics were in support of Catholic Spain against Protestant England. When Spain faltered in their support Queen Elizabeth sent her troops to Ireland. They unseated the Catholic Irish from their lands and replanted them with Protestant English landowners. English ships now raided coastal Spanish settlements and plundered Spanish shipping on the high seas. Sir Francis Drake was gaining fame in this vocation and was knighted by Queen Elizabeth for his actions. Spain sent a large number of ships to invade England in 1588. Their fleet was known as the Spanish Armada. These ships were large and cumbersome. The English ships were lighter, faster, more maneuverable and able. They severely damaged the Spanish fleet. The Spaniard's then retreated with the ships they could salvage. This ended Spanish power on the high seas for all intents and purposes. With the defeat of the Armada Spain lost its control of the Netherlands. Shortly thereafter the Dutch took control of Spain's holdings in the Caribbean and the colonies. England was now in control of the Atlantic and the master of the seas.

Between 1550 and 1600 England's population rose from three million to four million. Farmers were being pushed from their lands. Landlords began to enclose their lands so their sheep and cattle could graze. This left the farmers without land or the ability to feed their families. Consistent with the English bumbling of the time new governance laws were passed that made the situation worse. The Laws of primogeniture decreed that only eldest sons were eligible to inherit landed estates. Younger sons were cast out to their own fates. Many joined with the homeless and wandering farmers leading the wealthy to declare that England was overpopulated. This became the catalyst to find a solution to these homeless wandering people. That solution was obvious. Colonization would rid England of its excess population and provide earnings from their labors overseas along with tax revenue. It did not take long for the plans for off-loading the poor English to other shores to begin. In addition, the crown cast off their criminals to the colonies ridding them of that inconvenience and saddling these miscreants on the innocents trying to establish themselves and families in harsh situations. These criminals would prey on those not strong enough to defend themselves. This did not address the criminals lurking in high society or the government itself.

The funding for these colonies came through joint-stock companies. This called for a group of wealthy English to fund the colony until it was profitable. It was originally thought this funding would last a few years and then the company would sell to the settlers at a profit. If the colony was not profitable in that time colonists had the real threat of the investor abandoning them and leaving them to survive in this wild country on their own. Because the Spanish found gold in their colonies the English investors believed they would find the same in the English colonies. This would not be the source of success in these areas.

No gold was to be had. King James I granted a charter to settle along the James River in Chesapeake Bay. On May 24, 1607 a group of one hundred male settlers came ashore at this colony. The settling of the colony had many setbacks from shipwrecks to disease. Some starved to death or died of malnutrition or disease searching for the non-existent gold said to be there. Others died at the hands of the Native Americans or others from rival countries trying to collect all of the bounty the colonies could offer. At times their interests clashed resulting in bloodshed. The colony was saved by Captain John Smith. Shortly after his arrival he was kidnapped by Powhaten; a powerful Indian chief. He was to be ritually executed. Powhaten's daughter, Pocahontas negotiated his release with her father. This whole adventure seemed to be a symbolic gesture to demonstrate to Smith and the settlers the power of the Indian community in the area. It also was symbolic of their peaceful intentions and hope the settlers would find a peaceful way to co-exist.

1609 and 1610 was known as the starving time. Of the four hundred settlers only sixty survived this period. The mortality of the settlers would be discouraging. By 1625 there were only twelve hundred surviving settlers of nearly eight thousand who had landed at Jamestown.

The Native American Indians

Powhaten organized the small tribes and combined them with his own. With the Indian alliance he was the dominant power during the early years. The Indians and the settlers carried on a tense relationship. The starving colonists had taken to raiding Indian villages and homes and stealing their provisions to survive. In 1610 Lord De La Warr was sent to Jamestown with orders that amounted to a declaration of war against the Powhaten Indians. They immediately set out and began raiding Indian villages, burning their houses and stealing their provisions. They burned the cornfields and crops in a scorched

Earth type of campaign. During these raids they would abduct and enslave Indians including their women and children. With the provisions gone and the fields burned the Indians retaliated. A peace settlement in what was called the first Anglo-Powhaten War came when Pocahontas married the English settler John Rolf. It continued on shaky ground until 1622 when a series of Indian attacks left three hundred and forty-seven settlers dead including John Rolf. The Virginia Company issued orders for perpetual war without peace or treaty. This lasted until 1644 with the defeat of the Powhaten Indians. A new treaty was in place by 1646 that banished the Indians from their ancestral lands. By 1685 the English considered that the Indians in Virginia were extinct.

Early Slavery
and the Plight of the Indentured Servant

John Rolf's legacy to Virginia was not his marriage to Pocahontas. It was the development of its main crop. This crop was tobacco. Rolf found a process to take the bitter taste from the leaf and Europe's demand for it multiplied exponentially. They could not grow and export enough of it. The tobacco crop demanded large amounts of physical labor. There was a huge shortage of able-bodied persons to work at this time. This was the beginning of another institution that would tear the colonies and states apart in the future. Slavery was introduced to the Virginia colony in 1619 when a Dutch Warship landed in the Chesapeake Bay and sold nineteen blacks into slavery to work the tobacco fields. At this time the cost of slaves was too high for the poor settlers and few could afford such a luxury. By 1650 there were only three hundred such slaves in the entire territory. Labor needs could be filled by a similar institution called indentured servitude. In this version of slavery, the poor from England, Ireland and Scotland could obtain their fares to the colony in exchange for a pledge to work for a period of time for the contract holder or master. This was different from slavery because it set a definitive term of servitude. Each contract listed penalties of additional time for violations to be determined solely by the indenture holder. This was not always adhered to though. Many of these agreements called for the servant to receive a grant of land when he finished his years of service. To encourage a sufficient workforce both Virginia and Maryland employed the "headright" system. Anyone paying the passage of a servant to these colonies would receive fifty acres of land. Land became scarce as these numbers rose. The ability of a servant to obtain a land grant diminished and disappeared. These masters took advantage of their investments in land and servants to build their own wealth. This practice of "white slavery" would grow to one hundred thousand servants by the end of the century. Almost 75% of the population was made up of indentured servants to these rich merchant planters. The majority of those were from Ireland. The servants who misbehaved in the opinion of their masters would be punished by having their terms extended beyond their indentured term. When their terms were fulfilled most of these people found themselves to be penniless and had little option but to hire back to their master to survive once their freedom was granted. They had little legal recourse if they did not receive their land or other promises from their masters. The courts were made up of these rich landowners and they would seldom rule against the masters in favor of the servant. To do so would set a dangerous legal precedent. This left many homeless and wandering around when their terms were satisfied with no means of support. Eventually they would organize into revolt.

In these early years many of those that arrived on America's shores would go to their grave before they passed the age of twenty years. They would fight diseases. Malaria, dysentery, and typhoid would reduce life spans by an average of ten years. New Englanders had a better chance than the Virginia colonists. There were ready amounts of fresh water in New England and the winter freezes would kill off the microbes that caused disease. Of course, the harsh winters would take its own toll on the New Englanders and shorten their growing seasons limiting food supplies. These diseases were still a factor for the New Englanders but not as much of a factor as in Virginia. The southern colonists were working in rice fields and swamps where mosquitos and foul water would incubate these insects and microbes. In these times there were few women. It is estimated that men outnumbered women by a six to one ratio in the early years. Many women who survived the diseases would succumb to death during child birth. By the end of the 1600s the ratio would be reduced to three men to two women.

In addition to these adversities the colonies suffered at the hands of Indian uprisings. The Indians were decimated by the white man's diseases prior to the Plymouth landing in 1620. They had no immunity to the new strains of pathogens that they would face. It is estimated that 75% of the native population died of these newly introduced strains of disease to their villages and reduced their ability to stand in their own defense against these invaders. If the Native Americans had been able to sustain their numbers the history of the colonies would have had a much different outcome. Most likely it would have been a more peaceful and humanitarian effort at co-habitation.

The Early Government of Massachusetts Bay Colony

One hundred and two souls disembarked at Plymouth. Of those on board only about forty were from the separatist community in Holland and fit the Puritan mold. The other sixty-two consisted of a dozen servants and hired men with the rest being non-separatists recruited by the merchant company which financed the voyage. The forty Puritans took over a minority rule. They demanded that all aboard follow their religious practices. They gave themselves the name "saints" and called all others "strangers". Their sanctimonious attitudes with the crew and the "strangers" caused outrage and dissension. The "saints" were equally upset with the "strangers" for their intolerance of the "Saints" ways.

This original group came from the poorer working classes. Once on land the Puritans were quick to take control. The Mayflower Compact was written and signed. The Puritans coerced enough signatures from the "strangers" to pass this initial form of government for the New England colonies. It is likely that the "strangers" gave their votes because they realized that the group could not survive if it was divided.

They compromised in this initial phase to improve their chances of survival and the success of the settlement. The Puritan leaders were careful to word the agreement to ensure that only the Puritans would take power. Only "saints" were allowed to hold office. The Puritans did not truly believe in democracy. In fact, the Puritans favored communal living or what we would call communism. This could have been necessary in those very early days when so many were dying from starvation. No colonist outside of the Puritans would stand for it in the long run. Most came to the colonies to end religious oppression, avoid politics and the constant warring by the governments of Europe and for their own desire to hold land. Once ensconced in the new world and in complete control of political power the leaders of the Massachusetts Bay Colony favored the old forms of elitism.

Winthrop, the Governor stated

"If we should change from a mixed aristocracy to mere democracy we should have no warrant in scripture for it: for there was no such government in Israel . . . A democracy is, amongst civil nations, accounted the meanest and worst of all forms of government."

The Mayflower Compact

In ye name of God Amen. We whose names are underwritten, the loyall subjects of our dread soveraigne Lord King James, by ye grace of God, of Great Britaine, ffrance, & Ireland Hing, defender of ye faith, &c.

Haveing undertaken, for ye glorie of God, and advancemente of ye Christian faith and honour of our King & countrie, a voyage to plant ye first colonie in ye Northerne parts of Virginia, doe by these presents solemnly & mutualy in ye presence of God, and one of another, covenant, & combine ourselves togeather into a Civill body politick; for our better ordering, & preservation & furtherance of ye ends aforesaid; and by vertue hereof to enacte, constitute and frame such just & equall Lawes, ordinances, Acts, constitutions & offices from time to time, as shall be thought most meete & convenient for ye generall good of ye colonie: unto which we promise all due submission and obedience. In witnes whereof we have hereunder subscribed our names at Cap=Codd ye ~11~ of November, in ye year of ye raigne of our soveraigne Lord King James of England, ffrance & Ireland ye eighteenth, and of Scotland ye fiftie fourth. Ano Dom. 1620.

John Cotton wrote:

"I do not conceive that ever God did ordain [democracy] as a fit government either for church or commonwealth. If the people shall be the governors then who shall be the governed?"

The Indian Fraud

By the end of their first winter only forty-four of the original colonists had survived. The Wampanoag Indians led by their Chief Massasoit befriended the settlers. To the Indian's credit they tried to get along with the settlers. It was the settlers who showed aggression and thievery. When the Indians died off in large numbers due largely to the diseases introduced by the Europeans it was the settlers who moved into the lands that the Indians had cleared and made prosperous. They absorbed the land that the Indians left vacant by their deaths. The Indians did not know the concept of land ownership and saw all land as communal and shared. The English saw it as an opportunity to take advantage of their ignorance and claim ownership of the Indian lands with little friction and for little or nothing in compensation by instituting boundaries and deeds that were used in England. It was clear that the Indians did not understand the documents that they were signing or the details of the agreements being made. They had never before used or been approached in such a manner with such and alien concept. Indeed, an Indians verbal agreement was his bond and was sacred to them. Even by English common law concepts these agreements did not stand the test of a valid contract and therefore would not stand up in a court of law. It made no difference. Any that were of a different color or religion to the Puritans were thought to be of a lesser existence to them.

Squanto was a Wampanoag Indian of the Pawtuxet band. His Indian name at birth was Tisquantum. During his lifetime he was kidnapped several times by various white men. He traveled through Europe, Newfoundland and along the northeast coast of America in the company of the English. In this time he learned the English language. Through him the settlers and the Indians had a shaky peace. The Indians instructed the settlers on planting and land usage. They introduced the settlers to the use of maize (corn). Through their teachings and patience with the newcomers they singly turned the fortunes of the New England colonists around. These were the same Indians who shared the first Thanksgiving with the settlers. In 1621 Massasoit signed a treaty with the pilgrims. They had no forewarning of the later treatment that they would receive from those that they now helped to survive. Once again, the Indians through their own beliefs and kindness were to be taken advantage of for their own simple principals.

Over the next two decades more and more settlers arrived and pushed inland to the Connecticut River valley. This incursion further into Indian land and the cultural differences between these two unique cultural ideals created conflict. In 1637 the conflicts erupted into hostilities. Thirteen colonists and English traders had been killed by the Pequots. Governor Endecott organized a large militia to punish the Indians. On April 23 two hundred Pequot Indians attacked a Connecticut settlement killing six men and three women. They abducted two girls in this raid. After the death of an Englishman, John Oldham, on Block Island, Endicott sanctioned hostilities against the Indians by the colonists. The Pequot War had started. The Pequot Indians were in control of the area. They were one of the most powerful tribes of this time. In order to have success against the Pequots the English militia made an alliance with the tribes who were the enemies of the Pequots. These tribes were the Narragansetts and the Mohicans. With this alliance they marched on the Pequot Village on the Mystic River on May 26th. They burned the village of Missituck (Mystic) and shot the escaping survivors. The death toll for the Pequots was between four hundred and seven hundred. The following account of the battle is from the narratives of the Mystic massacre/battle written by John Underhill, John Mason and Philip Vincent. Their descriptions are all consistent with this depiction of the massacre/battle.

The fort is located on the top of Pequot Hill in Groton approximately ¼ west of the Mystic River. Pequot Hill is the highest hill in the area and is very defensible because of the steep sides. The fort was described by Philip Vincent in his narrative of the Pequot War (his account was published in London in 1638):

"They choose a piece of ground (that was) dry and of best advantage, forty or fifty foote square. (But this was at least 2 acres of ground.) Here they pitch(ed) close together as they can young trees and halfe trees as thicke as a mans thigh or the calfe of his legge. (They were) Ten or twelve foote high. They are above the ground and within (the ground) rammed three foote deepe with undermining. The earth being cast up (around them there) for their better shelter against the enemies dischargements. Betwixt these pallisadoes are divers loope-holes through which they let flie their winged messengers. The doore for the most part is entred side-waies, which they stop with boughes or bushes as need requireth. The space within (these walls) is full of Wigwams.

The attack began at dawn on May 26th (Old Calendar – June 5 New calendar) when the English surrounded the 2-acre village and fired a volley through the gaps in the palisade. The force of 77 English, 60 Mohegan and 200 Narragansett surrounded the fort and the English fired a volley through the palisade walls. Mason and Underhill, with twenty men each, entered the fort through entrances on the northeast and southwest sides. Their objective was to "destroy them by the Sword and save the Plunder" (Mason). Unknown to the English the fort was reinforced the night before by 100 warriors from other villages bringing the total number of warriors inside the fort to approximately 175. Within 20 minutes English inside the fort suffered 50% casualties. It was then that Mason said:

"We should never kill them after (in) that manner: WE MUST BURN THEM!" The English retreated outside the fort and surrounded it to prevent anyone escaping from the fort. Their Native allies formed a second line outside the English as depicted in the woodcut. The fire quickly spread from the northeast to the southwest forcing everyone in the fort to cluster in the southwest quadrant of the fort. Pequot warriors continued to battle the English from behind the palisade and the English fired at them through the gaps in the palisade.

"Captaine Mason entring into a Wigwam, brought out a fire-brand, after he had wounded many in the house, then he set fire on the West-side where he entred. My selfe set fire on the South end with a traine of Powder. The fires of both meeting in the center of the Fort blazed most terribly and burnt all in the space of halfe an houre. Many couragious fellowes were unwilling to come out and fought most desperately through the Palisadoes so as they were scorched and burnt with the very flame and were deprived of their armes. In regard the fire burnt their very bowstrings. And so (they)perished valiantly. Mercy they did deserve for their valour. Could we have had opportunitie to have bestowed it. Many were burnt in the Fort, both men, women, and children. Others forced out and came in troopes to the Indians, twentie, and thirtie at a time, which our souldiers received and entertained with the point of the sword. Downe fell men, women, and children. Those that (e)scaped us fell into the hands of the Indians that were in the reere of us. It is reported by themselves that there were about foure hundred soules in this Fort, and not above five of them escaped out of our hands" (Underhill).

http://www.mashantucket.com/pequotwar.aspx

On June 5 the allies attacked another village of the Pequots at Stonington. The villagers were again massacred by Captain Mason and his forces. The Pequot chief Sassacus tried to lead his people west but was caught near Fairfield Connecticut. He was defeated there in what was called "The Great Swamp Fight". Sassacus escaped with a few of his braves and sought refuge with the Mohawk Indians. Before he was able to reach the Mohawks he was overtaken by the Mohicans and put to death. Those that were captured with him were eventually killed. The surviving Pequots in the territory were sold into slavery. A handful of them joined other New England tribes. This slaughter successfully ended the influence of the Pequots in the area. It ushered in four decades of uneasy peace with the Indians. One unforeseen outcome of this massacre was the mindset that would be carried into the future. The English would see themselves as the civilized whites against the savage Indians. This would greatly hinder and in most cases eliminate the idea of living cross culturally with the Native Americans. This would be encountered throughout our country's history. It set a precedent as to how disputes would be settled with the Indians in the future. The massacre would not be the last throughout history.

The Puritans

In the 1630s John Winthrop made his way to Massachusetts Bay. The Massachusetts Bay Colony was situated on the site of modern-day Boston. Its inhabitants were made up of the more affluent Puritans and would grow to be the greater of the two colonies in Massachusetts Bay. They would expand their control to be the most influential in New England. Winthrop had accepted the offer to become the Governor of the colony. He believed that he had the "calling" and this was required of all Puritans who wished to hold office. The church agreed and Winthrop became Governor and held that position for nineteen years. The colony moved forward on the strength of their fur trading, fishing and ship building industries. With the Mayflower Compact firmly entrenched the Puritans wasted no time asserting their morals and religious beliefs on everyone who lived within the Puritan's realm. It was much like the rule of the King in England who had persecuted them there. It mattered little to them the desires or beliefs of the others. The Puritans persecuted and tortured non-conforming colonists. They were hung and buried alive in Boston Common. Roger Williams was banned from the colony in the dead of winter for becoming a Baptist. The timing of this banishment could have been seen as a death sentence in itself. In the winter of 1636 he left with his followers and traveled north establishing Rhode Island as an unchartered colony. William's God had watched over them on their journey and they survived the harsh winter. This had no effect on the Puritans. Thomas Hooker splintered from the group and started settlements in Connecticut. The Puritans had no tolerance for anyone that did not completely submit to their demands. It was an odd behavior for those that had experienced persecution. They now had the power to administer religious tolerance and understanding. Instead they became the persecutors themselves.

The Native Americans treatment at the hands of the Puritans was harsh. The Indians developed a hostile and distrustful relationship with the Massachusetts colonies. The Puritans would take the Indians captive and ship them to England as slaves. In 1633 they passed a law that no Indian could receive a land allotment or plantation unless they converted to Puritanism and were civilized by accepting the English ways of agriculture and life. The following is a reading of the law concerning the Indians in this time.

For the settling the Indian title to lands in this jurisdiction (it) is declared and ordered by this Court and authority thereof, that all the lands any of the Indians have in this jurisdiction have improved by subduing the same, they have a just right unto, according to that in Gen. I, 28, and Chapter IX, I, and Psalms CXV and 16, and for the civilizing and helping them forward to Christianity. If any of the Indians shall be brought to civility and shall come among the English and shall inhabit their plantations and shall there live civilly and orderly such Indians shall have allotments among the English according to the custom of the English in like cases.

http://www.quaqua.org/pilgrim.htm

The Crossing and Conditions on Board the Ship

The new world was indeed a harsh setting for many reasons. This was the world into which the boys were sailing and would be forced to live and survive. They were still too young and unaware to know what lay before them. These were Henshaw boys however and they were survivors. They would take what negative things their young lives had thrown their way, absorb them, react to them and come out stronger and successful in the end. This is how families survive for generations and prosper. The Henshaw line of ancestry would go on and make a difference in the world. Within each family exists the proverbial "black sheep" But a family moves like a wave from generation to generation. They would survive these "black sheep" amongst their families and miscreants within their ranks and deal with them in their own ways. Sometimes they would win and sometimes they would lose but they would march forward into the future nonetheless.

The storms of fraud and death had finally subsided. They had bashed both boys in the early years of their young life. The boys sat on deck and watched the clouds. The current weather was the first good weather they had seen since going to sea. The boys would set near the sailors and listen to their stories staying far enough away so as not to be noticed. To be noticed could mean ridicule or worse. This could be a bad experience for the boys if they encountered the wrong person or circumstance. The ship was not built for a comfortable voyage. It had nothing in the way of luxury. It was sea-worthy and stout. Mather was required to pay extra for the boys. The ship's officers did not like being responsible for boys of their age. After all they were sailors and not nannies. They were also men who were making the long crossing without the companionship of women. For this the boys would be at risk of being molested at their tender ages. The boys had to be watched. They had to make the crossing in good health and condition. If the boys did not survive the crossing the Captain would forfeit his extra money and Mather would lose his continued payments from Ambrose. Along with the boys came a large lump sum of money that was to provide for their education, expenses and to eventually finance a business or land holding for them. It was a pittance to the wealth they had lost to the Ambrose plot.

The boy's bedsteads were shared with many others on board the ship. The bed itself was roughly two feet wide and six feet long. This was the allotted amount of space for each passenger on board. The boys' fate was better than most. Being that they were two young boys who could share their two space allotments gave them a better space than most on board. This gave them four feet by six feet. Every square inch of space was used on these ships to maximize the profits of the journey. They would pack four to six hundred people on board. In addition to the passengers the cargo was tucked into every available cranny. In addition, the ship carried its own provisions that would be consumed by the Captain, crew and passengers at sea. Most of the ships carried slaves in the lower decks and under the worst conditions. In these early days the slave trade would include the Irish and captured enemy soldiers that would be placed into indenture or slavery. In these early days of the colonies the slave trade was a rarity unless headed to the Caribbean area. Many slaves would not see sunlight for the entire trip. All of those on board would live in misery for seven weeks if they had good winds. The normal trip was up to twelve weeks if the wind faltered and this was mostly the case. The stench of the ship was overwhelming. The odors came from vomit and human waste. These unclean and germ ridden conditions caused a myriad of sea maladies. These included sea-sickness, fever, dysentery, headache, heat, constipation, boils, scurvy, cancer and mouth-rot. Other factors would contribute to the misery. These included the want of clean and edible provisions, hunger, thirst, frost, heat, dampness, anxiety, fear, homesickness, injury, afflictions and lamentations. They all played their part in the journey. Joshua and Daniel had one advantage over the others. Mather could not let anything happen to them. He saw that extra food and medicines were stocked for the sole purpose to administer to the boys if they might become ill or malnourished to a dangerous level. He instructed the Captain to use these reserves if a life-threatening issue came about. He remembered his initial trip to Massachusetts. They had sailed into an Atlantic hurricane and for long hours thought that their judgement day had come. There was much praying and crying but eventually the storm blew by them and they had survived. Many ships did not make it all the way to the new shores and their passengers and cargoes would go to the ocean's floor.

Two weeks out of port the boys were required to help on deck. They befriended some of the old sailors who had taken a liking to them. These men took them under their wings and told them stories of the sea and of their adventures. Some stories were age appropriate and some not so. The boys were thrilled with them and it made their crossing much more bearable. These salty stories made them feel excepted and grown up so they did not mind them although they found themselves embarrassed and confused by them at times. The sailors told them about the Massachusetts Bay Colony where they had landed many times now. This was their indoctrination into their soon to be home.

Unknown to them their circumstances were already much better than most of those on board.

The Plight of those Indentured

The boy's passages had been paid for in full. Most of those aboard had cast their fate to the wind. They could pay only partial passage or none at all. It did not matter. They knew that their fate in leaving England was to go to the colonies and thus surrender their freedoms for a term as an indentured servant.

http://www.virginiamemory.com/blogs/out_of_the_box/wp-content/blogs.dir/5/files/indentured-servants/indenture001_it.jpg

They would be required to stay on board the ship upon their arrival in Boston Harbor until they were purchased. At times these buyers would come from as far away as twenty to forty hours to enter these ships and shop its inhabitants. Once the selection was made, they would negotiate the number of years the person would have to work to pay back the debt of their passage. This would range from three to six years or longer if the person did not know better or how to negotiate.

It was a buyer's market and they would take advantage of any weakness. In many of these negotiations the number of years in the indenture was decided by the age of the person, their overall strength or their unique skills. There was no real way for a person arriving on the ship to demonstrate a particular skill. These skills, even if real, were not often considered because they were hard to prove to those wishing to indenture them. There were many issues to these indentures. Those that were ten to fifteen years of age had to serve their master until they turned twenty-one years in age. Parents would sell their children off to these masters. In this way they could put their debt upon their children.

Mother and father could then walk from the ship unencumbered. In reality most children under the age of seven would die during the crossing and be cast overboard into the sea with no blessings and no grave. This system was not efficient. Many families would be indentured to different masters and would not be allowed to live together. It was not uncommon for a wife to be separated from her husband or children from their parents. It could be years before they were reunited. In most cases the family members were not told the location of each other or where they would be taken to serve their time for fear they would run off to find their family members. Many times they would never see each other again in their lifetimes after their separation. There were other drastic rules that came into play. If a husband or a wife died after completing the halfway point of the crossing the surviving spouse must pay for both themselves and the deceased doubling the term of indenture. If both parents of children died during the voyage after completing over one half of the journey and the children have nothing to pawn or pay with, they would serve until they were twenty-one years of age. If a man completed his term of indenture he is entitled to a suit of clothes and if it had been stipulated a horse. A woman completing her indenture would get a cow. If an indentured servant were to run away the person who would capture and return them to their master would receive a large reward. As punishment for running away the following formula was used:

If gone one day their term would be extended

by **one week**,

If gone one week their term would be extended

by **one month**,

If gone one month their term would be extended

by **half a year**.

Since the value of an indentured servant was much less than that of a black slave the masters would mate the white women with the black slaves to produce a half black child. This child could then be sold at slave rates and a profit could be made. There was no consideration of mother and child in this matter or for the father.

The boys were not out of the woods but they would not have to face the delays or the sale block upon their arrival. Those that came into port in ill health would obviously not be bought immediately and they might remain on board ship for an additional three weeks or more. Eventually the ship would have to leave port. Some of these sick would die from the delay in medical treatment. Many would have otherwise survived. This was a very rash and greed driven system. There was no humanity involved in the decisions that were to be made throughout the journey and their landing. For this to exist in a religiously based community is hard to understand.

With the weather they encountered at the beginning of the journey the winds played against them the whole first week. This would not be a short crossing. It was shaping up to be one of the longest crossings that would be made. They were out of port in Liverpool now for about two weeks. The boys were healthy after their first bouts of seasickness had passed. They tried to spend as much time on deck as possible to escape the stench and disease that was already starting to appear below decks. The sight of the sails full of wind thrilled them by their majesty alone. They were seeing some whales and dolphins playing in the waves and racing along with the ship. They worried about the storied sea monsters that were said to have swallowed ships whole or dragged them to the bottom. There were many tales that they had read about giant squid and monsters of the deep. Even the seasoned sailors spoke of them and showed fear now and then. Many of the sailor's stories that the boys overheard included the sea monsters.

Many of those that embarked to be sold into servitude did so as a drastic measure of survival. They were penniless with little hope of work or improvement to their lives in England. They had come to the ship malnourished and dehydrated. These passengers were showing signs of disease and sickness within the first two weeks. The meals on the ship left much to be desired. Warm meals were served only three times per week. Many of these were inedible because they were so fouled and uncleanly. To eat them would risk illness in itself. The water served was usually black and thick. The cups of this liquid were filled with worms. The ship served its biscuits which were filled with red worms and spider nests. Others became ill from the old and heavily salted food and dried meat. There was little or no vegetables or fruits that would help fight off such diseases as scurvy. Joshua woke one night in the cusp of a storm. The ship was pitching to and fro. This wasn't specifically what had brought him from his rest. He had heard the screams of a woman from her bunk. She was pregnant and her time had come to bring the child from her womb. They could not keep their footing to aid her. When the storms came the waves rose to the size of mountains and crashed down on the decks. The ship was thrown in violent motions. At times the ship would run up the wall of water and when reaching the crest tumble down the other side at great speed only to find the next wave approaching. There was uncertainty with each new wave if the ship would weather it and stay afloat. The passengers were pitched about the room and could not lay, sit or stand without being thrown about. It was hardly a scenario where a child could be born. Even the mother was tossed from her bed. The Captain was brought to the area and he sized up the situation. He had his sailors lift the woman and take her up the stairs to the deck. Those close to her were crying and begging the Captain to leave her. The Captain refused and they left with the woman. The family was distraught and tried to hold on to each other against the rolls of the ship in the violent waves. Joshua followed the Captain and when it was clear that he would not be seen he climbed the steps after them to look out on the deck. He got there just in time to see the two sailors lift and toss the mother and her unborn child into the sea. They staggered back to their work. Joshua was shocked and bothered. He had lived in a civilized world. The things he had been through and seen since his mother's death had set his ideas of the world on its head. Nothing seemed as it should now. There were no morals or empathy. There was only greed and self-preservation it seemed. Even a man of God and stature as was Richard Mather was not immune to the pull of sin and greed. All he had been taught in school and church made no difference now. It was a different world that he found himself living in. He would have to put away his teachings and meet it head on. It was his prerogative to write and rewrite his own rules so that he and his brother's survival would be assured. He would not rest until he had reclaimed what was his by birthright. He went below to be with his brother. Daniel could tell that his brother was somehow different and worldlier in his focus at that moment. In this minute he seemed distracted and deep in thought. It gave him a feeling of security and peace. He loved his brother and trusted his judgement. Joshua was the oldest and he was in charge. As the storm passed, they both drifted off to a peaceful sleep. As the storm ended the waves recessed. The waves would stay high for days after such a storm so sailing was very rough. Most were just happy that God had answered their panicked prayers for the second time since the voyage had begun. They had lost even more time on the crossing. Joshua learned that the ship had lost three crewmen that were washed overboard during the height of this second storm. Two of these men were ones that had taken the woman from their quarters and tossed her into the sea. He suspected that their loss was at the hands of the Captain to cover his actions with the pregnant woman. Others on the crew thought it was God showing his displeasure of their actions. Her husband and relatives were questioning the Captain and crew about her location and well-being. They would not get the answers they sought until much later. Joshua could not tell them. If the Captain had been behind the two men's disappearance, he would put himself and Daniel in jeopardy if he made what he had seen known. He remained silent. After all he could do neither the woman nor her unborn baby any good now. They had little contact with the Captain on the crossing. He stayed in his quarters and to himself. The few times that he met with them he avoided their questions to the largest extent. They were able to learn that they would stay at the Mather property on their arrival. There they would work for him to earn their keep. The Captain did not mention that Mather was receiving money for their care or that he had a lump sum of money that he carried with him to pass to Mather upon their arrival. He did not answer any questions about the status of their family's property in England or why they were sent to America instead of staying in their home. He would only say that it was God's will. The boys were constantly hungry and thirsty. They were warned by the adults on what things to eat or drink and what to leave on their plates for their own safety even if they were starving. Catching a disease from the fouled food and water could quickly lead to death. It was better to starve. In this way you might make it to landfall and then be nursed back to health. The Captain failed to tell them that they would not starve. He also failed to give them any of his tightly held provisions. He assigned a sailor to advise him if there were any pressing health issues with the boys. They had entered the cold northern waters of the north Atlantic. They would turn near the tip of Greenland. There was no real port there to stop and resupply. It was unlikely the Captain would have used it if it were there. More provisions would cost money and bite into his profit for the crossing. It was better to leave the passengers to their misery so he could collect a larger profit as he saw it. They shivered above decks and lay together at night to stay warm. The boys were abducted with nothing but the clothes on their back. They had no blankets or coats to wear. They were chilled constantly in this part of the voyage. When the winds would pick up the temperatures would plummet. The family of the pregnant woman who was thrown overboard brought the boys her blanket. There was no need for it now. They said that she would have wanted them to have it. The boys were grateful. Joshua thought about telling the man what he knew. He thought on it all night as he huddled in the blanket's warmth with his brother. He finally thought it was best they did not know what had happened. Their memory of her was good. The actuality of the events could foul their memories and cover them with bitterness and hatred. It could drive the man to such a state that he would confront the Captain himself and that could only end badly for him. He would not tell the man. Death on the voyage was becoming an almost daily occurrence at this point. Those that were ill were now cold and chilling. Others were getting sick from their exposure to those with contagious diseases and the elements. People were praying and wailing and begging for life. Many a husband and wife were at each other because of their conditions. The one that made the decision to sail was pitted against the one who did not want to leave England. Children were upset with their parents and crying. Most thought their survival was very much in question. Many did not realize that the colder weather and below freezing temperature could be keeping them alive. Many germs and viruses would die in the cold and keep those that were well from catching the festering diseases. There would be a rekindling of the illnesses when they reached warmer climates however. The body count had continued to climb on board. The Captain favored tossing the bodies over the side but the Puritans on board beseeched him to hold services for their loved ones. The Captain reluctantly agreed to these religious services to stay in the good graces of Mather. He was an influential person in both the colonies and England and brought him much profit and paid in full business. He wished he had more like him so he did not have to go through the time intense procedure of selling those on board. Slaves were a different business. He generally owned them and could sell them for a higher profit than just passage. Although they suffered it did the Captain no good if they were to die. The unhealthy or the dead did little for his profits when they came to port or the slave markets in the Caribbean. In these ways the slaves became a more valuable cargo than the indentured servants or those with paid passage. During this time the market for slaves in the colonies was not profitable. Few could afford the cost of a slave. The Captain granted permission to perform religious ceremonies before the dead were cast to the sea. He knew full well that this would highlight the number of deaths that normally would be disguised by simply tossing them over the rail like the daily trash. He hoped there would be no repercussions.

It was on the ninth week of the crossing that Daniel came

down with a fever. Joshua knew that he would soon have it too. He did all he could for his brother. When he was himself struck down, he continued to care for him over his own suffering. Their condition was becoming dire. The sailor that the Captain assigned to watch the boys reported this after several days passed and their condition had worsened. The Captain began to have clean water and good provisions sent to the boys along with some medicines that would see them through. This had to be done in strict secrecy. If others on board knew that provisions and medicines were on board the ship there could be mutiny until it was found. Tempers ran high with the amount of people packed into the filthy and anxiety producing quarters. This escalated with the miles traveled and would only be relieved when land was once again sighted signaling the end to their suffering in time. They did not consider the time it would take to be purchased or what the outcomes would be. To some the reality of the process would be a complete surprise. To others it would be expected. Those traveling alone would not have a worry. Those traveling as families would have many stressful decisions facing them. The boys were too ill to stand for three more days. They were on the mend when the ship broke into the warmer climates past Newfoundland. They were now on the last leg of their journey. They had finally spied land but that made the journey seem that much longer. It would still be weeks until they found Boston Harbor. Time would crawl with each land sighting as they ran the coast of North America. The boys were still weak and stayed huddled in their one blanket for most of this leg of the journey. As they landed the summer months were ending and autumn would greet them with a beautiful canvas of color. It would lighten the moods of the colonies newest inhabitants but would not accurately depict their lives. At least they would be on terra firma once more at that point.

The boys had kept count of those that had died on the journey below decks. Of the four hundred that had started the journey there were now only three hundred and forty-two aboard. The rest had been tossed into the waves to their eternal rest. Some were still alive when they went over the railings but most were dead at the time they were cast into the sea. Almost all of the children younger than Daniel had died. There was much sadness with their parents. Some mothers had thrown themselves over board to join their dead children and perished. The ship would not slow or stop to recover them. Joshua had spoken to the sailor who had befriended the boys on the voyage. He confided to him what he had seen after he knew he could trust him to keep the secret. He looked sad and said "Aye mate! It is a sad, sad thing that happened to that woman and her unborn. Ye' have to understand though that their fate was settled when she had the misfortune to begin her labors as the storm set upon us. As it was, and I have seen it many times, she would not survive the birth. The baby in calm waters would have been taken from her belly by knife and likely would have survived the birth. The mother would have perished. Without its mother to nurse it at her breast it would have died shortly of starvation or disease. At times and if there is another mother feeding her child, we can have her act as a nursemaid but for the most part this baby is not likely to survive without his mother. It seems cruel but when the Captain threw them to the sea, he only hastened what was to come and saved them a long period of suffering. I wish it could be a different way but that is the reality of being at sea in these ships packed to its gills with humanity. Profit for the Captain and the ships owners is always the guiding light that dictates all decisions. This one was for that purpose and for the benefit of the mother and her babe!" Joshua was astounded. He could not fathom what he had just heard. This would be something he would have to think on. It would dominate his thoughts for days. They were still two weeks sail to Boston and he would have time to do just that.

Daniel did not wish to think on it. Joshua told him what he

had learned from the sailor. Daniel could not justify the murder of these two-innocent people. He did not want to consider all of the factors. To do so would admit the true evils of the world that he would be forced to live in. Both knew that it was a primitive society and country. There were no real certainties here. There was no security, family or close friends to support them and help them to return to their homes. They still did not know what lie ahead of them and could only imagine what a man like Mather would do to them. They did not know what his instructions from Ambrose had been. Both knew of the hatred that Ambrose bore for the Henshaw family. They also expected that if he could make things worse for them he certainly would. Both men seemed to them to be of the devil and they could only turn to their faith they had known in their own life and not that taught by Mather and his Puritan horde. The Puritans would demand much more from them including amending their previous beliefs to abandon the practices of the protestant religion and the Anglican Church. The Puritans had their own ways and did not tolerate any others. Both boys vowed to keep this as an act of defiance to reject the Puritan teachings and stay true to those taught by their parents and family.

The Captain had begun to meet with the boys as they grew close to Boston. He instructed them on their expected behavior when they made port. He read to them a letter from Mather that detailed their duties at his hearth and to his church. He told them that if asked any question that they were to respond that they were the sons of Mather's friend in England. They were to say that they had come of their own accord to be schooled and apprenticed in the colonies. Any attempt to escape would be punished severely. The boys continued to ask their questions and the Captain continued to ignore them. Any question that did not address their current situation fell on deaf ears. It was as if their past did not exist except in some other reality that they were no longer connected to in any way. When the ship docked, they would be taken off the ship and on to the Mather carriage where they would be taken to their quarters at his estate. The boys were told that they would be educated and taken care of until such a time that they could support themselves. When pressed on what this meant the Captain responded by saying that it was not for him to speak for the Reverend Mather on these issues. His responsibility would end when they were delivered to the carriage on the Boston docks alive. Mather would decide what training they would receive and for how long. They were to receive room and board for their labors to earn their keep. The boys had discussed this and knew that they would be required to work at something. The colonies were not for slackers unless you held status. They had never been slackers at home. Their mother and grandmother insisted on them working along side their servants doing chores at the earliest age that they could handle the required tasks. Their father would have expected no less. They were no strangers to labor.

At the first sighting of land there was a feeling of relief that swept through the passengers. Even those suffering illnesses made their way to the decks to observe the land sighting for themselves. They did not want it to be a mirage or a false sighting. They could only satisfy their curiosity as a first-hand witness to the scene. There were cheers and cries of joy as they verified the sighting one by one. There was praying and singing and thanks to their God and the crew. It made the sick rise from their beds and brought them back to life. It brought them hope that they would soon be on land and get proper care for their illnesses and survive. The port of call was still weeks away. A day seemed like a week now. A week seemed like a month. To the ill it felt like eternity. All they could do now was to be patient. The days drug on. The boys had it better than most. They spent much of their time on deck in the warmth of the sun. The Captain did not like the deck too crowded but the boys were doing chores there. The weather was good and the sun was warm. They worked hard and it kept their muscles toned. They knew that each minute, each hour and each day brought them closer to the end of the journey. Finally, they could see the inlet to Boston Harbor. Those on board were celebrating. The moods elevated and excitement swept through the ship. The decks became crowded to get their first looks at their new homes or at least the first few steps to the new land. The Captain was on deck. He looked none the worse for wear. He had not lost weight like everyone else on board. It was apparent that he had eaten a full diet on the crossing. It was clear that he had generously borrowed from the extra provisions that had been stored aboard for the boys. As they pulled into the harbor the boys were preparing to spend their last night on board the ship. Others would spend from a few days to three or four weeks on board before the ship was cleared of its passengers through the process it took for the Captain to recover his fares from their new masters whoever they would be.

Competition for Human Goods and Services

The Captain was in a foul mood. This seemed to stem from the appearance of another ship that had pulled into harbor a few hours before. The word came down that the ship was full of Scotsmen. There were ten thousand Scots captured at the battle of Dunbar in 1650. They were marched from Durham to Newcastle after their defeat by the English. Many would die on the march from disease and starvation. The remainder landed in Newcastle. This was problematic. The quartering and feeding of this many soldiers was quite expensive. One week after the battle the Council of State, the new governing body under Cromwell, passed the authority to Sir Arthur Hasellrigge. He was to decide their fate. Many would be passed into indentured servitude. Among those were requests for one hundred men with interests from New England businessmen to man the iron works and saw mills. This was quickly approved and one hundred and fifty men were put aboard the ship "Unity". The ship's Captain lived in Charlestown and made the crossing on a regular basis. John Becx and Joshua Foote contracted with the New Englanders to bring these men. They had to be in good health and absent from wounds. Becx and Foote purchased these men for five to ten pounds each and intended to sell them at the end of the journey for twenty to thirty pounds each. This would be a huge sum of money for the two. They could figure that about twenty percent would die on the crossing but they would still land one hundred and twenty men. In the worst case their profits from this human trafficking would be twelve hundred pounds and in the best case three thousand pounds. The men would be distributed as follows:

15 or 20 of the men went to Richard Leader for services at his Saw Mill, at Berwick, on the Pascataqua River, in Maine.

62 went to John Giffard, the agent for the Undertakers of The Iron Works of Lynn (Saugus).

The rest of these men were indentured to local residents.

The term of service for all of them was seven years.

These men were in much the same position as the boys. The difference was a matter of age. They were all soldiers and of legal age. They had many skills and their youth and strength would make them very desirable purchases by those in the market. Since they were soldiers the Captain knew that the interest would be drawn to the other ship in direct competition to his own because of its superior cargo. That would mean a delay in emptying the passengers from his ship. This would cut his profits and delay his return trip by weeks.

The market was flooded. When the colony began in 1630 the population was at twelve hundred people. By 1650 the population stood at two thousand. There were others in the Plymouth colony and some spread out in other areas. The desirable factor of the men on the other ship was that these men were soldiers and those skills would be needed in case of attacks from Native Americans or others from competing countries. They might have left one battle but could be battling the same foes on different ground before it was over.

The Mouth of Boston Harbor

http://search.aol.com/aol/image?v_t=keyword_rollover&page=5&q=boston+harbor+pics+1652&s_it=topsearchbox.image&oreq=86ac

Making Port in Boston Harbor

With some seven hundred souls arriving on the two ships the Captain was worried about what the market would bring to pay off the fares and secure the release of those aboard his ship. It was clear that his anticipated profits had taken an adverse position. It was now guided by the laws of supply and demand. This was a question that Joshua and Daniel did not have to worry about. They were served their last meal. It was galley biscuit and brackish water. The boys did not eat or drink either so they would not risk illness. They would wait to get ashore and try to eat then. They were sure to be able to get clear and clean water immediately after they disembarked. The ship anchored in the bay that night. This allowed the Captain and crew to get organized for the docking on the following morning. They would identify those that had paid their passage in full. Next would be those that would be bought quickly because of their size and general health. They would triage the sick to see which could be sold and those that would not make it and probably die on board the ship. They bargained with the passengers. In this they would bargain with those that would trade their children for passage. Then they would bargain with those that would be responsible for additional passage because of the death of their spouse on board the ship after the halfway mark of the journey.

Boston Harbour Circa 1650

http://upload.wikimedia.org/wikipedia/commons/2/22/Boston-view-1841-Havell.jpeg

The next passengers were those that had paid a part of their passage and owed a balance to the Captain. Some would offer their belongings to the Captain in barter to pay off their passage or to offset part of their balances. It was a market for freedom and the prices were high. They slept fitfully that night. In the morning the ships bells were ringing and the crew was a riot of activity. The ship was heading to pier to be tied off. Shortly thereafter the gangplanks would be dropped and those that were paid up would disembark.

Meeting Richard Mather

Mather had arrived on the pier with two carriages. He expected to have a substantial stock of unused provisions on board. He could have left them to those poor suffering passengers below decks that were to be held on board until their futures became clear. These provisions could have saved some of those stricken with illness. Mather sought out the Captain to complete their business. With one look at the Captain he knew that his provisions would be much less than he had expected. Mather had them removed off of the ship and onto the carriages parked on the docks. He would not part with anything of value although he preached just the opposite. He disembarked with a large sum of money that the Captain passed into his hands from Ambrose. His final business was to settle his accounts with the Captain. He was to pay half of the passage and settle up on any additional expenses that might have arisen on the crossing. He questioned the Captain about the amount of provisions that had been loaded onto the ship and their disposition. He did not receive satisfactory answers. He deducted what he felt was reasonable and paid the Captain a greatly reduced amount. The Captain roared with anger but slunk back on board under a withering stare from Mather. He was a man that was not to be trifled with in his own surroundings. The Captain would have to take the loss. The boys looked out at the city of Boston. The population was now a little over two thousand citizens. The city was built on a hill and had a port. The port was different from Liverpool. The water was much clearer then the muddy waters of the Mersey River delta. The city was very similar except the houses were not as well built. There were fewer businesses there than in Liverpool. The boys were heirs to many of those businesses that were left behind in their homeland. Any one of them would dwarf the businesses that they saw here. The wildness and rumored dangers of the colony were not apparent from this viewpoint. The Indians and the wild lands were outside of the town. There was relative safety in this large gathering of settlers and in these urban settings. The boys were on the deck waiting for Mather's porters to load the carriages. They were witnessing more of the dark side of Boston society. Below on deck they heard the cries of families as the realities of this life set in. Some of the buyers were on board the vessel and deals were being struck as early as they could come aboard. There was an advantage to be first on board so the buyer would get first choice of the available servants. Sometimes this was granted to friends of the Captain and sometimes it came in the form of bribes to the Captain or crew. Those who were negotiating their fates were pleading with the masters not to split up their families and to buy all of them as servants. Much of this fell on deaf ears. Occasionally there would be the empathetic buyer who would try to negotiate on the families behalf but many were looking for just one servant or specific types of servants and having children or adults that did not fit their needs was just an extra expense to them. Joshua and Daniel felt very bad for these people. They were angered at these supposed religious people who would act so inhumanely to others. They watched as parents stole away from the docks leaving their children behind to work off their passage for all of their childhood years. It could not be determined by either boy if this was by design or unfortunate circumstances. It did not take a stretch of the imagination to know that some of these parents bore children as barter for their own passage. These were the ones that would steal away from the ships and settle away from Boston in other locations. In this way their neighbors would not know the true nature of these miserable and self-serving people. In short order Mather was loaded and ready to go. His demands took priority over any others. He gathered the boys and took them off of the ship. Their legs were wobbly and their heads were spinning. It had been many weeks since they had been on firm ground. Mather could wait no longer. He was feeling his hunger for a noontime meal and good food and drink. It just so happened that near the Boston docks was an ordinary called "Bunch of Grapes". It was near the water and at times the waves nearly touched the Inn's door. Its proprietor was one William Hudson who was a baker by trade. He was one of the earliest settlers of Boston and very active in his community. Mather always used his standing in the community to his advantage. He made strategic acquaintances and used them. He would not waste a time like this one with such a need in his belly and two hungry boys to feed. He had the carriages stop at the door and escorted the boys into the establishment. They were seated. Mather was a big man. He did not allow hunger pangs to dally too long before quenching their demands. The boys would be fed here and given good drink. There were many dishes. There was domestic beef, pork and lamb. There were the wild meats of boar, turkey and other fowl. In 1648 the harvest was bad and the colony survived by eating passenger pigeons. There were usually harvests of corn and grains in most years. These originally came with the help of the Indians in the early days of the colony. The merchants traded for rice from the Virginia plantation to add to their diets. The drinks of the day were tea, wine, ales and coffee from the West Indies. The boys would have a feast this day. It would not be repeated for many years however. Mather was a different man in public than in private. With the boys in tow at the "Bunch of Grapes" he put on quite a show for the populace.

He portrayed himself as a mentor and savior to these poor boys. He craved the attention and the opportunity to paint himself as some sort of philanthropist to the poor. He was quick to stop any questions thrown out to the boys about their family or what conditions brought them to New England. They quickly understood that disclosing the true nature of their abduction could leave them homeless and in this destitute harsh new world in which case they would surely perish. They were totally immersed in their meals and drinks at this time anyway. Mather noted that he would have to have a strict discussion with them about disclosure outside of his family. After their meal the boys were loaded in the carriage.

Bunch of Grapes Ordinary

A second carriage followed behind with Richard Mather's provisions and gifts from England for his family and church. Dorchester Massachusetts was the site of Mather's home. He was seated in the church there and would remain so until his death in 1669. The boys would live with the servants in their quarters and share a room. In this way Mather could control his expenditures on their upkeep and make a maximum profit from his agreement with Ambrose. It promised to be a money-making venture for him. Dorchester was about five miles to the south of Boston. By carriage it would take a few hours to get to their destination. Mather took this time to school Joshua and Daniel on their behavior, their religious beliefs, their church obligations and their discretion when around those not of the Mather household. Of course, his wife would know of the circumstances of their journey but Mather would prefer that his children and those of his church and town be left in the dark. His behavior could cast dark shadows on his standing in his community.

A depiction of the Mather House

http://search.aol.com/aol/imageDetails?s_it=imageDetails&q=bunch+of+Grapes+Ordinary%2C+Boston+pics

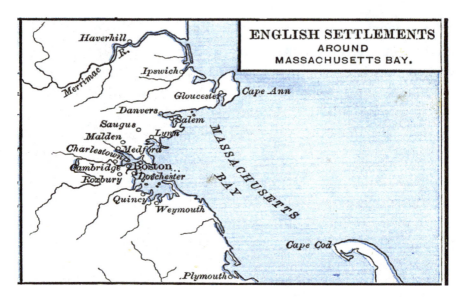

About 1652, the orphans Joshua and Daniel were *"fraudulently abducted"* and sent to New England. They came to Dorchester, Mass., where they resided during their minority. According to family tradition, they were in the care of the Rev. Richard Mather, who came from Lancashire, England, and was responsible for their care, and for the money sent with them for their support and education, and for setting them up in business. The two boys were shipped off to America by their caretaker, while he reported that they had died during an epidemic that had then just recently raged in England. In the meantime, the boys grew up in the colonies under the care of Richard Mather, the famous New England patriarch of a family of preachers and civic leaders. A descendant, John C. Henshaw, has explained in his journals that it was by no means easy going for the boys. They became servants upon their arrival in America, and had to work off their term of indenture like so many others in a similarly impoverished state.

http://www.rawbw.com/~hinshaw/cgi-bin/id?186

The Boys New Living Arrangements

The boys arrived at their new home. The servant's quarters were dismal but the boys made easy friends with the servants right away. They were determined that if their new friends could live in these conditions that they could too. They were not allowed to discuss their previous lives with these people but they were not there long before they heard the gossip among these people. They did not know the boy's story but they knew that there were elements of their lifestyle and unknown history that did not align with Mather's religious beliefs and teachings. It was clear that the boys were not brought there simply to serve as servants. It was clear that there was more to the story and that the boys were from a much different station than the other servants. These people were not fooled at all and knew that something was unsavory with Mather's dealings in this matter. The boys would do chores and then report to the church. There Mather had arranged for one of his associates to school the boys in private classes. By colonial standards the boy's education was already to the level of most children. Mather used this education to indoctrinate the boys into the Puritan ways. The boys had been raised Protestant in the Anglican Church of England. The Civil War in which their father and grandfather fought and died stemmed from religious differences between Charles I and Bishop Laud against the Scottish Covenant. In short Laud was pushing changes in the church that included expensive items, changes in the religious books and what was believed to be a movement towards Catholicism. Charles wife was a practicing Catholic and practiced her religion in the Palace. After the overthrow of Catholicism and the issues it had caused in England's history there were large wounds in the populace that would not heal. Catholicism was a hated institution. The Puritans were Christians who wanted the Church of England purified of any liturgy, ceremony, or practice which was not found in Scripture. They believed in a literal version of the Bible and that its teachings applied to all walks of life. Their movements started during the time of Henry VIII and his reformation of the Church of England. With the death of Henry his sister Victoria came to the throne. She persecuted the Puritans and many fled across the channel. She was known as Bloody Victoria. During her reign the leaders of the Puritan movement were burned at the stake along with many others. Queen Victoria died in 1558 and Elizabeth took the throne. She was brought up Protestant. She wished to return the Church of England to the Protestant religion but wanted to also appease those of the Catholic faith that had allied with Victoria. The Puritan movement called for more reforms to move it further from Catholicism. It was a full-blown movement by 1560. Puritan was a negative term for the movement but was adopted by the population. Through the next years at various times the Puritans were persecuted by the church. Eventually the leaders concluded that they would have a better outcome in New England and the migration started. Their hatred for the Catholics never wavered. The colonization in Maryland was almost exclusively Catholic in its citizenry. The truth was that the other colonies were not tolerant of Catholics living among them. The solution was to have a colony that was exclusive to that religion. In fact, the Puritans became intolerant of any other religion as the years went by. They were fanatics by the time they took control of their own fates at Plymouth Plantation and under the Massachusetts Bay colony charter. The boys found themselves amidst this fanaticism in their new lives. The changes that were demanded by Mather to alter the boy's beliefs were an affront to their family. Their father and grandfather died fighting against the King's proposed changes and now they found themselves under the control of fanatics trying once again to force change in their faith. This was a change that their father had resisted and they too would resist it. Their faith was all that they had left of their family legacy and would not go quietly into the night. This would be the basis for their rebellious attitudes and cause conflict between them and Mather in the years to come. The idea that they had been up rooted, moved and robbed of their heritage was also behind this rebellion. The servants were not a part of it however. Joshua and Daniel were raised Protestant and they were happy to learn that these people were of the same background. They were not intolerant of others and they certainly were not Puritans. In the colonies only church members were recognized to govern or vote. Those that lived among them not of their faith were powerless. They did not control their own destiny. Those that were bought as servants were in their fold for their terms of servitude. They would be free to leave once their indenture was fulfilled but many lacked the funds to relocate. Mather's two sons, Eleazor and Increase were older than Joshua and Daniel.

Codman Square, Washington St Second Cong. Church, Dorchester, Mass.

http://www.dorchesterhistoricalsociety.org/blog/wp-content/uploads/2011/10/1648-Second-Church-smaller.jpg

They were not a fixture at home and were being schooled at Harvard in those days. Richard Mather took the pulpit at the First Congregational Church in Dorchester. Upon Graduation from Harvard and a time in Dublin with his brother, Increase Mather returned to Boston and took the pulpit at the Second Congressional Church in Boston in 1661. He was ordained there in May of 1664. He was the youngest of Richard Mather's sons and was five years elder to Joshua Henshaw.

The Death of Peter Ambrose, His Will and Mather's Deception

The boys were going to have to develop their life and friends through their interaction with the servants, church members and acquaintances that they would meet throughout their duties and interactions in their daily routines. They were not a part of the Mather family and did not attend their functions. They worked hard, studied hard, ate little and slept in a single room for this part of their lives. Fate was not through with the boys yet. They had been with Mather approximately a year when Mather received word of the death of Peter Ambrose. It came in the form of a directive from his Will and Testament.

> *Peter Ambrose, the boy's steward, is suspected of having been responsible for sending the boys out of England for the purpose of getting possession of their property, for before they were sent away, they had been in his care for several years, and after their departure he retained possession and died in the occupation of the estate. Peter Ambrose supposedly claimed that Joshua and Daniel had been sent off to school in London, where they both died of the plague. However, when Peter Ambrose died about 1653, he left the following provision in his will:*

Also my will and mind is and I hereby give and bequeath to Joshua and Daniel Henshawe, late sons of William Henshawe, late of Toxteth aforesaid deceased, who are now in New England, so much money as shall make up what already hath "ben" by me laid forth for them and expended for them for their voyage to New England and otherwise, the sum of thirty pounds, to be paid them at such time as they shall have attained full age and shall give a sufficient discharge for the whole thirty pounds.

http://www.rawbw.com/~hinshaw/england.htm#Joshua

The Ambrose estate sent a sum of money to Mather to be spent on the boys. His original agreement included a sum of money deposited with him for the voyage and for future expenditures on their behalf. The monies sent thereafter were to educate the boys and to establish them in business when their age, education and training called for emancipation. Ambrose had thought that these allotments would discourage the boys from ever returning to England and laying claims against the holdings that had now passed to his son Joshua Ambrose. If they were soundly established in their lives in Dorchester it would lessen the chances of this happening. It was up to Mather to see that it did not happen. Now Mather had a crisis on his hands. He had counted on continued deposits in the boy's accounts from Ambrose in England. He did not think from the stern wording in the Will that this stream of money would continue. He had a large sum of money in his hands though at this time. He would need to rethink his obligations to the boys and how they related to his own family's needs. The boys had no clue that Mather held money on their behalf. Ambrose had taken the bulk of their holdings in England and set them adrift with this initial allotment that Mather held close to his vest. There was now additional money being sent to ease Peter Ambrose's conscience on his death bed. In his own rationalization of his actions Peter

Ambrose was attempting to buy his way into heaven with his ill-gotten gains. An admission by Richard Mather at this time would go a long way to the boys recovering their legacy and rightful standing in their community in their rightful home in England. The time that had passed by since their abduction was brief. A return to England and the filing of a suit to recover their property could be completed at this time with little problem. Another steward would have to be appointed for the boys since Peter Ambrose was no longer in that position. Joshua Ambrose, Peter's only son, was left in possession of the entire estate and would likely fight to keep it. He was of an age that would require someone to oversee the estate also because he was in the same age status as the boys. This would likely come from the distant relatives from the Stanley family, Katherine Houghton's grandparents. These family members stood to gain from keeping the holdings with the Ambrose family.

Richard Mather was aware that exposing the Ambrose plot would be a painful and complicated matter. He would be implicated for his part in this diabolical plan. It could derail his standing in his community, church and family if it was ever to be made public. Under the right circumstances it could get him imprisoned for the criminal he was. The current circumstance with the passing of Ambrose had never been considered. He sent a letter to those in control of the Ambrose estate to expose Peter's plan. It gently mentioned the repercussions that could be expected to the family and Joshua Ambrose if the Henshaw boys would establish their defense to recover their interest in the estate. He further suggested that with proper funding he could most likely keep the boys in New England thus keeping them far from the courts of England. The result would be that they would not assert their legal rights to this estate. Establishing them in a life and business in the colony would encourage them to stay in New England. Their return to England would stir up a hornet's nest to the discredit of those behind their abduction. Mather had nothing to lose in this attempt to extort additional payments. In essence he was restating the agreement he had struck with Peter Ambrose. The worst that could happen was that they would deny the additional funds or his part in the affair would be exposed. He ran that same risk with the release of Peter's Will. The best that could happen would be the continuance of a stream of income from his criminal enterprise. He would not tell the boys any of these things. They had no contact with their home in England now and those that would contact them were long immigrated to Ireland or dead. The boy's fictitious death had been announced in the community so no one would be looking for them. It would have ended with this outcome except for the Last Will and Testament of Peter Ambrose. Their death would now become an issue because in his own spike of conscience he had admitted their death was a hoax in an accepted legal document. Of course, someone would have to notice his recanting of this death claim. He readily admitted that the boys were alive and in New England but gave no detail as to where they were located. There was no mention of Mather's name as the guardian of the boys. He would keep it that way. He could not have the boys running off to England to expose him for the fraud that he was instead of the revered figure that he had presented in his own community. Joshua was the firebrand. If his actions were to be discovered it would be through Joshua. He did not worry as much about Daniel.

Richard Mather suffered his own loss in 1654. His wife, the former Katherine Hoult, died in the spring of 1654. He would remarry Sarah, the widow of his friend John Cotton, in 1656.

Daniel's Condition

Daniel seemed to be acclimating to the colonies well. He had come to accept what had been dealt to him. He did his work and school assignments. He spent his free time with Joshua and they tried to relive the things that they had done at Toxteth Park in happier times. The forests, outside of the populated areas of Dorchester, was where they liked to go. It could be dangerous with wild animals and angry Indians. Not all Indians were this way but coming upon one in the woods always came with a feeling of trepidation and a chance of harm. It was sure that the Indians most likely felt the same way. They were somewhat restricted in their play and free time for this reason. At times they would go hunting or fishing with the servants or their children. They were pleased that there was a husband and wife working for the church that had children their age. Some of the congregation had children that were in the boy's general age group. Nobody knew what status they held in the Mather house so some looked at them as being of a lower class and withheld their children from their company. The boys found enough friends for the limited amount of free time that they had. They were grateful to be together. Daniel had set his mind on progressing in the colonies. He had no desire, after a while, to return to England. What was there for him except for material things? It was not even known when and if they could ever be regained. He had serious doubts that it was possible to overcome the tidal wave of bad fortune, lies and betrayals that had drowned them in Liverpool. There was no one there for them anymore. He was the second son. Any inheritance would be in the control and ownership of Joshua. He would have no legal stake in it.

Joshua's Condition

It was Joshua that caused fear to rise in Mather's belly. Joshua was angry. He wanted revenge. He wanted to be placed back at the head of his fully restored family in their family estates and to see his family restored to their rightful state. He was distrustful of Mather and anything that he told them. He was confident that he would be able to establish himself and make a go of the new world. He was his father's son after all and the Henshaw's were stout of heart. If they set their mind to something it usually got done. The more adversity that came their way the better they dealt with it. This was true of the virtuous family members. Unfortunately, it was also true of those family members who were less virtuous. These were the ones that were involved in their abduction. They too would survive but their survival was like that of a parasite. Their survival came from the hard work and success of others. These people would draw the family into their toxic souls and bring drama into their lives. They only cared for the end game. Their goal was to take all they could seize or steal from others. Like a parasite they would bleed them dry before they would stop.

Joshua considered his religious upbringing. Like all children he would have rather been a thousand places doing a thousand other things than sitting in the church pews on Sunday. Before all of these things had happened to them he believed in the teachings he had learned in the Protestant faith. His parents lived in its graces. His father and grandfather defended it with their own lives. Joseph Henshaw was the Bishop of Peterborough. What was their reward? This made the demands that Mather was making of them to renounce their religion and adopt his beliefs a terrible slight to his parents and only made his anger rise. Their mother and grandmother were selfless souls and would help any in need. Their mother acquired the plague while working in the makeshift hospital to soothe the sick and dying. It took her to her reward much too early. His grandmother was the same type of woman. The loss of her husband and the drain of the constant conflicts of the times eventually took her to her grave. Joshua pledged that these things would not defeat him. He pledged that he would return some day to reclaim his family's holdings and restore them to his family. He pledged to find justice although it is a fleeting thing. Justice in this time was really not justice at all. In truth justice at any given time was the result of who was in power and whether or not you supported their positions. There was nothing just about it. Justice could be bought and sold in the courts. It had been this way for centuries.

Mather's Condition

Mather trudged on in silence. He wondered now whatever possessed him to enter into such a lewd agreement with such a man as Peter Ambrose. He did not want the boys to be aware of the funds he held for them. This gave him the option of using them for his own needs if needs arose. If the boys did not know of the money and its intended use they could not claim foul. He would struggle with his rationalization and try to reconcile them to his Bible. Anything could be rationalized. The Puritans would prove this many times throughout their religious history. They could bend the scriptures to fit any situation and justify their actions from either side of the argument no matter how ungodly the issue. It seems that the public Mather and the private Mather were two different people. The public Mather would harp and rail on another person for their actions while acting in the same manner himself. As long as he was complicit in the boy's abduction he was a hypocrite. The private Mather rationalized his position to make it acceptable behavior in his own mind. This was the way of people of his ilk. Even though it was apparent that what they were doing was wrong they had to twist it in their own minds to make it seem right. They put themselves and their needs in front of all other things including their religious beliefs and teachings but would forever condemn others.

Life in Puritan America

Living in Puritan America was a bitter life. There was little joy. Things that caused joy were usually sinful. This is the conclusion that the boys made from what they were taught. They observed the people that now surrounded them. Those dubious souls now dictated their lives for the present and near future. The only respite came when they could steal time alone with themselves or among their non-church member friends. The boys worked hard every day except the Sabbath. On that day they were expected in church for activities that lasted long into the day. They were depressed and tired. Living in this overwhelmingly dark style only exasperated their condition. They craved their adventures in the woods and playing or fishing there. If they had a good catch it was less likely that they would be denigrated by the elders for wasting their time. Of course, their catch would be taken for the enjoyment of those in the Mather house. There were times that the boys would stash some of their catch and cook it in the woods to enjoy their nutrition and the bounty of their good fortune and skills. Sometimes they would give their catch to the servants to cook for their families. It was rare that any food of this quality would be passed down to the servants. The prime cuts of meat, fish and game was always kept for consumption in the main house. The innards, tough cuts and scraps of the cuttings were sent to the servant's quarters. A good cook there could turn these things into fine eating however. The English were keen on eating organs from the animals. They ate hearts, kidneys, stomach, tongue, gizzards, hoofs and brains along with other parts. They made a pudding from the blood. They were allowed to plant gardens and these brought variety to their diets. They had gatherings of wild berries, roots, varieties of wild fruits, herbs and plants that could be eaten in season when found. The herbs and spices found in their natural form gave these lesser meat cuts their flavors and savory textures. They made ales and wines from these offerings. They would gather various things of nature to make medicine, ointments and salves for the sick or injured. Many of these foods and medicines were learned from the Indians or from old wives tales. The proof of the effectiveness came with their successes or failures. The Indian medicines were usually more effective because they had a greater knowledge of the local plants and medicines. They knew what effects and doses to administer from knowledge passed down through centuries of trial and error.

The colony was drained of all joy. It was replaced by fear that someone would be watching every move and then reporting it to the church elders. The punishments that followed were severe. At this time a colonist not in the Puritan faith had little or no rights. They could not vote, could not hold colonial office and they were looked down upon. If they were of a different belief they were in the early throws of radical persecution. They were not just shunned. Some of these poor souls were exiled from the colony; some were maimed with branding or cropping of their ears. Some were hung, buried alive or burned at the stake.

Under such circumstances minutes trudged into hours, the hours trudged into days, the days trudged into weeks and the weeks to months. The boys had landed in the colony for a year when Mather received notice of Peter Ambrose's death and his admission in his Will that he was guilty of misleading the court and community about the boy's death. If anyone would delve deeper into the matter, they would have uncovered the entire plot. As long as Mather kept his secrets, he knew that Joshua Ambrose and his handlers would also. They all had nothing to gain and everything to lose.

England looked at the colonies as a subsidiary of the King's interests. The colonies were called plantations. The plantation system began in Ireland and was used there as a ploy to antagonize the Irish to anger and convert this anger to action. Irishmen were then stripped of their land when they would rise up against the injustice of the crown. With this history the plantation system carried a negative connotation and the word brought with it a distrust of those who governed it. The colonies were simply an enterprise to add to the King's coffers while contributing little or nothing to the work, equipment or expenses of creating this wealth. Leading up to the period of the 1650s the English government and monarchy had their attention drawn away from North America by a constant series of civil wars, religious upheavals and their battles with Spain and France. With the majority of these issues now settled they had returned their focus to the governance of their possessions. The pursuit of the riches, taxes and goods from the colonists became important to offset the losses from the Civil War. New England and Old England represented two points of what was known as the Atlantic Triangle. This included the colonies on one point, the Caribbean and West Indies trade on the second point and England on the third point. The colonies would have a hard time accepting changes. After this large expanse of time the colonists operated unencumbered by England. England now seemed more like a foreign country instead of a mother country. Since settling North America in early 1607 in Virginia and 1620 in Massachusetts they had been left to their own means by the English throne. They had established their own way of doing business that included raw materials, supplies, trade partners, transportation and labor. These had been practiced in the colonies for almost a half of a century and were embedded in the colonial way of life. People hate change. In the Puritan way of life change was even more despicable.

Troubling Times for Massachusetts Bay and England

In the early 1630s troubles were beginning between the Massachusetts Bay Colony and England. The Puritan intolerance and their habit of expelling those that did not agree with their positions had filtered back to the Privy Council. The Puritans and the Crown did not have good relations from the beginning of the movement. It was the Council's duty to oversee the laws and governance of the foreign plantations. They were focused on the Plantation in Ireland for quite some time in order to exploit the Irish for troops or to confiscate Irish lands as punishment for disobedience to the crown. As the issues of New England came to their ears they were forced to address them as well. Massachusetts seemed to be the source of most issues that filled their agenda during this time. Already before them was a petition of grievance from two gentlemen named Georges and Mason against the Massachusetts Bay Colony. In the meantime, the Massachusetts Plantation had banished two more gentlemen and sent them back to England. Thomas Morton and Philip Ratcliffe had started the process to file a grievance objecting to their removal. In another issue Sir Christopher Gardiner had gone to the colony. He had a history of troubles there with those that governed the colony. He had booked passage and returned to England himself. Here he met up with Morton and Ratcliffe. They filed their grievances against the plantation. As the number of complaints increased it was apparent to the King that things were not well with the Massachusetts plantation. In December of 1632 these grievances were heard by the Committee on New England. The Council was favorable to the colony in their resolution of these grievances but this ruling caused a backlash and the regeneration of the Committee of New England as a result. The King reorganized it in April of 1634.

The committees name had been changed to the "Commission of Foreign Plantations". Its original membership was as follows: William Laud, Archbishop of Canterbury; Richard Neile, Archbishop of York; Sir Thomas Coventry, the Lord Keeper; Earl of Portland, the Lord Treasurer, Earl of Manchester, the Lord Privy Seal, Earl of Arundel, the Earl Marshall, Earl of Dorset, Lord Cottington, Sir Thomas Edmondes, the Master Treasurer, Sir Henry Vane, the Master Comptroller, and the secretaries; Coke and Windebank. The Earl of Sterling was added after this original group. A meeting of a group of any five of the members in council was considered a quorum which allowed for some political maneuvering. Many of the names on this committee were the same names that had caused the turmoil that led to the civil war. This was the same civil war that took the lives of Joshua and Daniels father and grandfather. They were much hated names in the Henshaw household and their control of the

Commission could portend nothing good for the plantation itself.

The commission held extensive and almost royal powers over the colonies. They had the power to make laws and orders for the governance of the English colonies and foreign plantations. They could impose penalties and imprisonment for offenses in ecclesiastical matters. They could remove governors and require an accounting of their government, its expenditures and the collection of taxes. They could appoint judges and magistrates and establish both civil and ecclesiastical courts. These courts could hear and determine a wide variety of complaints from the colonies. They had power over all charters and patents. They could revoke those charters or patents they determined to be covertly or unduly obtained. These changes came about because of the continued immigration of Puritans to New England. The English did not trust the Puritans who had left the country for Holland and then once again for New England. The number of complaints generated from the Massachusetts Bay Colony attracted the attention of the King and his councils. The perceived sense of independence from England caused concern and was brought to the attention of influential people with the ear of King Charles I. The Puritan's attitudes and behaviors were becoming their own worst enemies. The New Englander's perceived this commission to be the twin to the Star Council. The Star Council was used to coerce cooperation or to intimidate non-compliant citizens or groups to comply under the King's will. As a deterrent itself in New England it was ineffective. These many years of non-interference from England did not readily entice those in power to give in to these changes. They would under no circumstances reduce their own importance in any way. The colonies were many miles from London. It was three thousand two hundred and eighty miles (2850 nautical miles) between the two. During these times they were simply out of the King's reach. This committee did little in its existence. At the end of the English Civil War and the unseating of Charles I the commission was replaced. In 1643, when Parliament assumed power and became the executive head of the kingdom, the committee was again reformed and renamed. Among the earliest acts of Parliament was the appointment of a parliamentary commission of eighteen members on November 24, 1643 that authorized this commission to control plantation operations. At its head was Robert Rich, Earl of Warwick, and among its members were Philip, Earl of Pembroke, Edward, Earl of Manchester, William, Viscount Say and Scale and Philip, Lord Wharton. It was loaded with well-known Puritan commoners as Sir Arthur Haslerigg, John Pym, Sir Harry Vane, Junior, Oliver Cromwell, Samuel Vassall, and others. This commission carried eighteen members but only four were required to have a quorum. With the prominence of the Puritan figures embedded into this commission the Massachusetts colonies were assured a period of peace and non-interference once again. England could not see or understand the predisposition that the colonists felt for their own independence. With the lack of participation since the landings in Virginia in 1607 and Plymouth in 1620 an entitlement had grown to a way of life that they had established and settled into for many decades. Interference or governance now from abroad would be difficult if not impossible to establish. Even if it could be established the colonists would not accept the changes that would be demanded readily. It was a recipe for trouble.

Communications between England and the colonies would play its part in this independence. The crossing to New England took twelve weeks. The return trip was similar. Any letter, complaint or notification to or from the Privy Committee or whatever committee or commission would be received at the time of the communication's arrival to the ship making the crossing to the colonies. Then it would take twelve weeks to make the crossing. Upon landing there would be a period of time for the message to leave the ship and land in the hands of the correct authority. This could take from a matter of days to several weeks depending on the messenger and perceived importance of the communication. The committee would then review the issue. The time frame was determined by the complexity of the request or information. A formal meeting would need to be called. Dates would be set and reset until a quorum could be achieved to take the necessary action. Witnesses or complainants would need to be summoned and gathered. Some more complex issues would require debate and research. A time for this was indefinite. There were politics to be played out on each issue and gathering just the right people in acceptable numbers to vote the desired outcome. Once a decision or answer was found the edict would be sent to port to locate the next ship returning to the proper colony. At times these ships would sit in port for weeks to fill their holds and board its passengers. Finally, there would be a second twelve-week crossing. Many ships were lost during these crossings. If the ship was lost on the crossing to England the message would not get to its intended destination. If it was lost on its way back to New England the edict or answer would be lost at sea. There would be no way to know if a message had been sent or received from opposite sides of the ocean. A quick response would be six months but it was normally much longer. A military response with troop mobilization would follow a similar timeline. In the case of an offensive incursion or action the orders would land on the shores with the troops to cut this time in half

Mather Decides the Boys Fates

Mather had not heard a word from his inquiry to the Peter Ambrose estate. With Ambrose's death and the letter he received informing him of the clause Ambrose included in his Will admitting that the boys were alive made it look less than promising than he had hoped. As time passed it became more and more clear to him that no additional funds would arrive. This forced upon him a decision. He had a large lump sum of money in hand for the boy's education and funds to establish them in business that he had received when the boys landed. He now had an additional lump sum from Peter Ambrose's Will for allotment to the boys of another large some plus the thirty pounds each stipulated in his Will. His original agreement had likely netted him a large amount of personal money as a payoff for his participation in the scheme and his pledge to silence. History would find no definitive writing on this subject but much speculation as to the agreement and the sums involved. It was the nature of clandestine agreements to leave no trace or writings on the subjects that could be intercepted and used to incriminate the miscreants in the deeds described. Joshua and Daniel had no first-hand knowledge of the funds being held by Mather on their behalf. Mather had seen no reason to disclose this to them. This left him several options unhindered by knowledge by others that would bind him to his word and dubious contract on the subject.

The first option, most likely the correct one for a man of the cloth, was to care for the boys as contracted and see to their education, welfare and future business ventures.

The second option was to bring the misadventure into the open and send the boys back to England to reclaim their inheritance.

It was clear that these two options were out of the question. Mather would not gain financially or personally from either.

The third option was to find the boys apprenticeships to learn a trade. This was a standard practice among the Puritans but he would be required to pay a fee to the craft master and pay for the support and needs of the boys

The fourth option was to indenture the boys into the service of a master. This would reduce or eliminate his expenditures. The cost of education and the employment for the boys would be passed on to their master. Since the community was unsure of the relationship between Mather and the boys he could easily satisfy his commitments in this manner without raising any conjecture or gossip. It was the option that cost him less and delegated his responsibilities and expenses to third parties. This clearly would be the path of such a man as Mather.

Puritan Ways

In the Puritan community control of the colonists was of upmost importance. This was especially true of those that were "strangers". One of the ways this was accomplished was through community schooling and neighborhood monitoring. The first school was established in 1635. It was called The School of the Prophets. This was a divinity school that taught the Puritan ways. This became Harvard College and later Harvard University. The intent of this structured schooling was to manage the families, indoctrinate the children and prevent further shifts away from the Puritan's desired lifestyle by either the "saints" or the "strangers".

Taking this one step further, the Puritans settled on a system of social control. Many of their practices would be incorporated into the structures of Communist and Socialist Doctrine. For now the basics were in place for this type of development. A part of the beliefs of the Puritan family structure was keeping a platonic relationship with the family's children. It was encouraged that Puritans place their children in the care of other families at a very young age.

> *[There was a] practice common among English Puritans of*
> *"putting out" children--placing them at an early age in other*
> *homes where they were treated partly as foster children and*
> *partly as apprentices or farm-hands. One of the motivations*
> *underlying the maintenance of this custom seems to have been*
> *the parents' desire to avoid the formation of strong emotional*
> *bonds with their offspring--bonds that might temper the*
> *strictness of the children's discipline or interfere with their*
> *own piety.*
>
> *The Diary of Samuel Sewell, c. 1674-1729*

The Puritans clearly had control issues. Once they established their seats of power they became abusive. Laws were enacted that curtailed parental rights. They created community schools. They forced all colonists as a civic requirement to adopt Puritan practice. They imposed taxes to support the schools and their faith. They encouraged citizens and family members to report non-conforming relatives and neighbors. They used the separation of children from their parents as a tool of compliance. A member of the family could not rebel against the Puritan authority without running the risk of reprisal to themselves or other family members. Child abuse was on the rise and accepted in Puritan society. What drove the Puritans from England to Holland and from Holland to Massachusetts Bay was now being practiced by the Puritans against others.

In the early years the colonies had trades develop that met the needs of the settlers. Agriculture, logging, milling, weaving, mining and iron works were big producers needing much labor. The normal trade work common in England developed with the growth of Boston. Shipbuilding became a large industry. To a lesser extent were blacksmiths, silversmiths, pub operators, grocers, clergy, construction workers and servants of varying types that were needed as the colony grew. These crafts were harder to apprentice in because the number of these desirable jobs was limited by demand. Most of these apprenticeships were filled by the sons of the wealthy merchants as they desired this type of work over the harder work in the fields, mines and mills. With each growth period came the need for additional labor. The indigenous Indians provided some labor. It was a resource that was depleted early on during colonization with the huge amount of Indian deaths from diseases and annihilation by wars with the settlers. Indentured servants were recruited to provide the increasing need for labor. Captured soldiers and criminals were a source of labor during these times. There was a limited amount of African slaves and many in the colony could not afford this expense. The need for cheap labor played right into the hands of the Puritans and their platonic families. They could now justify the need for labor to ship off their children and put them to work. The abuses would start at earlier and earlier ages.

Mather's Decision

The Reverend Mather was not a man without means. He could find an apprenticeship if he wished. Usually the agreement required payment of a sort to seal the agreement. It was different with an indenture. Reverend Mather would receive funds and be relieved of all of his responsibilities to feed, clothe and house the boys for the remaining decade of his perceived responsibility within the agreement struck with Ambrose. They would be bound until their twenty first birthday. If he could negotiate some property and a horse at the end of their terms he would be able to save additional funds. The boys were young however and it was hard to tell what their interests were or their strengths and weaknesses. He had not spent much time with the boys since their arrival. He received reports from his servants. For the most part though he knew they were strong and healthy. Their studies were not a worry. They came to Massachusetts and could read, write and perform mathematical calculations. This placed them well ahead of many of the students who were much older and had reached a level to what most would strive to achieve as their total educational goal in the colony. Reverend Mather simply checked their education off on his list of obligations to the boys as complete. They did attend the highest school available to them and were quite bright. Sadly, they did not learn much from their studies that their mother and grandmother had not already taught them. Mather did not want the boys going to the same household or indenture. He wished for them to be separated so they would grow independent of each other. In this way they would develop different interests and a different circle of friends. This would discourage their pursuit of their lost inheritance if indeed they considered it at some point in the future. He felt that the separation would keep the boys from acting upon each other's emotions to join into any plan to return to England together to make their case. What Mather knew of the family was that William Henshaw, the boy's father, had interests in shipping and the textile industries. He would first pursue these professions for the boys. He knew those in both and would most likely have little trouble in arranging the details. He felt that Joshua being older and a bit more of an adventurer would be best suited on the ships. Daniel could then work in the textile industry. It should be a better situation for all of them in his mind and he could rationalize to himself that he had kept his obligations to them even though it was in essence a criminal conspiracy.

Joshua and Daniel's Journals and Settling into Life in the Colony

Joshua and Daniel were getting settled. They had made good friends among the servants. In their presence the fog of Puritanism was not so thick. In their privacy these people would break down and have normal relations and fun. This included music, dance and singing. The Puritans thought that all of this was the work of the devil. It was a good respite from the strictness of the hellfire and brimstone of the Puritan everyday life. The boys had been missing their home. They were having discussions almost nightly of their memories of the family and the old country. With time these memories had begun to fade. They agreed to keep a journal. They were able to get journal books that had been given them by one of the servants. He had been a sailor but had suffered a severe leg injury that took him from the sea. With his departure he took several journal books. He did not read or write so when he noticed the boys and recognized their intelligence he gave them the books. He told them how important it was at sea to chronicle the journeys so that nothing was forgotten. They might need to refer to them for information or directions or for other things. They learned to improve their safety on upcoming journeys through this journaling and shared their knowledge with other sailors. This was not lost on Joshua. If he documented the things he learned and experienced it could help him when he was able to make his way back to England. He would begin writing immediately. There would be a lot of writing to catch up on since their arrival. Daniel would also write his journal but would start with the current date. When Joshua was caught up they would share the writing and Daniel could add what he wanted to the earlier writings. They had made friends at the church. The young of the church lived in fear it seemed. The boys noticed that many of their friends did not live in their own home with their birth parents. It did not seem logical and their friends tried to explain. When they could get alone the mood would lighten and they could be children again. Their lives were severe but even in this radical atmosphere the happiness of childhood could sneak out for short periods of time. The children all dreamed of leaving the colony to return to England or drift into the wilderness where they would not be watched or threatened by the elders. They longed for a happier place.

Mather Makes His Move

Joshua felt a dread in his heart when word came to the boys that they were to meet with Reverend Mather at his church. They had been treated decently enough for their situation. It was not fair. But life was not fair. They had been called to meetings before. Some were for instruction on how they were to behave. Some meetings were to harp at them on the need for them to be discrete. These were early meetings soon after their arrival. There were meetings explaining the rules of the house and church. There were meetings when the boys would act up or Reverend Mather heard whispers of misbehavior from one person or another. Usually these arose from their times in the woods or the times they sought to steal away with each other. They, like their friends, longed to escape the prying eyes. They had never attended a meeting with Mather that was called to praise their good behavior or to impart good news. With this in mind they knew the odds of bad news or punishment would be likely. They ended their studies early on this day and trekked the mile from the school to the church. The Reverend Mather was in his office perusing religious texts that were in his library. He was constantly working on sermons and writings for the church and his government positions. He sat in a big high-backed chair behind a huge wooden desk. It was obviously expensive. His appearance, as they entered his room, resembled a King on his throne. In many ways the boys knew that Mather most likely saw himself as such. He called them to his desk. There were chairs there but they were not allowed to sit until he gave them permission. It was apparent that he did not want them to get too comfortable for this meeting. In fact, it seemed that he was trying to put fear into their hearts. He stood and walked to the window and stared out into the trees. He stood there for some time before returning to his desk. The boys remained standing. Mather returned to his desk but did not sit. He stared into the boy's eyes and then told them to sit down. He arranged and rearranged the papers on his desk. He had two pages that he picked up and glanced at for some time. He carried these papers with him and crossed to the front of the table. He told Daniel to stand. He rose from his seat. He was quivering a bit now. Mather looked at the paper. He said "Daniel! You have lived under my care now for just short of three years at my expense. It is time that you strike out for your future and you can hardly expect me to support you through your training. Tomorrow morning you and your belongings will be moved to the home of Walter Eggleston. You will stay in the Nanny house on Cross Street. The textile house is just behind. At times you will work the docks unloading wool from the ships. Other times you will work on the sheep herds learning about the animals and their shearing. In fact, you will work in a variety of locations as you are taught the textile industry." Daniel could barely remember his father's operations but what he could remember was that there would be a lot of hard work and long hours in this endeavor. Mather prattled on but Daniel was hardly listening now. Finally, Mather finished and said "Do you have any questions sir?"

Daniel stammered "Yes sir! Is my brother to accompany me sir?"

Mather stood silent and glared into his eyes. He finally said "No! He is not! It is time for you to stand on your own. You are dismissed! You may return to your quarters to pack or you may wait for your brother to be dismissed out on the steps. It makes no difference to me!"

Daniel said "Very well sir!" but his voice was shaking and he was very sad and near tears. He would not show this to Mather. He left the room and closed the door behind him.

Joshua was ready to burst. He wanted to take this man by the throat and throttle him. He was a pompous and pious man who in Joshua's eyes was a fraud to his God and his way of life. It was clear that he enjoyed inflicting pain and sorrow on those weaker and less powerful. Mather knew that Joshua would like to kill him and strip his hide to the bone. He pushed in close to Joshua so he towered over him. He did not ask him to stand so he could take this dominant position. He said "You Joshua will be moving to the docks. You will be learning the ship building trade. You will also at times be with the logging crews and at the sawmill learning all of the functions of building a sea worthy ship. I understand that your father was quite interested in this pursuit. He would be happy that this is where I decided you were to go. I expect hard work, obedience and no trouble from you over this arrangement. You are in my charge and I solely decide what is in your best interest. You cannot coddle your brother forever and it is time you both stand on your own two feet. The colony needs workers. There is a shortage and the two of you will help to alleviate that problem!"

Joshua said "May I ask the term of our service? I assume you have sold us off like a common slave! I would also like to state for the record that my father would not approve of the circumstances of our situation nor the part that you have played in it."

Mather slapped him across the face hard. He said in a voice full of hate "Do not speak to me in this manner. In England they already believe that your life has ended so if it were to happen in reality no one would notice your absence. Your service is like all others your age. You will be indentured until your twenty first year. If you run or cause trouble then the length of your term can be extended. I have negotiated that you and your brother be deeded fifty acres of good land and given a horse at the end of your indenture. You will see your brother at church and wherever your paths cross but you are not to visit during work hours. Do you understand?"

Joshua was red in the face. His anger was rising into his throat. He choked out his answer "Yes sir!"

Mather said "You are dismissed. I will keep check on your progress and attitude. Under my agreement with Ambrose I am responsible for you until you reach the age of emancipation and you become able to care for yourself. You may inquire of me as you need!"

Joshua was angry. He had never been so mad. He was concerned about Daniel so he did not tarry. He quickly left the church and found Daniel on the steps trying to hide his tears. He took his hand and they walked along to spend their last night together. Daniel said "Joshua! What will we do?"

Joshua answered "We will do as we are ordered to do. We are the sons of William Henshaw and Katherine Houghton. We are warriors and carry our coat of arms proudly. We are survivors. What we do here will establish the family legacy for our children and their children's children. We cannot fail! We will work hard at our duties. We will learn our skills and become the best there is at our endeavors. Reverend Mather said that when we end our terms we will be given fifty acres of good land each and a horse. Together we will make a life for ourselves here until we can return to England and reclaim our heritage!"

Daniel said "I will do my best Joshua!"

They walked in silence. That night Joshua and Daniel slept fitfully and stayed very close to one another. Joshua could not understand why Mather insisted on separating them knowing that they only had each other to rely on in their world now. There was little he could do in his current circumstance except comply with the current edict from Mather.

As the sun rose the boys did not want to leave their bed. They knew they could not linger there. They also knew that once they left the warmth of their quarters this day their life would be drastically different than when they lay their heads upon their pillows the evening before. Neither relished the change but knew it was inevitable. They made plans to stay in touch and connected. They would speak to friends to relay messages and report on each other's conditions when personal contact was not possible. The morning came and the boys packed their things.

They only owned a suit of clothes for church and two sets of work clothing. They were wearing one of those on their backs. They had one pair of shoes and they were wearing them also. They went to the church and were met there by their new masters.

Daniel in the Service of Walter Eggleston

Walter Eggleston was an older man. He was quite rotund and his healthier years had passed him by. He seemed kind however and this made the boys worries ease a bit. He introduced himself to the boys and told them a bit about himself. Reverend Mather was impatient during this process. He wanted Daniel to be off. Mr. Eggleston had arrived in a wagon. Daniel mounted the buckboard with him. Joshua took his hand and bid him farewell. He told him he would see him often. Mather took note of this to address later. Joshua did not know who would take his charge but would soon find out. Another wagon was in the church lane as Daniel's carriage was leaving. They stopped as they passed each other and there were pleasantries exchanged before moving on.

Joshua in the Service of Sam Wickford

The wagon was not new by any means. It was well used but sturdy. The man at his reins was in much better shape than poor Mr. Eggleston. He jumped from the seat and landed firmly on both feet. He was a sight to see. He was very tall and well built. He had a scar on his cheek and was rather unkempt to be visiting Mather's church. He looked Joshua up and down and felt his upper arms and back. He looked at Mather and said "A fine lad! He will do just fine!"

Mather just smiled. Joshua was soon loaded onto the wagon and off they went. Joshua looked back to the Reverend Mather and caught a sly grin growing across his face at the thought of his victory in passing his responsibilities and expense off to these two men. He turned and hummed a hymn as he returned to his office. It was a happy day for him.

They rode in silence for a while. Then the man stopped the wagon and said. My name is Wickford. Sam Wickford. My father was Henry Wickford. He was a judge in the old country. I am telling you this because he knew your family and your parents. Shortly before your mother passed to her reward he succumbed to the same illness. He had some holdings at his death and I had decided long ago to leave England and all of its problems. I am not a religious person but I am a person of some means and have my own faith. I sold my father's holdings and came to America. I used the money to start this shipbuilding business. I once worked for a similar business in Liverpool. Your father owned it and gave me my chance!" With that he drove on to the dock area. Joshua was struck. He didn't know what to say. Sam Wickford's living quarters were very small. He lived on the docks with his business. He was not married nor did he have a family so he did not need a large house. A simple space walled off in his shed would suffice. It could be heated well enough in the winter. The wind off the bay kept it cool enough in the summer months. His room adjoined his office. The only other walled in space was a work area where the ships prints and plans were kept, developed and produced. It was a sort of operations and engineering office. Sam hopped off the wagon and motioned for Joshua to follow. He said "Tonight you will sleep in my quarters on a pad on the floor. I have ordered my men to build some walls for your own private space. I figure I owe that to your parents. You will start to work on the morrow. It is best to learn from the bottom up. Initially you will do the hard work until you have learned it to my satisfaction. I have agreed to teach the entire process so you will be required to learn and perform many tasks and work from many locations. We will get to know each other for a while and then develop a good plan for our goals. For now, you can stow your gear in there and get on the broom and mop to clean up the dock area. I will check back with you later!" Off he went shouting orders and meeting up with another man that seemed to be in charge of one of the crews.

Joshua put his things in Sam's room. He located the broom and started sweeping up at the nearest area that needed his attention. He did not feel so alone now and felt a connection to his lost life through Sam. He remembered Judge Wickford and what help he had been to his family. He was sorry to hear that such a good man was taken by the Black Death. In many ways he and Sam were alike. Sam had escaped England with his inheritance however and did so by his own choice. Joshua was doubly motivated now to return and set things right with the Ambrose family. In his way of thinking they were a family of thieves. No better than highwaymen and probably worse since they could use their wealth and influence to manipulate these frauds with no repercussion to them from the law. It was true that well placed money could blind the eyes, deafen the ears and stifle the tales of those that received it. For now he would turn to his duties and the development of his skills in shipbuilding. He did not know of Daniel's conditions but felt encouraged after meeting Mr. Eggleston.

Daniel's New Life

Daniel arrived at the Nanny house with Mr. Eggleston. The ladies there were very happy to see him. He asked Daniel to aid him in carrying several bundles into the house. Daniel noticed that there was an assortment of groceries and supplies in the bundles. The women set to work on them as soon as they were offloaded to process them. Meats had to be dried or salted for long term use. Some would be prepared and canned for later use. Some would be prepared for immediate use in stews or portions for consumption that day. Daniel looked around the house. He could not figure where in this conglomeration of women that he could stay. Mr. Eggleston visited for a few minutes and then addressed this situation. "Young Mr. Daniel, you will not be required to deal with this female bastion of femininity. Your quarters will be in the carriage house in the back. There we keep the wagons, carriages and horses. The upstairs holds your accommodations. You are very lucky to have your own quarters. With your studies and schedule you will need your privacy and your rest. There will be chores in the stable to offset your living costs. Your meals will be in the Nanny House or at my home. When you are away overnight your food and lodgings will be supplied. For today get settled into your quarters and work here in the stalls. Reverend Mather said that you worked in the stalls at his home so you know what needs to be done. I will come back and pick you up for dinner. Mrs. Eggleston will want to meet you. I know this is all new to you and that you miss your brother and family. Rest assured Mr. Daniel that I have made provisions with your brother's master so that you will be together when it is possible. Please keep this between you and me though. I do not know how the Reverend would take to his wishes and demands being taken too loosely." With that he bid his goodbyes and left. Daniel found his room. It was not bad. It was small but had a comfortable bed with a reading table and supplies. There was a small closet for his clothes and belongings. He flopped on his bed to give it a test. It felt very nice. It was better than the bed that he had shared with Joshua. His door could lock so once he was inside he could keep the outside world at bay. He was not sure where he would bath or use the privy. These things would come to him. He heard voices below and went down the stairs. The stables were chaotic. There were several boys around his age scurrying around and working, Daniel stood in the center and looked around. One of the bigger boys came to him and stood there in a challenge of sorts. He said "Who are you and why are you here?"

Daniel said "I am Daniel Henshaw and I will be staying here and working with Mr. Eggleston!"

The boy said "Daniel huh?! I heerd ye was comin'. My name

is Mark. These are the others that are here most times. This one is Johnny, this one is Benny and this'n is Isaiah. There are others but they don't stay here like us. I am the biggest and the longest stayed so I am in charge. If'n you want to challenge that a fair bareknuckle fight can be arranged to settle the matter!"

Daniel said "That will not be necessary. I will be staying here but I don't know how much I will actually be here. Mr. Eggleston is teaching me the textile business."

Mark said "Well! La di da! We have a very important person amongst us boys. We won't be treatin' you any different though. Don't expect it. We earn everything we git so you have to earn your share if you want anything from us!"

Daniel said "We will have to figure what my share would be to be fair. I could be gone for days or even weeks at a time Mr. Eggleston tells me. I don't know yet what arrangement I will be able to make here with you."

Mark said "We will work it out. You got your own room. Maybe I will just take that!"

Daniel said "That you would have to take up with Mr. Eggleston. He made the arrangements. Until then I will be keeping it!" Daniel made a mental note to keep his door locked when he could. He asked the boys "Are you all in the church?"

Mark and the others laughed. Mark spoke for the group. "We are in the stables. We like to think that we keep company with Jesus where he was rightly born. He weren't no church person like these "saints" here. The church long ago lost interest in us! We are considered the heathens of the masses. Good only for our backs and not our minds. Some day we will break away like when Moses led the Jews from Egypt. We were sold into our positions in various ways. Some of us were sold by our Puritan families. Some of us were sold straight off the ships to cover our parent's passage. They bought their freedom from our sale. We will work here now until we turn twenty-one and that is if we can get loose then. These masters like to find ways to extend our time by making up things for punishments. They aren't known for keeping their agreements. We are not saints but we surely are not sinners either. We stick together and so we have some sort of family even if it's only ourselves. You have to earn your way here! You got Mr. Eggleston and he is one of the good ones! You are very lucky!"

Daniel said "Then give me my shovel and let's work together to finish the chores" Daniel was determined to fit in. He had not expected to have boys of his own age around him. He had never been around this many of his own age in his life. It would help with the transition to this life and his loneliness at the loss of his brother.

Mather's Changing Role

Mather spent some of the money to get the deal for the boys. He had to keep up appearances at church and in the community. He was forced in this manner to include the boys in celebrations and holiday gatherings at the church and his home within reason. Eggleston and Wickford drove a hard bargain but in the end he had gotten from their negotiations what he had wanted. The boys were under someone else's care. They were the new master's burden now instead of it being his own. He had much of their money in reserve in case he would need it at some time in his life and he would get a steady income for their labors. In these unstable times and places you could be fine one day and destitute the next. He had skeletons in his closet that could be the cause of his fall from grace and possible ruin if they came to light. He would monitor the boys closely to see to it that they kept their secrets as he had instructed them to do.

Joshua's New Life

Joshua had a long day. It was stressful being away from his brother. Stress always caused the burning of one's energy thus a day's normal work could seem like much more. The work day started before dawn and early in the morning by candle light. A worker would need to be at his place with first light so none was wasted. There were no lights except oil lamps and fires. Joshua would have just liked to go to bed but his mind would not shut down. He had many thoughts of what he had seen that day and many questions about his new circumstance that he tried to answer over and over to his satisfaction. The answers were not coming to him. It was a complicated matter and more thinking was required to understand it. He thought it a happy coincidence that he had landed in the care of Mr. Wickford with ties to his family. It was an omen he felt. He went to bed but could not sleep yet. His surroundings were unfamiliar and he longed to know how Daniel was doing at his new place. He yearned to know how his first day went. He felt his responsibilities for him. He was afraid he would fail him under these new circumstances. He would wait for that information for a time when he could see him. The here and now would have to be his focus. There was much to learn and do to master his new work. He felt a kinship to his father in this work. He remembered how his father and uncles had discussed the ships and their design and building of them. It was a love of theirs and would now be his focus.

Joshua's Journal

He dressed in his night shirt and scooted up close to the fire in the fireplace. The flickering light was enough. He pulled out one of the empty journals and wrote his name on its first page. He lettered the starting date and the other information on the journal page that it requested. He began to write. He decided to start at the time of his father's death and briefly describe how they came to be in the colonies. He wrote about the trip and the kindness of the strangers who gave them a blanket to keep them warm. He wrote about all of the things that he knew and heard about Ambrose and Mather and their plot to steal their property. He wrote of the conditions in Boston and Dorchester. It took him several nights to catch the journal up to the present time. Having finally caught up, pending Daniels review, he began to journal as time permitted by candlelight.

Today was a day like many others since our landing. I have not seen Daniel since our separation. Mr. Wickford is in touch with his master. He tells me that he is well. I am not treated like many of those in servitude in my position. The aim is higher. I am at my beginning in learning this craft. There will be many things to learn and understand. Right now, it feels a bit overwhelming to me.

I worry about Daniel every day. He is younger and I am supposed to watch over him. Reverend Mather has made this impossible. I am of the opinion that this separation was not necessary but by design of the divine Mr. Mather. To what ends I do not know.

So far my days are filled with menial labor tasks. I am twelve years old now and rather big for my age. I am as tall as many a man on the docks. The work they do on the ships and out in the logging camps is very strenuous but I long to put my hands to it. The sooner I develop my usefulness the sooner I will be able to return to England and set things right with that thief Ambrose. He will pay a price for his betrayal to my parents, Daniel and I. I have not spoken of our past with anyone except Daniel. Reverend Mather is quite powerful here and he has pledged to us that disclosing the events leading to our presence here would have serious consequences to us. I have considered having this discussion with Mr. Wickford since he had connections to my proper family in our good times. I have to weigh the good against the bad of this issue to make the proper decision. For now, I will give much thought on the subject to find some conclusions.

Morning comes early dear journal so I must retire for my rest. Be assured I will visit you again by candle light on the morrow!

Daniel's Journal

Daniel had a busy day. There was a rhythm to each day now. It had been less than a week since the separation from his brother and his new living arrangement. Mr. Eggleston was a good man. In his time with him he watched his interactions with his family, friends and customers. He was fair and amiable and seemed to be well liked in the community. He was a religious man but not made of the same brittle cloth as the Reverend Mather. There was a light spirit in him that reminded you more of the wee people of Eire than the stoic Puritans. He was jolly. That was the word that would describe him. He was honest, hard-working, caring and a man of good standing with his own version of God. Daniel knew he would be treated fairly by this man. He recognized that he was being groomed for something here that the others working for Mr. Eggleston were not. He understood the scope of what he was to learn. Every aspect of the mills had to be taught and mastered. This process had not begun as of yet. He had only been here for six days. He was excited about the prospects and his patience was growing thin. He did not mind doing the work that he was currently assigned to do. He just did not see how it could teach him anything about the textile industry. Daniel had come to an understanding of sorts with his housemates. He worked when there were chores to finish when he was present. His room and board was paid for anyway so he needn't worry of it. The others were there earning their way through their labor to pay their way. Daniel wanted and needed to make friends so he did not mind the extra work. The boys had become friends in this short time even though he was considered a newcomer and had a better path than their own. Daniel had promised Joshua that he would keep his journal and he had not started his entries. He was feeling guilty about procrastinating on his agreement to his only true blooded relative. He would start his entries this night after the chores were finished in the carriage house and then he would turn in. Like Joshua he would write by candle light before turning in for the night to recap his day. He had a little catching up to do so he would include his first days into his initial entry. With the chores finished the boys trudged up the stairs to the rooms above. Daniel bade them good night and entered his room and locked the door. He could hear the others moving around and talking. They were playing some sort of game. Daniel could join them but he relished his time alone in his room. He did not get to spend much time there. He lit his candle and took down his journal. He set up the initial information on the first pages and sat to write in earnest.

I will begin writing my journal pages on this day. Six days have passed since being separated from my brother Joshua and sold into servitude by the Reverend Richard Mather who was an instrument in our abduction from our lands in England. This he did in partnership with Peter Ambrose our supposed steward and guardian. For the most part we were treated better by the Reverend Mather than we expected to be. We continued our schooling, were clothed, fed and provided decent shelter. We worked hard to earn our keep. This did not in any way offset our loss of property from the betrayal and fraud wrought upon us by these people. In England we had lost our parents, grandparents and now our property. It is a bitter pill to swallow.

Joshua is perpetually angry and pledges to return to England to claim what is ours. It is assumed by Joshua that I will go with him for that purpose. The political climate has changed since our crossing. Cromwell was in charge but now Charles II has been returned to the throne. The Stuart Kings are once again in control. I do not think it would go well to petition the King's court for the return of our lands. Father and Grandfather both fell fighting against the Royalists. There is a known relationship to how the court would rule when the petitioner fought for his enemies.

I am different than my brother. I guess you would say of a gentler and more forgiving spirit. I cannot set my life's path based on revenge and the pursuit of a probable lost cause. I will build my life in Dorchester or its surrounds if God is willing. I do not want to disappoint my brother in any way but it is his battle and to him will go the spoils. He is the eldest son and would inherit all he seeks to recover. I would live at his will if I so chose to follow his course.

Mr. Eggleston seems to be a good man and well liked. I believe I can trust him. It will not be easy of course. There will be much hard work and learning to be done. It is my desire to have my own textile operation or a high position in Mr. Eggleston's business for my future. To this end I will work and study hard so I will be able to provide for a family in the future.

This Puritan religion is another thing all together. I was born in the Church of England. It was strict in its Protestant beliefs. The people who surround Reverend Mather are like none I have seen. They seek to tear apart families and foment distrust between its family members and the church itself. It seeks unnatural control over all that crosses their paths. I will practice my own brand of Christianity. I will not waver. In the church of the Reverend Mather this is called non-conformity. They have banished people in the dead of winter, hung them in Boston Common and buried them alive for these same infractions. They practice the same persecution of others that led them to leave Britain when they themselves were the subject of the persecution. In fact, this is a more extreme form of persecution than I knew of in my old land. I do not understand it all yet but I believe that now I am out from under the Mather roof and everyday control that I will get a fairer picture of this land and lifestyle from my new-found friends in my house and Mr. Eggleston who seems not so impressed by the divine Reverend Mather.

I am getting along well with my new housemates. It is early but there is a developing bond amongst us. We are all of the same social and financial standing so we can relate to our circumstances. They are very curious as to my family history but I have withheld this information under threat from Reverend Mather. I would like to share our story with my new friends. Maybe that will come at a later time. I know I could discuss it with Mr. Eggleston and that he would swear to secrecy.

Mr. Eggleston reports to me that Joshua is doing well at his new housing and trade. He hopes to arrange a meeting soon for us to spend some time together. He has spoken of a trip to the country to see a sheep herd. Much of our wool comes from these small operations and in trade with the Spanish that brings their wool to Boston market. The Spanish wool is far superior for fine cloth over the colonial supply I am told. I must turn in and get my rest. These days spend much energy and staying rested and in good health is imperative. I will be a devoted journal writer but will not make daily entries. It will come to me when the opportunity arises.

The Eyes of the King Turn to the Colonies

The King had now settled the disputes in England. It was time to turn his attention to the colonies. The colonies had turned to trade with other countries. Most notably they welcomed the Dutch, French and Spanish traders. England now focused on the lost profits from this trade with their natural enemies of the period. In 1651 under Cromwell the first of what was called the Navigation Acts were enacted. Originally, they stated that any goods bound to or from England or its colonies were to be transported solely on English ships or the ships of the country of the originating shipment. This would be the first legislation that caused friction between New England and the King. Although it angered the colonists for the most part, they ignored the acts. In response to the act an active black market and smuggling operations began in the Caribbean and up and down the Atlantic coast. It impacted Daniel's livelihood adversely. There were not enough sheep herds of quality wool in the colonies to supply their textile needs. They needed the Spaniard's wool and in its absence the cotton grown in the southern colonies. Many of these colonies south of Virginia were under control of the French and Spanish. The Dutch presence was in New Amsterdam or modern-day New York. The Caribbean Islands were also under their control. The textile industry preferred the wool of the Spaniard's sheep which was of a much higher quality than that raised in New England. The Navigation Acts were constantly amended to strengthen England's trading position. A decade into the Navigation Acts the law changed to demand that all tobacco, sugar, cotton, wool, dyes, etc. were to be shipped only to England. Products produced in England were the only exception. Those products from the colonies were exempt from the dictate. This was only because the import of those products would compete against and hurt the English producers. The colonies would have suffered under these laws except for the black market. These laws did not just target foreign countries. It targeted trade between the colonies themselves. The textile industry would have failed without its Spanish wool and southern cotton and indigo. As it was it would still flourish while flaunting open disdain for the laws. Seventy five percent of the textile industry was located in New York proper under Dutch control. The Dutch had settled the area in 1624 under charter from the Dutch West Indies Company. Most of the settlers went up river to settle in modern day Albany. Only eight settlers stayed on Long Island. Two years later they were joined by forty five more settlers and Fort Amsterdam was built to protect them from the Native Americans. They continued to grow to nearly one thousand settlers at the Long Island settlement. Peter Stuyvesant, as Governor, named the settlement New Amsterdam. In September of 1664 the Dutch were routed from their fort by the English. The Dutch had run into difficulties at home and the events in New Amsterdam mirrored the Dutch struggles in Europe. It was a bloodless fight. The fort was renamed Fort James after King James. The settlement was renamed New York for the Duke of York. The Dutch reclaimed the area for a short time in 1673 and 1674 and then abandoned their colonization in New England forever. They continued to colonize in the Caribbean however. The textile industry was under control of the English now. The textile merchants still engaged the black market for their raw materials. They would continue to do so disregarding the Navigation Acts almost completely. The habits of the colonial merchants had been established for several decades while England largely ignored their existence while they fought with France and Spain. Once the trade paths and business practices were established change would be hard to achieve even if the laws had changed the way they did business and who they traded with had not.

Joshua's Future and the Navigation Acts

Joshua's pursuits had found a bright future with the Navigation Laws. With shipping restricted to using only English or colonial ships to transport goods the demand for seaworthy ships had greatly increased and the business continued to grow and expand. Joshua had been introduced to Mr. Wickford at a very opportune time in this market. His learning curve would increase at a highly escalated rate than first thought. Mr. Wickford would need highly trained men to oversee his expanded operations. He would need men who he could trust. Greed was still a sin that was not easily overcome. Even in the Puritan colonies it was a sin much practiced by even those at the highest levels of church and society. Those that could be trusted in his business or personal life were few. Once he was prosperous, he would become the target of fraud or they would plot to remove him from his enterprise all together. The riches that went with these successes were greatly coveted by these pseudo religious vermin. Joshua was still young. Proving himself to Mr. Wickford each day became his mission. It did not hurt his position that Sam felt an alliance and fatherly intent towards both boys.

Joshua's Journal
24th, November 1654

Things are quite busy with the ships. The English passed new laws that bind the colonists to ship their merchandise to and from England only. They must use only English or Colonial flagged ships. I am told that this is to stop the competition of the colonial goods going to the Dutch, French and Spanish. The boon to the shipbuilding industry will be tempered somewhat by the continuance of the Black Market trade in goods with these same countries and colonies. We will still feel an increase in business. More and more ships are needed constantly. This was true even before these dastardly and limiting acts by the King.

Daniel tells me that the import on wool and cotton from the south is crucial to the textile industry could be in jeopardy. They get much of the wool from the Spanish and at a higher quality then what is available in the colony. Truth is the colony is not in a position to provide enough wool to keep the industry supplied. The ships and trade with those holding these goods is important. They get much of their cotton and indigo from the Virginia colony and it too is shipped to Massachusetts on the foreign flagged ships. It is wool that drives the industry today. Cotton is not used much. These laws restrict the trade between the colonies themselves. With this trade the colonists can see a profit and grow their wealth. Without it the colonies struggle to survive. The King and the English companies are then greatly enriched at the expense of those doing the hard work and taking the risks here. There seems to be an element of unfairness to these laws.

Mr. Wickford insists that I call him Sam in private now. Our friendship and bond continues to grow. It has grown so fast that it is dizzying. I still don't know who to trust after all we have seen and experienced. If anyone in my acquaintances can be trusted it would be Sam. I will be loyal to his mission and mine.

I have had to learn about another new thing here. The colonies have started to mint their own silver coins. There were many different types of coins being passed here including British currency along with Spanish, French and Dutch coinage. To a lesser extent even German and eastern European issues. Indian Wampum is used for exchange of goods and services with those of that persuasion. To add to the confusion were various private attempts at a means of exchange. There were accepted values of course but these values are argued and changed sometimes from transaction to transaction. I have few coins of my own but the loss of value of any coin could have the most impact on the poorer of us. Some transactions are bartered to avoid this miasma of values if the value of the goods being traded can be determined. This is easier for our industry because the prices stay fairly stable for our needs. It is the personal needs of imported goods that create the fluctuations. Sam wants me to learn and keep track of these coins because in anything I do I will need this knowledge.

The first coins were stamped in 1652. The coinage was made in the denominations of three pence, sixpence, and shilling. Our friend John Hull minted the first coins at a fee of one coin for each twenty coins made. They were simple coins and they were counterfeited easily by others. This was not anticipated in this community with its strict base in the Puritan religion. It was not a surprise to Daniel or me with our unique knowledge of the leadership here. I continue to learn my craft and I rather enjoy it. I do not see Daniel as often as I like but Sam and Mr. Eggleston are good about giving us updates on each of our well-beings and progress. Sam tells me that I am to go to the logging camp for a period soon. In this way I will understand the birth of the shipbuilding processes and the elements of trees and lumber that render them ideal material for our purposes. Not all varieties, sizes or lengths will work. I will be living in the logging camp for that period. Sometime after that I will work in the saw mill and learn those skills. For now, I will try to spend my time here learning and getting in as much time as I can with Daniel before my long absence.

New England Silver Coinage

Undated (1652) New England
(NE) Silver Shilling

1652 Willow Tree
Shilling

1652 Willow Tree
Shilling

1662 Oak Tree
Twopence

1658 Oak Tree
Threepence

1652 Oak Tree
Sixpence

1652 Oak Tree Shilling

1652 Pine Tree Shilling,
Large Planchet

1652 Pine Tree Sixpence

1652 Pine Tree Shilling,
Small Planchet

1652 Pine Tree
Threepence

The Continuing Fraudulent Dealings with the Indians

The Indian issue was in an unsteady period of relative peace. Sometimes the Indians would attack or steal from the colonists and sometimes the colonists would attack or steal from the Indians. They had opposing views on the ownership of land and how it was to be treated. The Indians believed that land was a gift from the gods. It was to be used communally as it had been used in the Indian way for generations. Their beliefs dictated that land was to be shared and every living thing was sacred. The colonists came from a much different system where the ownership and use of land was a symbol of wealth and security. They wished exclusive use of the land they cleared. They wished to hold a deed showing that the land was privately owned and controlled without infringement from the Indians or other colonists. They were symptoms of the colonial disease. The unnatural desires for greed, power and total control over others defined this disease. This was especially true if the others were different from themselves such as Indians, Africans, Irish, those of other religions and the poor.

With these two conflicting philosophies there was trouble on the horizon. The colonists passed their laws beginning with the Mayflower Compact. These extended English law and land rights with their charters. Then later they passed laws in the colonial legislation. They were so full of themselves that they never considered that those not associated with the colony would choose not to follow their laws. They did not consider that those there before them had made the laws of the land that they should have acclimated to and not force a new set onto the rightful inhabitants to fit their own mold. They did not know if they had the right to make laws for others outside of their control yet make them they did. These laws included that the Native Americans, the French, Dutch and Spanish settlers and others who came to New England or the other colonies were subject to their directives, demands and penalties. It could be argued that their laws could only govern those that attached themselves to the colony. The Puritan movement as limited as a group would find these laws desirable. After all they were the only ones that could write and pass the laws with no input from those outside of the community. The colonial governments took advantage of the Indian's trusting nature and lack of English education. They drew up many treaties and deeds and had the Indians sign them. In exchange they would pay the Indians worthless items or supplies. The Indians used a system of money called Wampum.

The foreign coins or currency meant nothing to them. They understood things of substance and things that provided to them the basic necessities of food, clothing and shelter. Even when the Indians agreed to these treaties their own understanding was that the land was to still be shared by all. The colonists made no effort to dispel this understanding before the signing. It only became known after the signings and much to the Indians dismay and disgust. They felt cheated and defrauded. By todays contractual standards this was indeed true. British Common law of this time would have found that these agreements and treaties did not meet all elements of a valid contract. Since the Indians were considered heathens by this pious group the standards were lowered to the colonists benefit. In this atmosphere of disrespect, fraud and mistreatment it is not surprising that the Indians were angry. The Indians distrust of the colonists grew quickly.

The colonists continued to infringe on the Indian lands. It was the dream of many of the settlers to stake out their own land and own it. This was not possible in England for most people. The earliest settlers came from the poor. As they crossed the ocean to religious freedom they carried with them their dreams of being landowners and choosing to live on their own. It gave them the powerful motivation to make the dangerous journey. Those that were indentured would seek land when their terms expired. In some cases, land was a part of the contract for completing the period of servitude. From the beginning those unencumbered with servitude in the colonies sought land. They could not buy it with money but they could stake it out in the wilderness or earn it through servitude. Some took over properties that once belonged to the tribes. These lands were once owned by the bands wiped out by disease or wars. For whatever the reason these lands stood empty and deserted. They were already cleared and tilled. There were dwellings there that could be used until shelters were erected if they were not in usable condition when taken with the land. The Indians found this disrespectful to their deceased and a misuse of the land according to their beliefs. As time progressed and the indentured servants gained their freedom they would set out into the countryside and begin clearing areas to farm. Most of the colonists had agrarian backgrounds. When they found their freedom, they wanted to do what they knew best. Clearing and tilling the land was hard work. Planting the seeds and keeping them healthy was even more work. Any number of things could affect the crops. Too much rain, too little rain, crop disease, pests, animals, storms or high winds, theft, attacks, war or the death of the male farmworker were just a few of the issues. It could ruin all of the hard work in minutes. The same issues would face the Indians. When hunger or starvation faces any man he will take drastic measures. They are driven to find food for survival. They could hunt and did. There was concern from both sides however that with the constant influx of colonists the supplies of wildlife would dwindle and would not be able to feed the ever-increasing amount of mouths that hungered for survival. When things get drastic the stealing and pilfering begins. As it escalates the violence follows. The Indians had shown that they would share what they had with the colonists and teach them their time-tested ways to obtain food and survive. They could feel the threat of the overcrowding and they knew it would only get worse as more and more ships landed in Boston Harbor. As the thefts increased so did the tempers and frustrations. It would inevitably escalate into murder and killing. Each side would justify their own positions for their actions as humans tend to do. No one was right and no one was wrong. No one would take responsibility for their own actions. To be clear though; it was the colonists who were the first thieves in this new land. They came to the colonies with very little in the way of possessions and the quickest way to acquire them was by theft or simply acquiring the abandoned properties and items of the deceased Indians.

Joshua's New Assignment

Joshua would be safe while in the logging camp. The dangerous times would come when they went into the forest to cut the trees. They would be exposed for long periods of time. There would be no one to stand guard as every man would be engaged in bringing down and trimming the trees for transporting to the saw mill. Joshua knew that Daniel would be equally exposed when he was working with the sheep herds and the shearing barns. Daniel's exposure could potentially be a longer one because they herded the sheep day and night to keep predators away. This had not changed in centuries. There were shepherds in biblical times doing the exact same work. Daniel found this comforting. Daniel would not work there forever but most likely six months to a year so he would know all there was to know about this part of the textile industry. He would learn about the breeding, rearing, shearing and care of the lambs and sheep. He would know how to butcher and cook the animals in this setting. Joshua knew he would learn his lessons well but prayed that there would be no attacks or abductions from the Indians.

Joshua would learn the harvesting of proper trees, the types of wood and grains in the wood. He would learn the hard woods and the softer woods and their uses. The loggers would harvest trees not only for ships but for the furniture makers and home builders, dock builders and others needing wood products. The time for the next shift in their lives and experience was near. They were learning some of their lessons from the others they worked with now. There was nothing like hands on experience to learn these skills and knowledge. That is the way it would be for the boys.

Daniel's Journal
December 10, 1654

I will continue to work in Boston until the spring I am told. It would not be a good time for learning in the dead of the New England winter on the sheep herd. I am relieved to wait until spring. Winters here can be very harsh and dangerous. With winter comes a scarcity of food and this always causes trouble. There are many dangers in this place. It is just a fact of life. I have lost my fear of it. If you focus on all of the things that could bring fear into your life there would be no room for joy, love, brotherhood or God. I have chosen not to dwell on it and focus on the future. If some unfortunate thing should happen then I am committed to address it as it happens and to whatever means it takes to survive. If I fail to survive, I will join my loved ones with God.

There was a story came into town this day that a settler was attacked on his homestead. The man was killed and the woman and children were carried off by the Indians. We have not heard what tribe or band was involved but there is death, abduction and pain to the families who lost loved ones on both sides nonetheless. These attacks have occurred on a continual basis and this seems to be increasing as more and more souls arrive from England and move into the forests to clear their land and establish their homestead. The Indians most likely see the attacks as a deterrent to the infringements on their lands or to just compete for the ever dwindling supply of food available.

I have encountered Indians on several occasions. I personally found them to be a peaceful and hard-working race unless provoked. I cannot say what starts these conflicts or what drives men to want to harm each other. It was the same in England. I will not ever forget the pain my family felt by the loss of my father and Grandfather for a senseless war. I did not know why then either. I was born shortly after their death. The pain and loss survived my birth and throughout my time in England. I saw the impact on my mother and grandmother and it was profound. The times in England seem to fade into the mist the longer that I am here. In my mind England holds nothing but bad memories for my lifetime there. Although a few good memories surface from time to time to enlighten my life with those I loved there. I hope that as things unfold here some good memories and things can happen. Joshua is of a different mind and I fear that revenge is the utmost in his heart. He will learn a skill here and he could practice his trade on either side of the crossing. I do not want him to leave me but I do not think his soul can rest until he makes right the wrong that has been done to our family at the hands of Ambrose. In this I wish him the best if this is his choice but in my heart I hope he can put it all to rest and find peace here.

Mather's Conundrum

Richard Mather did not miss the boys. What he missed was the free labor, the funds being sent to him and the control that he had over them. He constantly worried that he would be exposed by them for his part in their abduction. His sons were being educated at Harvard before their planned return to the pulpits of England. His youngest would graduate in two years. None of his sons now lived at his home. Three of them had returned to England and Increase was a resident of the Halls of Harvard. Mather's wife, Katherine Hoult, was showing signs of failing health. For the most part Mather would be alone in his house with his wife during this period. He had not heard back from England so his hopes of further payment from the Ambrose house had been dashed. He still held substantial amounts that were legally the property of Joshua and Daniel. He continued to hold the sums in escrow for them. He struggled daily with this money. It was a temptation to him. For now, he would simply put it away and try to forget it. He kept in touch with Wickford and Eggleston. He wanted to know the boys progress but he was also wanted to know if they had entrusted either of these men with the true story of their life and their crossing to New England.

He was sure if this had happened that it would get back to him in short order.

Market Day and Victoria Summers

Market days were a big part of colonial society. Everyone waited for market day. It was a day of shopping, meeting friends and catching up on the gossip of Boston and its outlying areas. Daniel and his friends looked forward to it. This was one of the best days for boys their age. There were goods to be had if they had any coin in their pockets. There were friends that they could only see during market day. There were girls of their age that came out to shop with their families or work the family stall for the day. The booths would sell their families wares. It was an important source of income and commodity for these families. As the boys reached their teen and pre-teen years their interests in girls would reach an ever increasing crescendo. Daniel knew that he would be likely to find his brother on those days also. The boys cleaned up and put on their better clothes. They walked the three miles from Dorchester to Boston to spend the day. Mr. Eggleston was glad to let Daniel have this day. He was a good student and worker and earned this time to spread his wings like an eagle. It was to him an immense feeling of freedom. Mr. Eggleston knew that it would instill to Daniel that he had gained his trust from him. Sam Wickford had made the agreement with him to release Joshua from his duties on these days so the boys could interact and catch up. With their upcoming assignments they would be apart for many months and not be able to see each other. It was important for them to stay close to each other and healthy for them.

Daniel and the boys arrived in town around nine in the morning. The wagons were still coming into town with their wares. In the town market was a huge building with permanent stalls laid out in them. The original inhabitants of these stalls would return to them on each market day. Newcomers had to set their market stalls outside and were thus susceptible to inclement weather and the hot sun. It was not likely that a stall inside would come to vacancy. They passed through families like an inheritance. If one did come open, they were quickly taken by others. In most cases one of the neighboring stalls would take it over and expand their own space before any new vendors could take control of it. These stalls were a statement of high standing in the business world of the colonies. These stalls by location, size and reputation established a sort of rating system of the businesses and vendors in the colony. The old families, like in church and society, held the most prestigious stalls in the market and they would never be relinquished to others. They traveled from family member to family member. In many instances shoppers would buy a lesser quality product from these old stalls for more money instead of buying a higher quality product from a new stall or one that was outside of the building. This was an act to show respect and satisfy the social order that was so important to the Puritans in the colony. The boys could care less. They rarely had any coin to purchase things anyway. They were looked on as a nuisance by the stall keepers and they kept watchful eyes on their merchandise when the boys were near. The stalls lost more of their merchandise to the colony's own leadership who felt it was their entitlement to help themselves to their wares whenever they passed them by or saw fit to take it. This was rarely accompanied by coin.

The boys wondered around the market taking in all of the sights and sounds. They scanned the crowd for familiar faces and when one would appear they would rush to their location for an excited greeting. Some of these acquaintances would join them on their journey while others were bound to work at their families stall selling their wares. Usually they were released from their work for a time to interact with their friends and see the sights. There were vendors who knew the boys' plight and would secretly set some food aside for them if they knew where to find it. There would always be some nonconforming fruit or vegetables that could not be sold or had to sell a a greatly reduced price. This would diminish the amounts of conforming product that they would sell if the buyers would settle for the flawed products at reduced price. It was good business to give these fruits and vegetables to those in need. The boys were showing Daniel where these vendor's stalls were located and what he needed to know to get fed. Some of them required a few chores and some just saw it as a Christian mission to feed the poor. The boys greatly appreciated it no matter what the requirements were for it. They had made the first pass through the market and had snagged some fruit from one of their regular friends. They did not take more than they were allowed but savored each bite. As they came to the back corner of the market Daniel was stopped in his tracks. At this isolated booth was the most beautiful girl he had ever seen. He had never really noticed girls before but for some reason this one stood out from the rest. He didn't know what to do next so he did a cartwheel and laughed loudly to draw her attention. She shyly smiled and turned her head. Daniel tried again to impress her. The other boys had now noticed his behavior and quickly focused on what was causing it. They teased him and slapped him on the back. The girl was now paying attention. She did not like them teasing him and rather liked the show of attention. She did not wish it to be interrupted by this boorish behavior. She walked into the group and straight up to Daniel. She smiled at him and said "My name is Victoria, Victoria Summers! At lunch time I get some time to go to market. I would appreciate it if I had an escort so I would not be accosted by ruffians or boorish young men who would turn on a friend!" Daniel was shaken. He had not expected to have such success at his first meeting. He especially was shocked that this girl in particular would take an interest in him. He had felt something when he had first laid eyes on her but thought it silly. Now he was not sure. He definitely wanted to follow the course that was unfolding so he quickly agreed to the escort. Daniel stammered "Sure, I will be your escort and see to your safety!"

Mark broke in and said "If it is safety you want then it should be me escortin' ya around. I am the biggest and strongest and could do a better job than this runt!"

The other boys laughed. Victoria said "I prefer one that is intelligent and a gentleman and from what I have witnessed you are neither. I will stay with my original choice!" The boys laughed even harder. Mark stood there eye to eye. He was angry but knew he had been bested. He said "Well then, have a fine time. We will be off! I will speak to you later Daniel! This isn't over!"

Victoria turned after they left and said "I hope I didn't cause trouble with your friends!"

Daniel said "Mark is Mark. He has to act that way for the others. We will be fine. I would have escorted you no matter!" I will come back at lunchtime for you!"

She said "You will have to meet my father before he will let you escort me so be on your best behavior!"

Daniel was nervous about this but said "Yes Ma'am! I will be on my best behavior!"

Daniel kept his word that day and escorted Victoria Summers through the market. He was introduced to her father and after a lengthy inquisition was thought to be fit to be in Victoria's company. They spent a pleasant time together and there seemed to be a friendship developing and maybe more. As they walked, they carried on a very natural conversation and became better acquainted. Daniel could not answer her questions about his past. She seemed put-off by it but they continued to talk and stroll through the market. They were followed by Mark and Daniel's friends. He said "It appears that we are quite of interest to my friends still. They have followed us since we left your father's stall."

Victoria said "Yes, I noticed that this Mark person is not good at listening and does not seem the kind to give up!"

Daniel replied "Aye, that is the case in most things he sets his mind to since I have known him!"

Victoria glanced over her shoulder to Mark occasionally. Daniel spoke again" In the spring I will have to go out to the sheep herds to learn about herding, wools, shearing and how to prepare the wool for market or the loom. I will be gone for six months to a year then. After that I will be going to the textile mills to learn weaving, dying and putting wool and cotton into their usable forms. I will be there about the same amount of time! I will then return to Dorchester and work with Mr. Eggleston in his business as his apprentice!"

Victoria said "You are under the oversight of Reverend Mather I have heard. I know of this man. I hear my father and others speaking of him. He has sold you into servitude if I believe what I hear!"

Daniel said "That is true! Mr. Eggleston and his wife are quite different than most. I have been accepted into their life and business. It was a matter of expediency for Mather to put his responsibilities on another. He does not have to fund my apprenticeship if I am a servant. It isn't a normal type of servitude however. I am truly treated as an apprentice and this will enhance my future possibilities to support myself and a family. I will have to study and work hard to achieve my goals though!"

Victoria studied him for a while. She said "You will be gone then for a long period with your training?"

Daniel replied "I will at that! I will write to you if that is agreeable?"

Victoria paused and thought. She said "I will write back to you when the time comes." They enjoyed the rest of their time together and Daniel walked her back to her father's stall at the end of the day. Her father greeted him and shook his hand. He said "Pleased to meet you Daniel. You seem to be a fine boy!"

Victoria broke in and said "He is going to be away father! To a sheep herd and then to a textile mill soon. He works for Mr. Eggleston!"

Mr. Summers said "Eggleston! He is a good man. You will do well under his tutelage. I have to finish my packing so we can get back home before dark. Again it is nice to meet a good boy such as yourself!"

Daniel was a bit embarrassed. He replied "Nice meeting you too Mr. Summers! I will be seeing you again!" With that he was off to rejoin his group. They were not far away so they were quick to find. They laughed and teased but it was all in fun. There was still some time to wander in the market and in short order he found Joshua. He was smiling from ear to ear! He said "I saw you earlier but did not want to interrupt your courtship!"

Daniel reddened and said "It is a bit early to call it a courtship Joshua. I have just met the girl and will be going away soon for a long period. It is not the best of situations when you first meet a girl!"

Joshua said "It isn't a good situation Daniel! If she is the one for you she will not mind the wait nor linger away from your affections. You will be a better man when you return and be able to support yourself at least. "

Daniel could only agree! Joshua continued "I will be leaving on first thaw to the lumber camp. Mr. Wickford said that the camp and your sheep herd are located about ten miles apart. There is a chance we can see each other on our time away from work. It will be rare. We will need to keep our journals and write post to each other when we can. I will miss you brother!"

Daniel said "I will miss you too! We will be back to Dorchester in time though and we will see each other often."

Daniel continued to see Victoria. It was the end of the year 1656. He was twelve years old now but looked much older. The hard work and the trials of his young life had the effect of aging him beyond his years. Victoria was impressed with his growth. She was a year older than he and girls usually matured more quickly than boys at this age. She was pleased that he was tall for his age and very muscular. They spent their time together when they could. This was mostly on market days but a few other occasions would give them some time. At other times they simply did not connect when opportunities arose. The winter was progressing quickly and the time for Joshua and Daniel to start their new assignments was not far off.

Daniel and the Ball Family

Mr. Eggleston did not want to waste time in Daniel's training regimen. During this winter he came to an agreement with the Ball family to have Daniel work with them. The family spun wool into yarn, wove cloth and dyed both at their home. The Balls had a daughter named Mary. (In some records the families name is listed as Bull) Mary was eight years older than Daniel. She did most of the work on the wool as her mother was older and her health in decline. Daniel worked with Mr. Ball in the first few weeks learning the dying processes and the handling of the fleeces to prepare them for spinning. This job was more physical than complicated so after he learned the necessary things he was assigned to work with Mary learning to spin the yarn and weave the cloth. This had to be completed before the dying process. The family would double their production with Daniel at work and the arrangement had its benefits for Daniel and the Ball family.

Mary was to be wed to Robert Pond in the spring. She liked Daniel and was impressed by his hard work and intelligence. As they worked together they developed a good friendship. Mary was twenty years old and Daniel was twelve. Mary found that she felt uneasy talking about her marriage to Daniel. She could not understand why. Daniel was still seeing Victoria. He felt that something was amiss. He would miss her at times when she was in town. She was nowhere to be found. Market days were different though and he would go into town and escort her on the free time her father would give her. The time was drawing near for both Joshua and Daniel to leave to their new temporary homes. Mr. Eggleston and Sam Wickford let the boys spend a lot of time together when they could free them from their duties. They knew that once this phase of their training began, they would have few opportunities to be together for the next several years.

Daniel Suffers a Betrayal

The time passed quickly. The weekend before they were to leave for the wilderness Mr. Eggleston asked Daniel to meet with him to go over their plans. He wanted to give him all the information he would need at the sheep herd and mill. Because of the meeting he told the others to go to market without him. Daniel would catch a ride with the Egglestons on their carriage as they went to market themselves. As the carriage arrived in town he jumped off at the end of the market where Victoria's dad had his stall. It was near lunchtime and he could escort her for their last time for a while around the market. As he came around the corner into the area of the market where her father's stall was located he was stopped in his tracks. He backed up behind a bush and watched as Mark was talking to Victoria. From their interaction it was apparent that this was not their first meeting nor was Victoria at all appalled at Mark's behavior as she had let on during their first meeting. He waited for Mark to leave. He was dismayed when Victoria took off her apron and left with Mark. To make matters worse they were holding hands. Daniel was hurt and betrayed. He had not anticipated this behavior and certainly not from Mark. Now he wondered why he could not have seen it. Mark was Mark and he would get what he wanted anyway he could. It did not matter to him who was hurt in the process. There was little Daniel could do about it with his long absence looming. He turned and left them to their own. He was processing things in his head when he ran headlong into Mary Ball. She was surprised to see him but happy. She said "I didn't think I would get to see you before you left to say goodbye and good luck. Now I will get to do both!"

Daniel said "Thank you Mary." She could tell something was not right with Daniel. She said "Aren't we a sad person! Is there something wrong?"

Daniel did not want to talk about it. He felt betrayed and upset. It was not bad enough that Victoria had found another but for it to be his friend made it worse." He said "Girl trouble. My best friend stole my girl!"

She said "That is terrible behavior on his part. Who is this girl I will have a chat with her!"

Daniel said "It will come to nothing if you did. I have suspected something out of place for a while now. With my upcoming trip and long absence I am afraid it is a lost cause."

Mary said "I am sorry Daniel. You keep your head up. There are many girls who would love to have a beau like you! Be careful on your trip and come back to see me when you return. I am sorry you will not be able to join us at the wedding. There will be lots of good food and fun!"

This made Daniel even sadder. Mary would be married while he was away. Victoria had been seeing his best friend and both had lied to him about it. He was hurt and felt betrayed by the most important people in his new life. He was used to betrayal. That is what landed him in this place. He decided that he should find Joshua and spend the day with him. Joshua was due to leave for the wilderness in three days. Daniel would leave in one week. They would see very little of each other until their return to Boston in about two years. Daniel thought with what had just happened the time away would be to his advantage. He found Joshua near the fish mongers on the far side of the market. He loved looking at the fish to see all of the varieties. The fishing industry here was the best they had ever seen. The waters were used very little before the colonists arrived and they were teaming with all types of bounty. Joshua knew immediately that

Daniel was upset. He walked with him to a quiet spot and they sat under a big welcoming tree. Daniel explained his despair and Joshua did not like what he heard. Joshua said "Where is this Mark! I will take care of this!"

Daniel said "It is nothing for you to involve yourself with now. We all have free will and she chose Mark. I will be away and it is likely that any future with Victoria would not have survived the distance. Mark will be right here. "

Joshua thought a while and said "There will be many more brother and probably better opportunities. I know Victoria's family and they are good people. She is known to be like a moor hen. They like to be free and they like to move around in the flock. It will be no loss for you. You will be working hard and focusing on learning your craft and developing your skills. When you return you will be fourteen and much closer to being a man. Being a man with a trade will open many possibilities for love and marriage. Be patient my brother. You will see!" They walked more and spent as much time as they could together until they were forced to say their goodnights. They hated to part this time because the upcoming changes would make times like today rare in their lives.

Joshua's Contemplations

Joshua thought as he walked back to his quarters. He had priorities in his life. At the top of his priorities was the return to England to deal with the Ambrose family. He wanted a family and children but he could not believe that his goals would be fair to them. Families of this time were large. It was not uncommon to see six to ten children or more in a family. Joshua would have to think on it some more also. He too would have lots of time at the logging camp to put his mind to pressing issues. He would put off any potential matches until he could clarify the subject in his own thoughts.

Journal Entry of Joshua Henshaw
15 March, 1656

I have spent this day with Daniel. I will leave in three days for the logging camp in the wilderness. It is a challenge but I am strong and in good health and up to it. I will have much to learn about living in the forests. I will face the elements, wild animals, both hostile and friendly bands of Indians and the dangers of the job. There are dangers of falling trees or shifting loads. There are dangers from the sharp axes and saws. I will learn to use these things properly so I will be safe.

Daniel was sad today over Victoria. He had seen her holding hands with his friend at the market. I think he had longings for her but they will pass. He will be gone a substantial amount of time. When he returns, he will be older and much more able to offer a woman a good life. He is bright and handsome. Any woman would be lucky to have him. He feels betrayal once again.

Sam Wickford has promised that they will arrange time for Daniel to come visit the camp or for me to go to him. It will be challenging since we have never spent this much time apart in our lives. We will become accustomed to this state. It will be easier as we get older. On our return I will be sixteen and Daniel will be fourteen. I will have five years left on my agreement then. This truly is not an issue as Sam is more of a friend to me than master. He will help me along I know. Daniel has the same type of franchise from Mr. Eggleston. We have been very lucky in our agreement. I will be traveling soon and getting settled in at the camp. It will cause a delay in my entries. I promise to make up for the missed time when I can

The next few days passed quickly. It went too quickly by the boys reckoning. They were eager to face their next challenges but not so eager to disturb their daily routine. As with all new things there was fear, excitement, dread and wonder. They knew their continued education was necessary and would accept it for its worth. On the third day Mr. Eggleston took Daniel by carriage to the shipyards. They joined Joshua and Sam at the "Bunch of Grapes" for a delicious lunch and to say their goodbyes. After lunch the boys were given a few minutes alone. With that Joshua was on board his wagon and they quickly pulled out of town to his newest destination in the new world. Daniel already missed him. It would be hard for a time but once his day came he would be too busy to worry about it. They would be together again in two years God willing.

Joshua's Disclosure to Sam

Joshua bumped along beside Sam on the buckboard. His belongings were packed in the rear along with his journals. Sam had purchased some additional journals for him just in the case he would fill them with his writing. It was likely that he would fill them considering the length of his absence. They talked about many things on the journey. Sam broached the subject of his time in England and the talk came to his parents and grandparents. Sam was not totally uneducated on their circumstance to Joshua's surprise. He was young when his father's graduation party occurred but he was in attendance. His father presided over the issues and brought what could have been a bad ending to a just and fair conclusion. He knew of Ann Ambrose, James and Peter. Joshua thought that he himself must have been an idiot to think that Sam would not know what passed through the gossip circles of this time. He was present as the murder of Thomas Henshaw was investigated and discussed between his father and the sheriff. He knew of the type of man that Peter Ambrose had become. The only thing he was truly foggy about was how Richard Mather came to be their guardian. Sam rode a ways in silence to give the impact of what he had disclosed to Joshua time to be absorbed and understood. He then asked the question "What brings you into the custody of the Reverend Mather? I was not aware he was a relation."

Joshua stammered a while and then answered "The Reverend Mather was in collusion with Peter Ambrose. Once my grandmother and then my mother passed he wasted no time. He contacted Mather and the plan was set in motion. He told our neighbors that he was sending us to school in London. Instead he kept us locked in our own rooms. On the night we were spirited from our homes. We were heavily drugged for days. We woke up on board the ship and could only watch England grow smaller as we had already set sail. We could see my father's holdings on the dock. They were already reflagged and renamed with the Ambrose "A" predominantly displayed. I must ask that you keep this our secret. The Reverend Mather has stated to us on many occasions that there would be serious repercussions if our story was shared with anyone here."

Sam said "He must not be a bright man. He is aware of my childhood and my heritage. It should have been clear to even this clod that the story would not have passed me by. I will keep your secret but I will make some inquiries back to my friends in Liverpool to follow up from there. I have heard that Peter Ambrose died just a year or two after your arrival. He left a will. It would be interesting reading I would say. It would at least detail the passage of the properties held in the estate he so blatantly stole from you." Joshua felt strange. He felt a release of these pent-up emotions. He felt like some demon inside of him had been pulled out of him and dispatched to the fiery place. Sam could sense the change. He said "Joshua, if you need to talk to someone about this my ear is always open to you. It was providence that put us together and we will discuss and plan your response when the time is right. One thing for sure is that the Reverend Mather will no longer have a say in you or your brothers lives. When he interferes, I will broach the subject of my own recollections of his time in Toxteth Park and his complicity in your abduction. I believe that there is nothing he wouldn't do to keep that a secret. I will lay a wager that we have a lot more to learn about the Reverend Mather.

Daniel's Revenge

Daniel returned to his room after market day. He did not come out except to work and take his meals. Mark was acting normally as if nothing had happened. Daniel knew that he only had days to go before leaving. He knew he would have to say his goodbyes but did not feel that he wanted to have a confrontation with Mark. He had not seen Victoria and would avoid her before his departure. Mr. and Mrs. Eggleston had him to meals with them for this period. They knew he missed Joshua and thought it would ease his sadness by being around others. On the final night they had a big meal with many of Daniel's friends in attendance. They had asked him to invite his friends from the stables but he had declined. They did not understand this but said nothing to him. He had his own motives they reasoned. The night arrived and he put on his best clothes for it. He sat to the right of Mr. Eggleston at the head of the table. The visitors began to arrive and trickled in over the next thirty minutes or so. There were trays set out with appetizers and drinks to feed them until dinner was served. They mingled and all was going well. Daniel was talking with some of Mr. Eggleston's competitors in the textile industry. Their competition was of a cooperative nature. They could not produce enough cloth in the colony to satisfy demands so what was good for one was good for all. Daniel was standing near the front door when there was a knock. The servant answered the door and their stood Victoria with her father. She was beautiful but Daniel immediately remembered the picture of her walking hand in hand with Mark. Victoria's father quickly found Daniel and came to him with Victoria in tow. He shook his hand and said "Hello Daniel, I haven't seen you around lately. I suppose you have been getting ready for your trip. Victoria has missed you! I will leave the two of you to catch up."

Daniel replied "Yes sir, I had a lot to do before I left. I saw my brother off on his trip just a few days ago."

With that her father walked off to the others to discuss their business. Victoria was uneasy. She could tell that Daniel was not acting in the way which she was familiar. He did not act happy to see her even. He said "Hi Victoria. I hope you have been well. I have been very busy and I know you have too!"

Victoria was dumbfounded. Daniel was always very attentive to her and she liked that sort of attention. She said "Even so you could have come to see me!"

Daniel paused. He didn't know if he wanted to get into the subject with her. He decided that he needed to let her know that he was no fool though in the end. He said "I did come to see you on the last market day. I had some responsibilities with Mr. Eggleston and came in to market around lunchtime. You can't imagine what I saw there!"

Victoria was now very uneasy. She replied "I can't imagine!"

Daniel continued "I saw my best friend Mark walking hand in hand with a girl that I thought had feelings for me alone. I saw that it was clear it was not the first time this had happened. I saw a large smile on your face with him that has been absent when you are with me!"

Victoria was silent. She did not know what to say. Finally, she stammered out the words "I am sorry! I didn't mean to hurt your feelings. Mark always has some coin and buys me things. You are going away for a long time and where would I be for that time without companionship?"

Daniel said "I understand. I said the same words to my brother about the situation. What I did not condone was the betrayal and the secrecy. That is disrespectful, embarrassing and just mean spirited. I thought you were better. I thought that you would not do that type of thing to someone that has respected you and put your needs and wants before his own. I don't have any coin usually but that doesn't mean I won't have it in the future. I am not sure I can say the same of Mark. He will always have a little but that will be his lot later in life also. I must leave to insure my future and to learn my craft. I am not short-sided enough to be happy with a few coins today when I can forego them now to make a good living for myself and a family later. I hope that you are happy with Mark. I will not be calling for you again. Of course, I will be gone for quite some time but when I return I will look elsewhere for a suitable match!" With that he turned and joined a conversation with some of the men who worked with textiles. Victoria had tears in her eyes. She stood in the corner for a while. She gathered herself and strolled to her father. She told him she was not feeling well and wanted to leave. He was disappointed but agreed. He came to Daniel before going. He said "Victoria claims illness so we will not be able to stay. I wanted to wish you good luck on your trip and I hope you will come see us when you return. I can tell that there is an issue between Victoria and yourself. Do you care to discuss it?"

Daniel just said "Victoria has chosen another. He was my friend."

Her father said "Are you speaking of the ruffian that has been coming to the stall with a group of boys?"

Daniel replied "Yes. His name is Mark. I saw her leave with him on the market day just passed. They were walking hand in hand."

Her father replied "She told me she was with you that day! She would not have been allowed to go off with the likes of him. I am sorry for Victoria's behavior Daniel. I hope we can stay friends though!"

Daniel said "I would have that no other way sir! You are a good man."

Her father collected Victoria and then left. It would be a journey that would not be to Victoria's liking. By going with Mark, she had betrayed her father's trust also. The punishment for that would be swift and sharp. There would be one more market day before his departure.

He had his things packed and ready to go the day Joshua left. He worked and did his chores at the stables. Mr. Eggleston assured him that his room would be kept for him on his return and no one would be allowed to use it. Nonetheless Daniel packed all his belongings including his journals to take with him. Mark had proved to be less than trustworthy and he did not care to risk the loss of any of his few belongings. He knew that Mark coveted his room in the stables and he would warn Mr. Eggleston of the possibility of Mark's behavior. He said "Mr. Eggleston, you will have to be sure to secure my room. Mark is desirous of making it his own and once entrenched he would be hard to evict."

Mr. Eggleston said "I own the Nanny house and the stables. Mark works for me. He will do as he is told and he will be told in no uncertain terms that he is to leave your room unmolested. I sense there is a tension between the two of you."

Daniel just acknowledged him. He said "It has to do with Victoria Summers. The issue is settled and I have capitulated to him. I will be away and would have nothing to say on it anyway!"

Mr. Eggleston nodded. He said "Oh the feminine wiles. Her father is very concerned of her behavior and her tastes with boys. He was very pleased that she had taken up with you. We have discussed it many times. He will be upset if she has taken up with Mark!"

Walter's Advice about the Indians

Daniel changed the subject. He asked about the Indians and if he would carry weapons. Mr. Eggleston looked amused. He said "I have a good hunting knife for you. I also have a musket that I will send. The men in camp are instructed to train you on its operation and use. They are good men and you will be happy in their company. They are looking forward to your arrival. You will learn much on that end of our business. They will instruct you on fighting if that need becomes necessary. The Indians fight in a different way than Englishmen. They do not follow our rules of battles so you will have to learn their ways to defend yourself if the need arises. For the most part the Indians in the wilderness are friendly. It is the actions of a few of our own that set them to violence or starvation. We have encroached on their land, their forests, their food supplies and their crops since we arrived. We have brought illness to them and yet they still wish to be our friends. A man can only take so much though and in the end they will rise up in anger and frustration. This I fear is the lot of our Indian friends. They have the firebrands on their side of the issue too. Do not be mistaken. You must earn their trust and they must earn yours. Once an Indian is your friend you will be friends for life regardless of any other problems. They are loyal to their inner circles and bands."

This made Daniel feel much better. He would try to make friends with the Indians. It would make his job and education much easier with one less thing to worry him.

Joshua's New Assignment

Joshua had a good trip with Sam. He felt like a weight had been lifted from his soul. He was not in fear of the threats made by Mather now. Sam and his friends could control him with their knowledge of the past and he would not have to deal with him directly. Like Sam he believed that they only knew a small bit of the true story of their abduction. They had arrived at the logging camp in the evening. Sam would stay the night to help him settle in. Like Daniel he had been given a large hunting knife and a musket awaited him in camp. The loggers had a good relationship with the Indians of the area. They shared some food and provisions with them and this was reciprocated as needs arose. There were always bands of Indians or rogues that would wander through an area and cause trouble. They would raid homes and barns and steal food or cattle. Sometimes they would kill the homesteader and abduct their children and wife for their own uses. These were the Indians that caused all Indians trouble. The foreigners placed the stereotype of these bad Indians on all of the Indians. This included the peaceful ones. It was more exciting to talk about the marauding bands than the Indians that lived in peace and thus their good deeds were ignored and the bad deeds amplified. As the years passed this would cause the death of many Indians and settlers over the next three centuries. It was clear to all that the colonists and settlers would come in great numbers and they would desire the Indian lands. For now the Indians were peaceful with his group. They were interested in the logging and the way the men built their structures. The Indians that counted on crops no longer traveled with the seasons and permanent structures were of much interest to these people. They lived in Tee Pees and other lodgings when they wandered the forests and hunted their food in the past. These permanent structures would offer greater insulation from the weather and better security against those that came into their world.

Joshua was shown to his bunk. He would share the room with eight others. There were groupings of small buildings housing equal numbers for the total complement of workers in the camp. There was a dining area and kitchen in one building for meals and there was an office of sorts for the logging operation. It had a few bunks tucked away in it also. The manager of the camp stayed in one and the other was for guests. This is where Sam would sleep this night. They sat to dinner right after their arrival and Joshua was introduced to the company. They all new Sam and liked him very much. Joshua was made aware that Sam's relationship to the camp was not as a customer but as an owner. He had deed to the land they logged and he had negotiated fairly with the Indians to get it. The Indians could continue to use the land in cooperation with the loggers or settlers. Any person on the land was made aware of the agreement and disputes were settled in the company office by the manager. He was a fair man and all of those involved abided by his decisions. It did not matter if they were English, French, Indian, Spanish or any other nationality. He had total authority over this land. He also had the duty of enforcing his decisions and keeping the peace. As with all populations there were some bad individuals that only looked out for themselves and rules meant little to them. Sam told Joshua that the following day he would get his musket and training on its use. He already knew how to use an ax. He learned from using these tools in his duties on the docks. He would be acclimated into a cutting crew in a short time where he would be expected to work as any other man in residence. His age and size did not matter to them.

The Overthrow of Mark's Reign

Daniel's day started early. Market day was upon them. He would say his goodbyes to his friends and get his last taste of life in Boston for a while. He walked alone to Boston that morning. After the first mile he was joined by Johnny, Benny and Isaiah. They ran to catch up to him. Johnny spoke for the group. He said "We will miss you while you are gone. In the time you have been here we see you as our leader. You are smart and fair. Mark is neither. He is just bigger. When you come back you will be the leader of the stable. We will support you against him. We know what he did and we don't like it."

Daniel said "Each of you is a leader. You have your own choices to make and your own mind and goals to keep. At your age you don't need a leader. You need to learn to live cooperatively so that all of your voices are heard and can live together. At the most you only need an arbitrator for disagreements among you and Mr. Eggleston would be glad to act in that capacity."

Johnny said "Mark says that now you are gone he is takin' over your room. I told him he wouldn't but you can't talk to him. He has his head set on it. He is very jealous of you Daniel!"

Daniel replied "Mr. Eggleston is aware of Mark's desires for my room. He will not get it. It is my room and paid for by my labors. It is owned by Mr. Eggleston as is the Nanny house. Mark could find himself cast out of the stables with his bad attitudes and bull-headedness. It is intolerable and you should make your stands against him as a group now even for the time when I am gone. There is power in acting in concert together. You will do fine and I will write to you about my adventures in the wilderness while I am gone. Sometime in the future I will work for Mr. Eggleston in his textile business or own one of my own. I will not forget my friends when that happens. You have been good friends to me and I appreciate it!" With that they had arrived at the market. Mark was nowhere to be found. Daniel suspected where he would be but was just as sure that it would not go well for him at the Summer's Family stall. The boys enjoyed their time. Mr. Eggleston had given Daniel some coin to spend on this day. He treated the boys to fruit, food and drink. He shared all that he had.

After their lunch they went towards the docks. As they approached they saw Mark coming their way at a brisk stride. It was clear he was angry and looking for trouble. Daniel braced himself and was determined to make a stand. Mark walked straight up to Daniel and got very close with his fists clenched. He shouted in his face with spittle flying. "You had no right to do that. She can make her own choices and she made it. It wasn't you. She chose me! You have turned her father against me and he has forbidden me to see her. It is your fault!"

Daniel stood calmly and did not back off an inch. He replied "You have a lot of nerve to talk about rights. You knew that I was with Victoria and you stole around like a thief to court her behind my back. You are no better than a thief. You certainly are not a good friend as I had once considered you to be. I had nothing to do with her father forbidding you. That was his own choice because he could see what type you were. You both lied to him and disrespected him as her father when you went off together without his approval. She told him she was with me those times and propagated more lies to him on your behalf while bringing me into a questionable position in his eyes. You can hardly expect him to trust you or his daughter with you when all you do is lie to him. You have cast your own fate and now you alone must live by it. Take responsibility for your own actions and quit blaming me or anyone else for your failures!"

With that Mark's temper exploded he struck out with his fist but Daniel was quick and ducked below his punch. He put his own fists together and landed hard in Mark's stomach knocking his wind from him and sending him to the ground in a crumpled mass. Daniel stood at the ready for him to get up. Mark looked up at him and saw his challenge. He could not answer it. The boys looked at him with pity. They said "We have been thinking Mark. We do not need a leader in the stables. We are all equal. We will make decisions as a group now. You are no longer the leader. If you have any objections you will have three of us to fight and from the looks of it you are not very good at it!" They walked off talking excitedly about their new circumstances and laughing loudly at the defeat of Mark in battle. Daniel was not proud. He had been goaded into this fight. He did not believe in violence except as a last resort. In this case he accepted it because it had other beneficial results. It freed his friends from their subservient role under this bully. Mark had been set in his place. They would have a much improved life going forward. Both Mark and Victoria had learned that there are consequences for their bad behavior. He was now ready to move on to his next assignment in gaining his manhood.

The Journal of Danial Henshaw
20 March 1656

On the dawn of tomorrow, I will embark on my next mission in my education. Today started out as a sad and depressing time but as the day wore on I was vindicated as were my stable friends. Mark has been unseated and his bullying is at an end. I will be eager to see how this has evolved upon my return to Boston in a few years. I am sure that the boys will rise to the occasion. I will discuss with Mr. Eggleston the overseeing of the situation and the establishment of an arbitration court for behavior within the group. My room is secure for my return.

I have left Victoria behind and do not intend to see her in my future. It appears that she will not be in Mark's future either. I am assured that my friends will be in better stead in their lives with the overthrow of Mark's bullying ways. They have made their stand

I will spend my time learning. I have promised to write to my friends in the stables, Joshua and Mr. Eggleston while I am away. I will keep my agreements and long for word from them in return. I am eager to hear from Joshua and his current circumstances and interests.

Joshua's Life at Camp

Joshua settled into life at the logging camp quickly. The men gave no allowance for his age or size. He was considered one of the crew and expected to keep up. Joshua would have had it no other way. With any new task there was a learning curve. This required Joshua to work harder to complete his expected tasks. He would achieve the required skills and work more efficiently and effortlessly as time went on. For now he was on a crew that would strip the limbs and leaves from the main trunk. The log then had to be chained to wagons to move to the mills. Surprisingly some Indians worked with them. They were cheap labor and were paid in food, provisions, tools and clothing that they could not produce themselves. They appreciated the work and Sam was one of the few that did not take advantage of them. He could have paid them in trinkets or worthless items but did not practice his business in this way. This was the case in the purchase of Long Island in the New York colony. Sam would have no parts of this behavior. The Indians got paid in kind for the work they did. Joshua was heartened by this idea and found the Indians to be great workers, strong, honest and loyal. These had been hard traits to find in many of the white men in the colony. It was especially true of the leaders of the Puritans. Few in the colony trusted those men and women.

Joshua and the Indians

Over time Joshua began to communicate with the Indians. This was difficult because each tribe and sometimes each band within the tribe had their own languages. At first he learned the universal sign language that was used by all of the tribes. This was necessary to avoid miscommunication when the bands would meet in their travels or dealings. There were several of the languages that were derivations of a main language. Joshua decided that his first language would be of the Lenni-Lenape tribe. This tribe was said to have been on this land for ten thousand years when the colonists arrived. Lenni-Lanape translated literally means "men of men". Another translation is "Original people".

The Lanape people were known to the English as Delaware Indians. They lived mostly in what are today New Jersey, Delaware, Southern New York and Eastern Pennsylvania. There were three main clans of the Lanape and three main dialects of their language. The three main groups were made up of smaller bands but their language came from the three main languages spoken in the territory. These all had some of their own phrases and words used in their groups. The three groups were:

The Munsee band (People of the Stoney Country) to the north

The Unami band (People Down River)

The Unatachtigo (People who live near the ocean) to the central and southern areas

The tribe held a high position with the other tribes in the area. These tribes called them "Grandfather" or the "Ancient Ones" Many of the other tribes found their origins throughout time from the Lanape. They were the mediators, peacekeepers and diplomats of the First Nation. The colonists and settlers held them in high esteem. Often times the Lanape would mediate disputes between the tribes, bands and settlers to avoid bloodshed and chaos. If the Puritan leaders would have bowed to their authority the shape of the country could have taken a different and more peaceful look for generations to come. Ironically Delaware, the Delaware River and the Delaware Indians were named after Lord De La Warr who was sent to Jamestown In 1610 with orders that amounted to a declaration of war against Powhaten's Indians. The Lenni Lanape Indians were from the south of Massachusetts Bay but it was common practice among the Indians to take hostages during their tribal wars. It would be the duty of these captives to escape the bondage. This would most likely have been the situation with those that Joshua had come in contact with at the camp

Joshua quickly learned the beginnings of the language:

English: Do you know me?
Lenape: Kuwahi hèch?

English: My name is Joshua Henshaw
Lenape: Ntëluwènsi Joshua Henshaw

English: Your friend (man speaking of man only)
Lenape: Kitis

The Lanape understood and made friends quickly. Over the next few months Joshua would study with his new friends to become conversant with the Indians. He would then learn the variations of the other languages so he would be able to communicate with any of the tribes with whom he would have contact. He learned the sign language also.

A strange thing occurred. They were visited by the Indian hunting parties on a regular basis. As Joshua's language skills improved he told them of his brother working with the sheep herds nearby. The visitors knew of the place. Joshua had asked them to carry letters and messages to his brother on their travels. They smiled and readily agreed. Daniel took out paper and wrote the first letter by Indian Post. They were very interested in his writing and wished to learn it. Many of the Lanape had converted to Christianity and there were those in each tribe that spoke and wrote English. Many had adopted the dress of the Quakers and others from their areas and traded for buttons and cloth to make these garments. The Puritan's took Indian children from their families and "civilized" them. In fact it is the only way a Native American could obtain a deed to land he already owned to insure his use and ownership of it according to the English system of land. He wrote the note quickly and the Indians were amazed at such a quick form of communications.

Daniel, I am well! I have befriended the Lanape that work with me at camp. There are bands of Indian hunters that come through camp regularly. In questioning them I find that they also journey to your location. I have asked them to make your acquaintance and I ask that you learn their language as you can. We will then have a quick method of sending our letters to each other.

The work here is hard but invigorating. The men have accepted me but expect that I keep up my own share of work. I am working doing the chores of a beginner for now but this will change as I gain skills.

I hope things are going well with you at your work and learning. I know we will return to Boston much stronger and brighter. Keep your health my brother.
Joshua

He placed the letter in a beaver pouch he had made and gave it to the Indians. He would now wait to see how his plan would play out.

Daniel's Arrival at the Sheep Herd

Daniel had arrived at the sheep herd in good time and health. The shepherds were of calm attitude and a slow lifestyle. It was amazing to see the changes that came over them during shearing time and the processing of the fleeces. The speed that they took the wool from the sheep was unbelievable. Daniel had to wonder if he would ever achieve the skills of these men. They kept a few sheep away from the others during their mass shearing operation. These would be held in a pen and the men would instruct Daniel on this process. The fleeces themselves would be available for that training.

At first Daniel struggled getting used to the feel of the tools and the method of their use. With practice the work improved. By the end of his training he was of intermediate skill that would improve with each shearing session. The sheep were now sheared for the hot summer months. Their wool would grow now until it was ready to be harvested once again. Daniel learned to handle the fleeces. This was much easier than the shearing.

The fleeces were thoroughly washed. This was done outside in large tubs. The washing was a long process. The wool would be washed, rinsed and dried two or three times to get it in the condition it needed to be to spin into yarn. It would be placed in bags that had the appearance of fishing nets but the holes were much smaller. These were then compressed by walking on them or using stones to remove most of the water captured in the fleece. The fleece would then go back outdoors to catch in the breeze in a shady spot until it was completely dry. It was a very hard and time-consuming process. This was just the first process. Next the picking of the wool would begin. The wool was picked and picked until all of the debris was removed from it. Sheep in the field would accumulate stems, seeds, dirt and debris that would get down into their wool. This all had to be removed. The first process of removal was this picking process. While picking the wool it was pulled apart. This opened the wool some to help with the process. Next the wool is carded. This in reality is using a brush to go through the wool and eliminate all of the other particles left in it. It is important not to wash all of the lanolin and oils out of the wool. These add to the way wool is spun into yarn.

Each fleece had to go through this process to be sold to the mills. Mr. Eggleston did not have to complete this process at the sheep herd. Since he was the user it could have been just as easily done at the mill. The reasoning was that the shepherds had the time to do the work and watch the flocks. This was captured labor that would otherwise be lost. To Daniel it made perfect sense to process the wool before sending it to spin at the mill.

Daniel Meets the Indians

Daniel awoke one morning to learn that there was a band of Indians asking about him in the clearing near camp. He took a shepherd with him who spoke the Indian language. This could be complicated because of the number of different tongues spoken throughout the tribes and bands themselves. The Massachusetts Indians were a part of the Algonquin tribes that moved to the area from the west and southwest of the North American continent. They were originally hunters and fishermen with no agriculture. It is likely that some of the bands were related to the Beothuk Indians of Newfoundland. The Algonquin bands moved further and further east pushing the tribes of that area farther to the coast. When the coast was reached, they annihilated the survivors or absorbed them into their realm. Once settled some of the bands turned to agriculture. The Indians were storytellers and there was a story for their turning to agriculture. This story involves a crow. It is said that the crow brought a grain of corn in one ear and a bean in the other. The great god, Kauntantouwit, from the southwest had planted these seeds in his own field. The crow flew down and took the seeds and brought them to the tribes in the East to ease their hunger. This story is a part of the Algonquin history passed from generation to generation. It speaks of the introduction of agriculture to those bands that immigrated to the Massachusetts and Connecticut areas from the west and the south.

These Indians lived mostly from the sea. They ate what could be caught from the near shore. In 1578 there was an estimated one hundred European ships whaling and fishing the New England coast. They traded with the Indians in peace. It was evident that the foreigners and the First Nation could live in harmony. As the Massachusetts Bay Colony came into existence there were proponents of peace from the Indian community. Samoset and Massasoit worked to establish a good relationship with the colonists. John Eliot was doing his work to establish this cooperative atmosphere between the colonists and the Indians. He converted many to Christianity and translated many religious works into the Indian languages.

During this time there were seven tribes of importance. They were the Massachusetts, the Wampanoags, the Nausets, the Pennacooks, the Nipmucks, the Pocumtucs, and the Mohicans. These tribes had different personalities and behaviors that connected some to the colonists and labeled others as hated enemies of the white man.

The Massachusetts: This tribe was dominant during the early years. They controlled the territory that circled the towns of Boston Harbor, Charleston Harbor, Maiden, Nantucket, Hingham, Weymouth, Braintree and Dorchester. Their dominance pre-dated the first settlers. There numbers were diminished to around 500 by that time from the plagues. They were gathered into villages. They were turned to Christianity in this setting. They were identified as "praying Indians".

The Wampanoags: This tribe was similar to the Massachusetts tribe and shared much of the history.

The Nausets: This tribe was friendly to the white man. They lived mostly in Cape Cod and its outer islands. They converted almost in their entirety before the later wars. They were known as peaceful and cooperative neighbors and allies.

The Pennacooks: This tribe was one of the tribes that caused problems with the colonists and settlers. They raided around Massachusetts during this period and in turn were raided and killed in response. They allied themselves with the Abanaki band from Maine. This tribe was particularly troublesome. After the later wars this tribe crossed into Canada to live.

The Nipmucks: They lived with Boston on their east, Bennington Vermont on the west, Concord, New Hampshire on the north and Connecticut and Rhode Island on the south.

The Pocumtucs: They established a village near the town of Deerfield and controlled the Connecticut Valley in Massachusetts.

The Mohicans: Lived in the Housatonic Valley of New York. This tribe was also reduced because of the plague. It moved its council fire to Stockbridge, Massachusetts in the latter part of the 1600s.

When one came upon Indians in the wilderness care had to be taken to identify the tribe. This would also determine the forms of communication that would be used. There were friendly tribes and hostile tribes. If one was schooled in identifying the difference the interactions could be much safer for the white man. There were variations in clothing, hairstyle and weapons between the varying bands. This group that had come to camp and sought out Daniel was led by a Delaware Indian. They were rare to the area and were generally from the south of Massachusetts. He was the spokesman seeking a counsel with Daniel. The translator and Daniel went to the clearing on the edge of the camp to meet with them. Daniel soon learned that they were carrying a message from Joshua and that they were friendly Indians. Daniel read the message, answered it quickly and put it back into the beaver pack. Joshua had posted his message in this pack and it would be used as a means of exchange. In essence it would be their personal mail bag going forward. The Indians were given food and drink and a lasting friendship had begun. The Delaware tribe had been converted to Christianity. This Indian went by his biblical name he had adopted. His name was Paul. Over the years they would learn much about Paul and his life. For now they would learn to speak the languages to communicate clearly. Joshua and Daniel would teach the Indians English and they in turn would teach their languages to them. Daniel was grateful for the letter. It meant that they would be able to post to each other much more frequently. The translator told Daniel "Paul says that with your agreement you are bound to each other. He will watch after you and you him. It will be the Indian way and not that of the townspeople with the sour faces.

He is your friend!"

Daniel replied "Thank you Paul. We will never betray our friendship!" They started their first lesson that very morning. The Indians camped for about a week on the clearing. The lessons continued during any spare hours. They could now communicate the basic greetings and wants and needs to each other.

Joshua and the Logging Camp

Joshua was working in full now. He was growing quickly and his muscles were becoming hard and manly. He was outworking many of the men. Logging was hard work.

In this time there were no mills near Boston. Most were in New York or Maine. Since there was no method to transport the fallen logs to the saw mills the colonists used more primitive methods. An individual settler with an axe and a wedge could cut enough usable lumber with his own sweat and muscle to supply his needs for housing and personal use. As villages sprung up in these areas more lumber was needed. With these came the demand for building material. One of the products in demand from these villages was ship timber. The villagers were not interested in this pursuit because they occupied the better paying and easier jobs of professional men. Some of the poorer settlers would work in this industry. The rest of the needed labor was supplied by indentured servants.

With no sawmills available the ship timber was acquired by hewing out logs and then squaring them by a broad axe. It required a level of expertise to handle the tool and achieve the desired results. Back in England this was the only method of cutting ship timber. Any efforts to build sawmills there was met by an outcry from the unionists. Within a short time after a mill was built it would be torn down or burned by the angry union mobs wishing to protect their jobs in the status quo. Any automation, they had come to learn, meant less workers and jobs. With the population booming jobs were in short supply. In the colonies it was different. The need for timber and lumber for all purposes was more of a need and the more that could be produced the better.

Trees were selected to be felled for ship use. They needed to be straight and thick. Different types of trees had different features. Some were taller or shorter, some were thicker in the trunks or thinner, some were hard wood and some soft. It didn't matter. Each type of wood had its use. Once a tree was selected it was felled by a saw or axe. This was a dangerous part of the job. Being in the wrong place at the wrong time could be deadly and dangerous. Inattention to what was going on around a person was not acceptable and usually proved to be unsafe.

Once the tree was brought down it had to be bucked. First it would be trimmed of all of its limbs so that there were no protuberances from the log itself. Once the log was laid out and stripped of its branches it looked like a long cylinder of wood. Bucking the tree was an important process and required the Bucker to know the trees. It was this person's job to maximize the amount of lumber that could be harvested from the log. Most board cuts were divisible by four. This was accomplished by what was called the flip-board method of measurement. The Bucker would cut a four-foot piece of wood. In it he would make a cut every two feet to resemble a crude ruler. In addition, he would make a cut six inches from each end. In practice he would lay this board on the log and flip it to measure out the feet. An additional six inches was left on the end for any cutting errors at the mill. It gave them a measure for error. The tree was marked after this measure and cut to length.

Once the logs were hewn and squared they were put to a process of pit-sawing. The tool for this was a long saw with cross-handles on each end. It took two strong men to operate this saw. The process went like this. A squared log was placed over a pit on an elevated platform. These could be trestles or another suitable appliance to elevate and hold the weight of the squared log. One man stood atop the log and pulled the saw in its upward motion and the other stood below and pulled the saw back on its downward motion. The more talented of the two men would be the top man. He was called the Pit Man. He would guide the cut along a chalk line on the log showing where the cut was to be made. This manual sawing was duplicated within the automation of a Sawmill when they came into being.

This work was hard and demanding. It could break a lesser man let alone a boy. Joshua was a boy. He was strong and large for his age and his body quickly adjusted to the hard work. His muscles grew stout and strong and his body built to resemble that of the older men he worked with. Many in this profession were injured or killed from accidents with the saws or being caught under a falling tree. Some were killed in the wilderness by raiding Indians while others died of illness. Those who survived worked their bodies hard and their abilities faded much earlier in life than those with softer jobs. It was a young man's profession. Many called it a day and hobbled away with debilitating injuries or crippling wear and tear on the body. This left them little they could do to support themselves or their families if they had them. Many loggers never married because they were aware of what their futures likely held for them as they aged under the heavy workload. Joshua would do this work for a few years including his work in the mill. He would then return to Boston and learn the building of the various ships of the sea. When this training was complete he would manage the builders or own his own business. It was his hope that he could partner with Sam and take over his business as he aged. He had not yet given up the desire to return to England to set things right. He never would. It was his hope that the ship building industry could be run from both Boston and the port of Liverpool upon his return. During this time he had not ruled out the possibility of focusing on the profession and leaving the past to the past. It was the first time he had pondered such an outcome. It tore at his soul and gave him sleepless nights.

The Sawmills in New York and Maine were the only ones in operation when Joshua went to the camp. Sam contracted to build a Sawmill in Massachusetts Bay in the interim. When Joshua finished his stint at the logging camp he would be learning the Sawmill business from its infancy in the colony. This had its advantages but it also had its drawbacks. He would learn from those who built the mill and its works. This would be invaluable to him and those that worked at the beginning. The disadvantage was that there was no one with any experience to maintain and teach the process. They would all be learning the operation at the same time. Joshua was schooled and intelligent. It gave him the advantage over the others. Sam had counted on this when his plan was made. If the Sawmill had problems, he could send Joshua to the mill to troubleshoot and fix the issues. It was one of the initial acts of trust that Sam had given to Joshua. Joshua would not realize it for some time yet though.

Daniel and the Sheep Herds

Daniel had taken to sheep herding. They stayed in the fields all day. Night watches were kept to keep the wild animals or thieving Indians or settlers at bay. Daniel liked these times in the spring and the summer. The nights were cooler than the days and the stars painted a portrait in the skies. Daniel did much thinking during this time. He questioned his faith and all that had happened to him in his life. He found a path of acceptance and forgiveness for those who had done wrong to him and his family. It was his deep faith that allowed him this respite. Daniel knew that Joshua had faith also but knew he lived by his own set of beliefs. He had focused on scriptures that called for vengeance and retribution for these wrongs delivered to them by his own hand. Daniel preferred to believe that God himself would punish those that had woven this web of deceit and greed. Daniel had accepted his fate and resolved to move forward with those things that his God provided to him in the here and now. He would make the best of what he could now hold in his hand and not what lay a sea away from him and in doubt. He wished that Joshua could see this solution but knew he would have to resolve his own path and decide his own actions in the matter. No one could do this for him in any way. Daniel did not want to force a decision. If his own way was best or if Joshua's was the path to follow would make itself known to each of them individually. He just knew that what was right for one was not always right for another. Each individual was unique to himself. God made us this way when he entrusted us with free will and it was not for him to question this or to try to change this uniqueness in his brother. Daniel understood that if Joshua did return to England and come to see all of his goals achieved that he would be fair with his brother in the family's legacy. Daniel truly did not judge his life by seeking out riches and power. He was content if his basic needs were met and if he progressed in his profession to its highest levels. Riches would follow this path but it was not truly his goal. It was a side product of success and being the best he could be.

Daniel Thwarts the Indians

Daniel was this night in the field on watch. They kept a number of fires burning around the herd. This kept the wild animals away and lit the area to provide good sight if the herd was under attack by human predators. The sheep stayed within the ring of fires and the shepherds patrolled the perimeters on regular intervals. Other than those duties they were free to sit and ponder and meditate. Daniel was brought to attention from a noise he heard in the forest surrounding the clearing where the herd lay. It was a rustling sound that was abnormal in its voice. There was no wind or gusts and the rustling should not have been disturbing the rhythm of the night. He heard a series of animal calls. These were random and spread out around the area.

Most predators ran in packs and would not be spread out in such a fashion. Indians would use the animal calls to communicate during their own raids and Daniel was sure this is what he was hearing. It was the beginning of a renegade raid. Whether it was white men or Indians it mattered little. It was Daniels duty to protect the herd from loss. He quietly went to the others in camp. He had a plan.

Daniel had the others spread out in the shadows between the fires. They would find cover and hide themselves. Whoever the raiders were they would not want a confrontation. They wanted to slit the throats of the sheep and carry them off for food. They wanted to get in and out quickly and with little risk. When all of Daniel's shepherds were in place Daniel made a loud call of a hoot owl. This call was answered by other hoots from those in hiding. The hoots came from all around the clearing now and they were just clear enough that the raiders in the forest knew that they were discovered. The number of hoots increased and moved. Daniel knew that there were only a handful of men in the shadows but with them hooting and moving to other covers it appeared to those in the forest that they had stumbled upon a larger force of defenders of this particular herd. The animal noises in the forest increased and finally they started to fade away deeper into the trees and away from the camp. Daniel's ruse had worked and there would be no losses from the herd on this night. As dawn broke on the clearing the others faded back into camp. At first they were quiet and then they began to talk. It started slowly. They exchanged their stories of what they had done and what they had seen or heard. Eventually it dawned on them that they had tricked the intruders. They liked to believe that there were Indians in the forest on this night. It was a much better story with Indians involved. They were known for being stealthy and dangerous. They were known as smart hunters and even smarter foragers. To better them through such a ruse was a story to tell in camp and back in the civilized world when they were at their cups at the pubs. A search of the woods found footprints and some evidence of the presence of those with evil in their hearts from the night before. Daniel saw it first. It was a colorful feather tucked in amongst a bush near the clearing. With it was as collection of footprints and prints of a body sitting in the dirt to watch for their chances to strike. It was not one hundred percent proof of Indians but the feather was enough to convince those that wished it to be that way to make their story a good one. It was decided that it was indeed Indians in the trees and that they had bested them at least for the one night. Daniel was a hero to the men and his reputation started to grow. It wasn't much but Daniel's actions gave them something to talk about for many campfires and pubs for many months in the future.

Joshua Contemplates his Future Course

Joshua heard of the adventure through his Indian messengers. They told the tale with much laughter and were pleased that Daniel had disgraced the renegades and drove them away. At first, he was concerned for his brother's safety but then realized that he knew Daniel was capable of his own affairs. This was a relief in ways but it also made him sad. The boy's relationship up through this time had been Joshua as the protector and overseer. It had changed. This event had simply highlighted the obvious. It had never entered Joshua's conscience that someday Daniel would not need him to play this role with him. He had not anticipated that the day would come so soon. He would have to adjust his own thinking to see Daniel as his equal now instead of someone to watch over. It would be a change that he would both like and hate. Their lives and growth had been greatly accelerated by the events that had taken place. Joshua knew from all of the old teachings that he would take his place as the head of the household and oversee a great deal of land and riches. This reality had faded away to nothing at the hands of Mather and Ambrose. It meant nothing. He had to earn his way from the beginning. No matter what the circumstances later this fact would not change now. He did not mind. All of the Henshaw men had the work ethic. They did not shy away from hard work or long hours. They thrived in it. It was in their blood and would carry through the centuries with them. Of course, there were always those like the Ambrose family who would look to take advantage of others hard labors and save their own backs from the burden. There would be those miscreants of his family who would not fit the mold. There were those in every family. The Ambrose men were loosely related through blood from the Stanley side of the Houghton family. They were nothing like the Henshaw family. They were lazy, dishonest and felt an entitlement to things that others had earned. Joshua could not take to their kind and his hatred for what they had done rose. His life here in the colonies had been happy for the most part. It was happier now with Sam Wickford as his guardian. The separation from Richard Mather had been good for both Joshua and Daniel. If things were different, he could stay in Massachusetts and make his life. The ties to avenge his treatment at the hands of Ambrose and Mather were simply too strong for him to overcome. He had to try to undo the wrong. It was an internal driving force that he could not shake. He had to make it right if he could. He realized that Daniel and he were two different and unique individuals. They still loved each other but they were moving apart instead of closer together. He felt that this was Mather's goal. This was caused partly by Ambrose and his abduction. It was partly caused by Mather's plan to separate the boys in servitude. Joshua knew that the largest cause though was simply their growth in age and responsibility. He was having the feelings that most parents have when their children leave their home to strike out on their own. In this day and age many would never be seen again once this flight occurred. Communications were poor and if a child left the Bay area it was rare to keep contact.

Joshua's Time at the Logging Camp Ends

At this point in time the boys had spent their two years at their duties. Joshua had grown strong and studied nature and the characteristics of different woods and trees. He knew all of the things he had set out to learn when he came to the camp. The men there respected him and some even looked up to him. He helped them write their letters to family and loved ones and taught them to keep their personal books so they would not be cheated. They had nothing to fear from Sam. They did need to know these things when they traveled into towns or traded with the many Indians or French traders that came through the area. The Dutch traders in the towns and villages were known to drive hard bargains and in this process a man without knowledge could be taken advantage of in his dealings either intentionally or innocently. Some of the men had asked Joshua to teach them to read and cipher. Joshua did so with relish. He would be missed in camp and that meant a great deal to him to be accepted by these men.

The Journal of Joshua Henshaw
15 April, 1658

My time at the camp has come to an end. I have learned much about trees, nature, the characteristics of the different trees and the lumber they will produce. I have learned the suitable uses for each of the different types of lumber and timber. I have learned to measure the logs to length and to capture the most timber from each. I have grown during my time here and have achieved a size and weight equal to any man in camp. My body has grown hard and strong. My mind is clear. I have made many friends here. They have taught me many things and in turn I have taught them their numbers and reading and writing if they had the urge. Daniel has flourished during his time away also. I have been able to see him irregularly over this time. It is clear he is growing in both mind and body. He too will leave the sheep herds for the next phase of his learning soon.

I am told by Sam that I will be going back to Boston for a short period. There I will see Daniel for this time and we can commiserate on our time apart. I have many stories and much knowledge to tell him and from what I have heard in camp he has many stories to tell me. I have met friendly Indians and learned of their life and language. I can speak almost fluently with them now. I have made many native friends both in camp and out of the camp. There are some renegades that make their appearance and cause problems from time to time that cause much strife but I do not believe that we should group all of the Indians into that category. The Indians, much like the colonists, come from many tribes, bands and areas with different beliefs, skills and tolerances. It can only cause bad things to happen if we cannot live together in peace and except our differences while building on our individual strengths. We can teach them much. They can teach us even more of this country we have pilfered from them since our arrival here.

It will be a great time for Daniel and I together before we start or next period of time apart. Daniel will be going to the looms to learn to spin the wool and make it into cloth. I will be going to the new Sawmill upon its completion to take the logs I have helped to harvest and learn to cut them into lumber and ship timber. There is a huge need for these products as more and more souls arrive on the shores of the colony. They must have housing and shelter from the cold and weather. The ships must be built to meet the demands for imports and exports to England. They will also meet the needs of those who dabble in the black market along the coast, in the Islands of the Caribbean Sea and the West Indies. Daniel's products have a large impact on the colony too. Warm wool and cotton cloth are necessary to make the warm clothes that keep the body warm in those cold winter days and nights. They are made into sheets and blankets to warm those while they sleep. The way I see it we both contribute much to the success of the colony and the King.

I am packing for my trip to Boston so I must end my entry now. I will continue to journal and write soon.

Daniel's Time at the Sheep herds Ends

Daniel too was getting ready for his departure. The men, women and children of the sheep herds had grown fond of Daniel and like Joshua he had taken time to help those who desired to read and write. The children were a particularly blessed distraction from Daniel's work and trials of his life. He grew fond of each of them and would spend hours reading stories and later just making them up to tell them as they sat enraptured of his story telling abilities. In this day a good story teller was like a movie star or a rock star and provided the entertainment to those around them. The Indians had storytellers as did the colonists. Daniel began his story telling whenever there was a gathering. Inevitably they would want to hear the story of the night the Indians were outfoxed by the owl hoots. Daniel developed a way to tell the story with some theatrics of his own. Later he wrote down some of the stories that the Indian's told in their powwows. Powwows were the meetings that the Indian bands or tribes would call for the Indian community to come together. There would be food, music, dancing and storytelling. They had many good stories and would tell them over and over but each time was something new to them. Some business would be conducted by the tribal leaders but this was completed quickly and efficiently so the celebrations could get underway. Daniel attended some of these events when they were nearby at the invitation of his Indian friends. He found them to be very enjoyable and the stories particularly drew his attention. They were almost like bible stories and explained many things in nature and Indian history. The way the storytellers told their stories drew a person into them and made them feel like a part of them. It would be something Daniel would always remember and carry with him. He began to develop his own stories about his time in England and his adventures on the trip to America. He had his own versions of the biblical stories that he adapted to the Indian way. It would be frowned upon by the likes of Richard Mather but Daniel no longer cared how he was received by these men. He had found a more profound truth in the world through his work, relationships with the herders, Indians and nature. His time had been well spent and his mind and inner peace were restored and his essence expanded upon. He came to Boston with a new found feeling of security and progress. He would share this with Joshua.

Journal of Daniel Henshaw
30, April 1658

I am looking forward to spending some time with Joshua in Boston before my posting to the textile mill. It was a good surprise to find out that I would return to Boston for a short time. It has been two years since I have been there. The Sawmill where Joshua will find his next challenge has yet to be completed. He will go there before its completion to learn how to split the logs into lumber by hand before the Sawmill is running.

I have learned much about the sheep, their wools, the preparation of the fleeces and more. I have not worked with cotton as of yet but this training will come to me at the textile mill. Mr. Eggleston has decided that it would be financially repressive to send me to Virginia to work on the cotton farms and processing barns. We would not have a need to know how to process the cotton from that level. We would need to know the process to spin the wool once it was delivered in the bales. I can learn to tell the quality and put a price on the bales from Mr. Eggleston when I return to Boston. In the meantime, I will begin to prepare for my time learning to spin the wool into a finished product for market.

I will say goodbye to my friends here and the Indian friends I have made. They have been a great help in my communication with Joshua during my stay. I will see many of the Indians at the mill and in Boston where they trade their pelts and other things with the colonists from time to time. We have developed a lasting friendship. I will see how those pompous Puritans receive my friendships with the Indians. I assume that it will not be a thing they would wish a good Christian to do.

I will be busy in Boston during my stay catching up with old friends and spending as much time as I can with Joshua. There will be duties there in preparation for my departure. Mr. Eggleston tells me that there will be an important meeting with Joshua, Sam, and himself on my return. I do not know the substance of this meeting but it seems to be of an interest outside of our normal affairs. I am eager to hear the news

Joshua Returns to Boston

Joshua was the first to make his way to Boston. Sam made the trip in the wagon. He delivered some supplies to the camp and picked up some things there to transport back to Boston. Joshua and Sam caught up on the news of Boston and England. There was a lot to catch up on after two years. Joshua was aware of the meeting with Mr. Eggleston and Daniel that was of importance to him and his brother. He could not figure what it was about and Sam was not forthcoming during the trip. Joshua thought that he would know soon enough. Daniel would be in town on the following day and the meeting would proceed. It was a pleasant journey through the forests and towns returning to the Boston docks. It was the first time in two years that Joshua felt like he could relax a little bit. Since leaving England he had begun to find a sense of home in his room on the docks. The work had been hard but satisfying. He felt a sense of achievement from his experience and that was the goal of the trip. He also felt a sense of sadness in leaving those he had met behind to this hard life. There was some guilt from a sense of betrayal in his leaving that stabbed at him. He reconciled this by deciding that once he had the power and wealth he would find ways to help these families and those he had befriended during his time. He discussed all of the things he had learned with Sam. Sam was pleased to hear how he had applied himself to his task and his education. The news of the substance of the meeting would be that much more important now.

Daniel Returns to Boston

The following day Daniel began his journey into Boston. Mr. Eggleston did not pick him up this time. There was a supply wagon going to Boston to pick up a load and Daniel rode along. This saved Mr. Eggleston the hard trip. They would have time to catch up when he arrived. His room in the stables had been held for him so he would feel right at home. He had a lot to tell Mr. Eggleston about his time with the sheep. He was excited. He had enjoyed his work there. It was time to move on to the next step of his training and he could hardly wait to get started. Mr. Eggleston was getting up in age now and travel was difficult for him. Once this part of his training was complete, he would be taking a more active part in the running of the business to help Mr. Eggleston lighten his load. It was a bright future for him.

Daniel found his room intact. The boys were glad to see him. They had grown and changed in these past two years. Their lives had changed quite a bit after Daniel had left. With the new structure to life in the stables their daily lives had become more bearable. That was more bearable for Johnny, Benny and Isaiah. Mark did not like it at all. He sulked around the stables for a time and was very unpleasant. He tried every way he knew to reestablish his dominance but that had failed. He saw Daniel's room as the prize and the thing that would prove to the others that he was back on top. He went to Mr. Eggleston and tried to strike a deal. Mr. Eggleston rebuffed him. He then went about taking the room by force. The boys caught him prying the lock open and they too rebuffed his attempts. The room was just out of his reach it seemed. After a few months Mark could stand it no more. One morning when the boys awoke they discovered that

Mark and most of their personal things were gone. He had robbed them in the night and taken off to his own fates. The boys thought it was likely that he would seek out Victoria for his future but it was not likely that she would be interested in keeping Mark. It was a sure thing that Victoria's father would not welcome him into his home. The three watched Victoria's house and stall for a time but Mark did not appear. There were things Mark could do for a living as Joshua and Daniel had just experienced. He could work at the camps or with the herds. They did not see this happening. Mark had different ideas. He saw himself with his own land or business and being his own boss. This was not an easy task in the colonies at this early time in the country's history. Most likely he would fall in with those wandering bands of freemen that finished their indentures and traveled around to find food and shelter at subsistence levels. They would live by legal or illegal means to meet their own needs and try to find their fortune. There was the matter of Mark running off without completing his indenture which would not go well for him if he was caught. At the very least he would be indentured for a significantly longer time depending on how long he was gone before he was discovered or returned. Even with their anger at his thievery they wished him the best. To do anything less would be to deny the possibility that they themselves would find their dreams. Without dreams there was no hope. With no hope there was no future. Daniel had told them that if he was successful he would not forget their plight. The boys had tied their futures to Daniel's fortunes with that declaration. They trusted that Daniel would find success and keep his bond.

Daniel's return was like a bright light to them all. He had not forgotten them and they would now hear of the progress he was making for himself and their own hopes. Daniel was glad to tell them what he had learned and the stories of the wilderness. They listened to him completely immersed in his stories. They especially liked the story of the night that Daniel outsmarted the Indian raiders. It made him a hero in their eyes. Daniel was glad that he made them happy. At least for this short time they could focus on something other than the stables and hard work and enjoy themselves. Like the Indians he had met these three were true and lifelong friends that Daniel could count on.

Joshua's Arrival and Reunion with Daniel

Joshua arrived in town in the early morning hours. Boston was fast asleep and the morning mists hovered on the bay in a light fog. Those he needed to see were in their beds so he retired to his quarters to rest. He noticed that in his absence Sam had expanded their living areas. Joshua now had a room adjacent to his sleeping quarters. They had a cooking area and a basin to wash in. Sam had put a second story onto the living areas and this was where he now lived. It was a vast improvement to the living arrangements he had left two years prior. He snuggled onto his bed and slept like a log. He would not awaken until well into the next day.

Daniel was waiting for his brother when he did wake up. He was sitting in the new room reading some material that Mr. Eggleston had shared with him on the prices and a tutorial on how to judge the quality of the incoming bales of raw materials. Joshua washed his face and hands and splashed water on his face to help the waking process. Daniel noticed him at once and they gave each other a hug and a pat on the back. They were speechless for a moment. Neither knew where to begin. They spent the morning and early afternoon hours reminiscing about their last two years and catching up. As the evening quickly approached Daniel came to an abrupt realization. He said "Joshua, I forgot why I came. Sam and Mr. Eggleston have a dinner planned for us tonight at the Eggleston house. We will need to leave right away to make it there on time."

Joshua just laughed and grabbed his beaver hat he had traded for with the Indians at the camp. He said "Well then times a wasting. Are you ready to go?"

Daniel laughed and away they went on foot. They had a pleasant walk and continued to make up for the two years apart. Time passed quickly and they found themselves at the end of their journey. As they neared the Eggleston house Daniel asked "Have you been informed that we are to have a meeting to discuss something of importance?"

Joshua answered "I have heard this but I have no idea as to the substance of the meeting. It has been kept very quiet. I would imagine that we are about to learn what it is all about."

Daniel said "Indeed!"

An Important Meeting with Sam and Walter

They walked down the lane leading to the house and were greeted at the door by Mr. Eggleston's house maid. She escorted them in to the sitting room where they joined the Eggleston's and Sam Wickford. The conversation was light and they were served some light food prior to their main meal. The boys discussed their time away and Mrs. Eggleston, who was rarely a party to this type of discussion, was enthralled with their adventures and learning. She had many questions for them about the Indians, lumber and sheep. Sam and Mr. Eggleston were amused. Mr. Eggleston said "Madam! You seem so interested we could probably arrange for you to have an internship of your own if you wish!"

She replied "Mr. Eggleston, don't offer things that you intend to take back. You might very well get a positive response on the question!"

He was amused "I stand corrected. I could not do without you here running my household and meeting my needs. Perhaps a visit to see these things would be more appropriate!"

Daniel said "We have many Indian friends. We would be glad to introduce you to them when they come into Boston to sell their pelts. We even learned to speak their languages!"

Mrs. Eggleston was very impressed and wasted no time in sealing the promise. The boys knew they would make an introduction of Mrs. Eggleston to their Indian friends when the time presented itself. They retired to the dining room for their main meal.

The food was excellent and first rate. They were used to cooking on the fires and eating what they could trap or hunt. Usually it was a meat only diet but this meal had vegetables and some fruits to accompany the steak. They ate and ate and when they were entirely full they were offered desert. They managed to eat their share of that also! After some time, Sam said "We should retire to the library and begin the business part of our meeting. I suspect this should happen before the food and desert set in and put you boys to sleep. They arose and excused themselves from Mrs. Eggleston. They adjourned again in the library. The boys took their seats. Sam and Mr. Eggleston took places on the far side of the big desk and Joshua and Daniel in the seats in front. Sam began the meeting. He said "Since Walter and I have taken over your tutelage and accepted you into our homes and lives we have come to think of you as something other than our servants and outside of the arrangement that was made with the Reverend Mather. We feel a kinship to you boys and hope that is agreeable to you. As such I have decided to make inquiries and have done so with full disclosure to Walter as to the discussions we have had and the history of our families in Liverpool. These inquiries have traveled back to England and I have hired an investigator to track any possible clues to the misdeeds of Peter Ambrose and our own Mr. Mather. Surprisingly they were not that hard to turn up. A drunken ship's captain and a Will is what I speak of now. So let me get to it. Shortly after you boys arrived in Massachusetts Mr. Mather received a letter. This letter informed him of the demise of Mr. Peter Ambrose around a year after your abduction. This post contained news of Ambrose's death and a portion of his Last Will and Testament concerning the two of you. In it he admits that you are alive and living in the colonies. He does not go so far as to name his accomplice. He left to you thirty pounds each to be distributed to you by the Reverend Mather when you reached your age of emancipation. The wording seems to refer to amounts above and beyond the thirty pounds that was previously transmitted to Mather in addition to these funds both in the past and with this post. There was an unknown sum that made the trip with you that is also in the care of the Reverend. Ambrose seems to have felt the need on his deathbed to admit to his deeds thinking it would buy his way into heaven after all of his evil doings. There is more. I had one of my Captain's investigate the circumstances of your removal from England and he was able to find the name of the ship and it's Captain that brought you here. It was then easy to get this Captain into the Pub and ply him with ale to loosen his tongue. He was a part of the plot and was paid handsomely. He was quite proud of the money he made and the care he took of you on your journey. The lout thought he had done something to be rewarded. This was not the interesting part. The interesting thing was that he carried with him to the colonies on your behalf a large purse that was to be used for your schooling, living expenses and money to establish you in a chosen business. This sum is undetermined but was described as quite substantial. He said it was in excess of five hundred pounds and more was to come to Mather over time as he cared for the two of you. The Captain wanted accolades for not pilfering it for himself and passing it along untouched to our Reverend Mather where it now resides. As we all know the Reverend Mather has supplied no money for your living expenses, education or establishing you in a business or profession. In fact, once he received the letter of Ambrose's death, he quickly put you into your current agreement to cast off the debt he had accepted on your behalf. He therefore has some serious explaining to do about the whereabouts and use of those funds. He will not risk being exposed so we have somewhat of a bargaining tool to our advantage. Walter and I have sent a messenger to Reverend Mather that we seek a meeting tomorrow in the morning hours in a discreet place. That place will be in the forest beyond the church. There will be no one around to hear us there. He is not aware of our knowledge of these revelations and could be in bad humor when he understands the repercussions of what this demands."

Mr. Eggleston said "Boys, we will be there to support you every step of the way through this. We will recover these funds from Mather. He has no right to them. If he does not relent, we will expose his deeds to the community thus ruining the man and his family. It is our hope that he still holds these funds in his control and has not disposed of them in any way. This we will know during the meeting. If he has disposed of the funds than he will be required to make reparations equal to the amounts to you!"

The boys were shocked. They had no idea that there were funds. Their earlier opinions of Mather, which weren't by any means good, were further tainted by what appeared to be an attempt to convert their funds to his own use. These funds would go a long way toward assuring their futures and restoring them to their previous lifestyle in England. Daniel felt a surge of relief and happiness. Joshua felt this too with one exception. He now had the knowledge that Ambrose had at least partially admitted to his misdeeds and this opened the door a crack to recover the family's holdings in England. Even with this admission it would still be a difficult mission to accomplish.

The Confrontation with Richard Mather

The night passed quickly with only fitful sleep. Both boys knew this would be an ugly confrontation with the man who had betrayed them while they were friendless and helpless in their youth. They now had friends here. They were powerful friends with the means to make some things right. Mather was powerful in his own right. The Puritans had used the odd weapon of the church court to battle their enemies. Many of the convictions and sentences that came from this body were baseless and nonsense but quelled those who would rise up against them in the community. A favorite charge was blasphemy (speaking against God's word) and witchcraft. It took very little to originate a charge. A lucky coincidence, a strange occurrence or even an out and out lie would do the trick. For this reason Sam and Walter had sought out their circle of friends and confided to them the information that they were about to confront Mather with on this morning. In this way there would be witnesses and those who would step forward in their defense if Mather or his minions would attempt their court shenanigans. He could not risk the information getting to the public. It could destroy not only him but the structure and power of the church in the colony itself.

Joshua and Daniel rose early and met on the road to the church. They walked along at a brisk pace hardly speaking. Their nerves were on edge. They heard a wagon approaching from behind and were pleased to see Sam and Walter mounted on the buckboard headed for their destination. They pulled up beside the boys and said "Hop on! It is a stronger vision if he sees us all arrive as one. I am sure he will be watching!" The boys jumped in the back of the wagon. They continued to the church and went past it up the path and into the woods beyond. There was an old logging road that wound up into the woods behind the church. It was where the timber to build the church had originated and the path used to bring it to the building site. At the end of the road was a large clearing that the church used for outside worship. The general membership was never invited to these gatherings and those who were not akin to the Puritans whispered of devil worship and occult meetings taking place there. The one clear thing was that there were fires and circles and many things that in appearance alone would leave that impression. It was rumored that the local witch coven secretly met at the clearing in the face of the Puritans. The place was uneasy and restless and just the type of place that this confrontation should occur.

As they found the path they turned to the north and followed it to the clearing. The boys could see pairs of eyes peering at them from behind the trees. Mather had not come alone or unprotected. This added a threat to the proceedings. Sam and Walter knew that once Mather was aware that others possessed the information and that they had possession of official documents to support their story that they would be discussing that Mather would abandon any plan to abduct or injure them. He could not risk it. He had put himself into an awkward situation by having extra ears and loose lips around during the meeting. As they approached the clearing Mather stepped forward with two armed men. He had protection with him most of the time. It was a dichotomy. If he was the religious icon he claimed to be he would have faith in his God to protect him. Sam was convinced that Mather would be facing an angry God over his part in the mistreatment of the boys. Apparently, Mather thought the same. The wagon slowed and came to a halt. Mather stood in its path. Sam and Walter started to dismount and the boys jumped out of the wagon. Mather told them to stay in the wagon but he was ignored. Sam knew that it was the first volley from Mather to control the meeting and he was having none of it. Sam said "Reverend Mather! We are here to discuss some issues that you might want to keep to yourself. I will leave that decision to you. For our part we will speak our piece in the manner we deem fit and you will listen. When we are done, we will discuss your questions. I doubt that you will have any however since the issues you already know very well!"

Mather said "You come here to my church to dishonor me and treat me with disrespect. I will say what happens here and how it will be done!"

Walter spoke up and said "We do not come to dishonor or disrespect you unless the question of honor and respect comes into question from your own actions now or in your past. Respect and honor sir are earned and not given freely. You will not dictate to us. We are not a part of your church and the more we see of it the less we would wish to associate with it. The issues here stem from your time in England and the acquaintance of a Mr. Peter Ambrose. You may have a moment to decide who, if anyone, you wish to hear our discussion. I doubt it will take you long to decide!"

Mather said "Follow me! You two stay behind and give us our privacy."

They walked farther to the fringes of the trees and away from prying ears. When Mather stopped, he turned to face them. He said "Now, what is all of this about?"

Sam spoke for the group. "As you know my father was a judge in Liverpool about the time you left for the colonies. He was associated with Peter Ambrose and the Henshaw and Houghton families. I was of acquaintance to them also. Imagine my surprise when the sons of William and Katherine arrived in the colonies without their parents. I put out some inquiries and have found out many facts that could paint an unflattering picture of you and Mr. Ambrose. Mr. Ambrose, God rest his soul, has his respite in death leaving only you to face your God, congregation and possibly the courts of true justice to explain your actions in this haughty affair!"

Mather shouted "Watch your mouth sir! You are very close to blaspheming!"

Sam responded "…and you sir are way past the act of blasphemy and have dishonored your God and church. We are aware of the part you played in the abduction and theft of property from two poor helpless orphans those many years ago. I should say 1652 to be exact. You got your thirty pieces of gold just as Judas did and more. We have been informed that you are in possession of certain funds belonging to Joshua and Daniel Henshaw. We demand to know where these funds are."

Mather stammered out his answer "I sir do not know what you are talking about and would not honor such slander with a response."

Sam smiled at him. He said "This is your story?"

Mather said "It is and you can prove nothing else or you would!"

Sam smiled even bigger now. He had him right where he wanted him. He said "First I will present you with this document. It is a copy of the Last Will and Testament of Peter Ambrose. To make this short it states in the Will that he sent to you thirty pounds for each of the boys from his estate. What say you to that?"

Mather replied "I know nothing of such funds!"

Sam smiled again. He pulled another paper from his coat and handed it to Mather. He said "This is a witnessed statement from the ship's Captain that brought the boys to Massachusetts. In it he states that not only were you paid for your part in this crime but a substantial amount of money was sent with him to be held by you for the boys. These funds were to educate, pay living expenses and seed funds for a business or career to secure their future. These funds were turned over to you upon their landing here from England by the Captain and he swears to this act."

Mather said "He is a liar, a drunk and miscreant."

Sam's voice rose in anger "Sir, you are the liar. These are legal documents and prove your culpability in a crime. The very fact that you acknowledge knowing the Captain and his habits points to the facts of your involvement. You can turn the funds over to Walter and me for safe keeping or be exposed to the community, your church and the crown for your part in this deed. You can decide this now. Which do you prefer? Surrender the boy's funds or be exposed for the man you truly are!"

Mather was dumbfounded. He could not speak. He did not

find himself in subservient roles often in his life. When he did they did not go well for him. Finally, he replied after long thought "What do you plan to do with this information?"

Sam said "That all depends on your actions. We want a total accounting of the funds that were sent with the boys from England and the thirty pounds each sent on the passing of Peter Ambrose and any other funds due to them either from Ambrose or their earnings here in your employ. There is to be a refund of such to Walter and myself for monies we have paid out to you for our agreements which you had no legal right to make. This too will be added to the boy's funds. We believe that interest on the money is due because of the circumstances of it coming into your hands. There should be a payment to the boys to compensate them for your trickery and deception in this vile event. I would say another five hundred pounds."

Mather said "That is pure theft. I have no such funds to cover that amount."

Sam continued "Whether you do or don't you have assets that can be transferred to the boys. As for the claim of thievery your actions deprived these boys of their entire inheritance. It was substantial and much more than the payment I have stated. I assume that the court of the crown would see it that way also if the boys would wish to pursue it. I can tell you without hesitation that they do wish to do whatever is necessary to recover all of their family's holdings or payment in lieu of their losses. You have land, houses, carriages, livestock and valuables. It is sure that these total to much more than the needed funds. Reverend Mather you live in the lap of luxury compared to others here. It is nothing for you to produce the funds that were sent here for the boys benefits and through your generosity produce this other stipend to help them establish their lives as you agreed. The community will believe that you have been magnanimous and will know nothing of the shady business that you engaged yourself in with Mr. Ambrose. I would stipulate as a part of this agreement that you cooperate with the boys if and when they decide to attempt the recovery of their lands in Liverpool and England. We will be sure to keep it discreet.

Mather was angry. He paced around the clearing for some time and finally returned to face Sam and the boys. He said "I will do as you ask. Not because I have wronged these boys. They were orphans and likely to lose their holdings to the King anyway. There will be no discussion of this issue in the future!"

Sam said "There will be no discussion of it when the funds are received and you honor your bargain to speak up in the courts of England when called upon in the future. In fact I would like a written statement of your involvement and knowledge of the events surrounding the boy's abduction that I will place in my safe for keeping. This will insure that the boys have your total cooperation. Additionally, there are others that we have shared the facts of your behavior with that are sworn to secrecy. If you have any idea of silencing the boys or Walter or myself with trickery then you should be aware that those with this knowledge are instructed to come forward and expose you and the plot both here and abroad!"

Mather said "Very well, you shall have it!" With that he stormed off to his associates and they mounted their wagon and left the area. The boys grinned from ear to ear. There was a feeling of emancipation from their previous situation. Joshua said "Daniel and I would like to thank you Sam and Mr. Eggleston for your help." They were sure that they had made their last visit to Mather's church. The welcome mat would not feel so welcome to them going forward.

The Boys Gain their Freedom and More

Mr. Eggleston said "From this point forward you will call me Walter! You boys are like our own sons and we could not have done anything less to overturn this dire injustice done to you by these villains."

Joshua said "Nonetheless, Thank you very much for your help. We are forever bound to you for that!"

Sam said "Speaking of being bound. Walter and I have both decided that your indenture period will be ended early. In fact it has ended with this meeting. It is your choice if you wish to continue to work with us and to continue your training. Now that you are men with funds we will discuss business matters with you as an equal. If you wish you can buy into our ventures and be our partners or you can strike out on your own. You may even pursue other interests if that would suit you better but we hope that you would continue on with what we have started here! The choice is yours!"

Daniel said "I will continue with my education and learning of textiles and their weaving! I would be honored to be a business partner to you Walter! We can discuss the terms further!"

Joshua said "I feel the same and will stay the course with you Sam. I cannot rule out a return to England to right the wrongs there at some later time however!"

Sam said "I would have expected nothing less from you Joshua! Maybe we should take the wagon into Boston and have a good feast to celebrate this day. It is a big day for the both of you and these things need a proper welcome!"

With that they rode back into Boston to their favorite establishment. They ate and laughed and the boys took their first pint of ale. It was a good day. It was the best day they had experienced since their mother had died.

The Journal of Joshua Henshaw
24, May 1658

This day has seen a turnaround of our fortunes. Both Daniel and I have come into substantial funds that hither to now were unknown to us. Our dear friends, Sam Wickford and Walter Eggleston have discovered them through an investigation conducted in England of their own accord. This will enable us to invest into the businesses that we are currently laboring in under our indenture. Another surprise came to us this day. We were informed by Sam and Walter that we have been released from our indenture by them to pursue whatever path we wish. Daniel and I both decided to continue on our current path. Daniel wishes me to abandon my quest to return to England and with our new circumstances I will try to do this for him. The look on the Reverend Mather's face when the realization came to him that he had been discovered in such a way and his risk of exposure was an epiphany.

The truth is that there are demons inside of me that demand vengeance and justice. They are forever haunting my dreams and my thoughts. Allowing the theft to stand seems as a betrayal to my mother and my father and to my heritage as a whole. I have read in the Bible and find many pertinent verses that call for forgiveness and the evil of riches. But I also find passages about vengeance and setting things straight. The violation here though is from a deeply base premise. These men took advantage of us in our weakest of times. They disrespected my mother, father and brother while I was at the helm of the family arms. It is a great defeat for me personally and I know I will have to fight these demons until the day I die to stay on track with my promises to Daniel this day. I will do my best. With the revelations brought forth in the Peter Ambrose Will I feel that I am closer than ever to being able to prove my case in England. It is a hard cross to bear but I will try to honor my pledge. There is still the visage of an Ambrose sitting in my families rightful estate flying his flag of fraud and larceny for all to see.

Daniel and I have been offered the opportunity to buy into business with Sam and Walter. We have decided that this is a good use of our new-found wealth and we would see it grow further. We wish to own our own land so money will be held aside for that purpose. It is the dawn of yet a different day in our lives. We will be in the good hands of our dearest friends to mutual benefit. We will work tirelessly to make the best of our good fortune and thank our God each day for his deliverance from our circumstance and his sage guidance in the path of our future decisions.

Daniel's Visit at the Ball House

Daniel visited the Ball house the next day. He enjoyed his time there and Mary was a devoted friend. She had been married to Robert Pond a few months after Daniel's departure. The prior year she had given birth to their first daughter, Mary Pond, on July 14, 1657. Daniel was in awe of this little girl and her happy play. Mary was a proud mother. They had delayed further children at this time however. Mary and Robert welcomed Daniel into their home. Daniel was warmed by the thought that Mary was in a good circumstance and happy. He wished that he could have been available to marry but she was his elder and her time for marriage had come before he was old enough to contend for the honor. They would remain friends. Daniel spent much time on the floor playing with little Mary. She loved the attention and was a very pretty little girl. She was bright and happy like her mother. When his time came to leave, he was both happy and sad. It was understandable with the feelings he hid deep inside of his own heart. Daniel was now fourteen years old. He was feeling the pangs of puberty and a keen interest in those of the opposite sex. They would visit many times before he left for the textile mill.

Joshua's Decisions

Joshua had decided to delay any relationships. He knew of the sadness that his mother had suffered with the passing of his father. He did not wish to feel that pain. If relationships ended like those of his parents and his grandparents it was just not worth it. He failed to see the good times and the happy years and events that they shared. He was just too young to remember much of those times. Poor Daniel was born after the death of his father so he did not know him at all. Sam and Walter had said that they thought of the boys as their own sons and that was heartwarming. He had his first feelings of having a father when he made the acquaintance of Sam that first day. It was a different circumstance than most would understand but those deep feelings were starting to boil. He would bask in the time with Sam as they grew old together. He would focus on learning his trade. These things he hoped would drive the need for vengeance and repatriation far from his heart. He could not trust the church here in Boston. The Reverend Mather and his lot had their hands in every chapel and all things religious. Joshua longed for his old church and beliefs in England. They had made simple sense to him and those in the church seemed to be earnest in their devotions. These Puritans seemed to have other agendas outside of religion. These were wealth, political power and community standing. The mix of religion with these things set men on a dangerous path. Joshua could see this at work in the souls of these supposedly holy men. The devil was at work in their souls and they hardly recognized his efforts. Instead they seemed to wallow in its evil and except this into their own lives. In the meantime, they used this very premise to persecute and punish those that opposed them. Their coming to the new world changed nothing for the common man. It only brought different corrupt men to power and influence. Joshua would follow his faith in a solitary path and on his own. Doing otherwise would put him in danger of following the devil's own will as was being taught by the deeds of these religious icons. He would not fall to that temptation. He had spoken to Daniel on the subject and on this issue they both agreed. They would continue to search for those who thought likewise and offered a different option closer to their faith and beliefs. There were many of these groups in England but few had journeyed to the colonies. The Puritans were quick to expel them when they attempted to settle among them in Massachusetts. Some had taken to meeting secretly in their homes and they would move the meeting place each Sunday to avoid detection. The Puritans themselves introduced the rumor that those involved with this type of faith were indeed under the control of the devil or they would have no need to hide. In many conversations they were accused of devil worship in their meetings. These people were used to this treatment because it had been much the same in England and other places in Europe. It was rumored that there were large settlements of this strange religion that had settled in Pennsylvania. Indeed, the boys Indian friends started to show up in strange clothing that they had received from these Dutch settlers. They spoke of strange rituals where those in attendance would shake with the spirit inside of them. In England there was a group called "The Shakers". Daniel remembered that in reality they were of the Quaker religion but did not know that much about their religious practices other than to know they were certainly not involved with the devil. They simply wanted to practice their beliefs without interference from the organized church or government. With his life in turmoil both in his faith and living conditions he did not want to bring a mate into the fray until these things were settled in his own mind. He knew that many would follow and populate the community. With this growth the Puritan influence would be diluted over time. This was the hope of many. The Puritans had gotten on many people's nerves with their judgmental and demanding natures. If they did not dominate the political offices, they would have been put out long ago Joshua thought.

The Deals and the Future

They had two weeks to talk with Sam and Walter and to hammer out their agreements. There were no real areas of dispute. Walter was aging and would need someone to take over his company in the near future. His health dictated it. With no heir he had to find one and his feelings Daniel fell right into this role as heir apparent. Sam had the same feelings but his needs lay more with expanding the company and producing more ships and products for sale. Either of these circumstances made a good case for Joshua and Daniel taking a large part of both men's companies and futures. All of the parties stood to gain much. With the influx of cash from the boy's windfall there were many things to be done. It was agreed that the boys would be equal partners in the businesses and be treated as family by Sam and Walter.

Sam would use the funds to build the sawmill he so needed. It would provide standard sized timber for the ships and be of higher quality than the hand split pieces that they currently used. It would improve the amount of timbers available and the quality of the ships they built. There would be money left over for other improvements on the docks and to construct additional space to build more ships.

Walter would use the funds to bring the Spanish wool to the colony. He had learned that the sheep themselves were held closely by the Spanish royals and none had been exported from Spain. Trade would be established to accommodate their needs. This would improve the quality of the wool and expand the types of cloth they could weave. The better wool would provide a bigger profit with the same amount of work. There would be new looms and an expansion of the textile mill. Sam and Walter had discussed the purchase of two ships so Walter could transport his own products to foreign markets. Joshua knew that these two men resembled the vision he had of his own father. He had expanded into other businesses and shipping and missed no opportunity to get into other areas of industry as they presented themselves. To see Sam and Walter forge ahead with these great plans made him feel closer than ever to them. The boys would give their money but they were all big winners when it came to their futures and welfare. They all fit together now like some big puzzle. Joshua knew it was God's hand at work.

Daniel Rewards his Friends

Daniel had not decided if he should tell Johnny, Benny and Isaiah about his good fortune. In the end he could hardly hold it in. As they were sitting around the stables one-night Johnny jokingly said "Well Daniel! Has Mr. Eggleston made you a rich man yet?"

Daniel laughed with them and then said "In fact he had a hand in it!"

They all stopped laughing and got very quiet. Daniel continued "Sam and Walter were able to negotiate a sum of money from a past debt to my family that has allowed my brother and I to buy into their businesses. We will continue our training and learning but we are no longer indentured. Our indenture was voided giving us the choice of what we would do with our money. There was really no question to it. We will put our fortunes with Sam and Walter. They are like family to us both and the only family we have known since the death of our parents some years ago. The three of you at this table are family too. There is a kinship I feel with all of you."

The boys were in awe. Benny said "Well, don't forget your good old friends when you live with the wealthy merchants!"

Daniel said "I have told you that I will not forget you and I won't. I will be away another two years learning the mill. After my return I will not forget my friends. If you wish I can talk with Sam and Walter to see if there are positions that you can work in now. We will be expanding the businesses with this money so there could be some work there."

The boys shouted "Talk to them now. We need the work if we are ever to get out of the stables and have families. You are a good fellow Daniel. We will not forget what you have done either. We are bound to each other for life and are your loyal friends." With that Daniel brought on a veritable feast for them all. There were meats, vegetables and fruits for all. They had ale and a good time of it. The ladies in the Nanny house did all the cooking and preparation and Walter had paid them well for their help and shared the bounty with them. These were days of wonder and splendor for both boys. Joshua did not have the friends like Daniel had. Most of those were out in the logging camp now. They had set up a fund to help their Indian friends and help supply and feed their families. They were unaware of this now but they soon would know the quality of friendship that the boys offered to them.

These weeks of respite soon passed. The boys would leave for their next commitments the following day. Daniel had the shortest trip. The textile mill was just outside of Boston. He would stay in a cabin there that had been built on the property. It would be his first house that he lived in alone. He would be very busy though and spend his off hours sleeping there. The textile mill would be very busy in these times. There was much demand for cloth of all kinds in the colonies and England. The King expected that the colonies supply the crown with high quality goods and textiles. These products were one of the mainstays of the colonies exports. He had packed. He traveled light and had few of his own belongings. Their discussions with Sam and Walter had gone well. The two of them would procure some prime land for the boys to homestead on when the time was right. Until then it would be held in trust for them. He went to his duty with a different outlook on his life now. He was no longer bound by anything except his own fates and this was the way a man wanted it. He had spoken to Sam and Walter about Johnny, Benny and Isaiah. He was told to have them introduce themselves and they would find them a place as soon as it was expedient. This made Daniel happy and he rushed back to the stables to inform them of their good fortune.

Joshua leaves for the Saw Mill

Joshua was packed and eager to leave. His time at the Sawmill would be two-fold. Early on he would be splitting timber and board by hand with the help of hammer and wedge. Later as the Sawmill was built, he would learn to saw timber and board on the machinery installed there. In addition, he would be in residence as the mill was being built so he would know every nook and cranny of the facility and how it all went together. This would make him an expert with the mill. Sam would count on him for its smooth and steady operation in the future. Joshua relished this type of reliance on him. It replaced the lost title as the head of his household and bearer of the family arms to some extent. He would make his name through his own hard work and not through inheritance after all. In practice he still was the bearer of the family arms and this would play heavily on his future decisions. For now, he craved the learning process he was about to begin.

On the next morning the boys rose early and met with Sam and Walter at "Bunch of Grapes" to eat and discuss any unresolved issues before their departure. There were very few. The boys knew they were finally in the company of honest and hard-working men that only sought out their best interests. They were excited when the discussions turned to the available parcels of land that had been identified. Daniel said "I wish to be near a river or creek so I can have my own mill of sorts adjacent to me. Joshua believed that this was a good idea and wanted the same along with many acres of good timber to use for his home. There was a certain prospect of barter here. Joshua could construct the buildings on each property and Daniel could keep them all clothed and warm. Neither of them realized yet that they would have sufficient income to dress in the finest of clothes available for purchase. It seemed safer to each of them to rely on one another instead of outsiders. They now added Sam and Walter to their circle. Dealing with outsiders had never worked well for them in the past.

Friends with Benefits

Daniel was surprised when he left "Bunch of Grapes" to find

Johnny, Benny and Isaiah sitting on the front stoop awaiting them. Benny stood up as a sort of spokesman and said "We came here to introduce ourselves as you telled us Daniel!" Daniel laughed and took them to Sam and Walter.

He said "This is Johnny, Benny and Isaiah. They are the lads I spoke to you about. Apparently, they are eager to get started!"

Sam said "We will have a discussion with each of you tomorrow morning. Today we have to get Daniel and Joshua to their new postings and ready for their new training. I want you to think of what you would like to do keeping in mind that there is a wide variety of work to be done in the textile and shipbuilding industries. Come to us tomorrow with your plan if you would!" The boys were ecstatic and could hardly hold themselves in. They would have some planning to do. They had not counted on being asked this question so they would retire to the stables and discuss their options while doing their work. They thanked Sam, Walter, Joshua and Daniel and rushed off to chart their course for their lives. Daniel had no idea how it would turn out.

Joshua's trip to the mill was uneventful and he dove right into his work. He was not afraid of the physical labor and enjoyed it immensely. His elders complained and groaned about it. Joshua was now to be a leader of these men over time so he knew he must set the example. No man should point to him and say he never did the hard work of the lowest man. Joshua wanted them all to know that he would work in the most menial and the hardest of the jobs so he could effectively lead them later as his role in the company evolved. There are various titles for those who work with wood in the process of splitting the wood from the logs. These titles are joiners, turners, coopers and other titles for specialty types of woodworking. To split a log into timber or lumber a process is used called "Riving".

Riving uses an assortment of tools including a large maul or sledge hammer as we know it, wooden or iron wedges, a froe, a beetle (or froe club), a break (or holding tool) and a hewing hatchet to name a few. The log selected must be of high quality, straight grained and free of knots. The log is split in half on the first split. This is done by inserting the wedges into the grain at the halfway point and then striking the wedges with the maul until the split occurs. This can be done on the end with small logs and on the top for longer logs. Short logs are usually used for furniture or barrels and long logs for ship's timber or lumber. A longer length of the log produces a log with a wider diameter. The logs have been measured and cut when they are felled to the desired length allowing an extra six inches for error in the

riving process. The log is split into halves, quarters, eights and so on so long as the material produced meets the requirements of the end product needed. At this point the material produced can be brought into the shop or barn to continue the process. At this point the riving continues using the froe. A combination of froe and wedge might be necessary to cut the longer logs into ship timber or lumber of longer lengths. As the froe and beetle are used the wood begins to split and this continues until the desired piece is separated from the original log. The pieces are always split in halves and then halved again until all of the stock is used up. For the longer pieces a holding tool is used called a break. This holds the pieces in place while the riving process continues so the log does not slip or turn. The froe is moved back and forth to widen the split as it moves through the material. This gives added leverage to force the split. When the splitting is completed any waste wood is removed with a hewing hatchet. This shapes and squares the wood into the desired product for use. This is all very hard work and requires much time and effort.

Each piece of lumber or timber must go through this process by hand without a Sawmill to do the work. Sam and Joshua saw the benefit of learning this process in its most natural form. This gave them an understanding of the wood and the labors it entailed. Each log had its own personality and traits.

It was much like a person. The Indians believed that each tree had a soul of its own and that they were a living thing to be respected. Joshua liked this aspect of the Indian beliefs and the thoughts of this made him see things differently from the time he had made his acquaintance with the Indians at the logging camp. Even in his hunting and trapping he did not waste any part of the animal or tree. The cuttings from the trees were used to burn for heat or to produce other cutting used for furniture or other needs. There would be no waste of anything of nature under Joshua's management. Sam had not considered this prior to Joshua's practice. It was true that each of them had much to learn from each other over time.

On their hunts they would use what they could and give the rest to the Indians for their use. They made many items from the bones, sinews and other parts that the white man did not use. The meat was usually shared with the Indians. In this way good relations were maintained and they had a cooperative spirit between the loggers, the mill and the Indians. There was no trouble between them.

Daniel's Work at the Textile Mill

Daniel had left a few hours after Joshua to his post at the textile mill. He would have the same attitude and would start in the lowest of jobs to enable him to learn every aspect of the business that he now partially owned.

Christopher Columbus brought a hearty meat sheep to Cuba and Santa Domingo to feed his crew. These were known as Churros. They were not good wool sheep however. He left some in Cuba. Later the descendants of these sheep were taken to South America by Cortez. In fact, Queen Isabella used profits from the Spanish sheep industry to finance Columbus's 1492 voyage to America. The basis of the industry was the Merino Sheep. These were brought to Spain by the Moors and Spain held a relative monopoly on the breed until the late 17th century.

The sheep produced short-stapled and ultrafine wool needed to make fine clothes. By 1526 there were an estimated 3.5 million Merino Sheep in Spain. The wool and woolen goods were a major export for the country. It was traded in the West Indies and by extension in the colonies even though England had forbidden trade with foreign countries under the Navigation Acts of 1651. Like all goods that are embargoed or in short supply a vigorous black market arose to fill the need. The offspring of these sheep would be the breeding stock for the Rambouillet sheep breed.

The first sheep to appear in the Massachusetts Bay Colony were Southdown sheep. Governor Winthrop himself was said to keep a flock of these sheep. There were roughly 1000 sheep in the area by 1643. Britain did not worry when the sheep were used for meat to feed the colonists but wanted no part in a competition in the textile industry. Soon they specifically restricted the import of wool and the establishment of the textile industry. The Southdown sheep had coarse wool that was not suited for many applications such as clothing. The Spanish sheep wool was the answer. Sheep were not the only items that were woven into thread or yarn. Flax, hemp, cotton, silk and animal hair were also used for this purpose. Cotton had not yet made its worth known. It was hard to spin and clean and not widely used. Flax was woven and planted by many of the settlers and woven in their homes for their needs. Hemp was widely used but was not good material for clothing. Hair was used in areas where cloth was in short supply. The hair of horses, rabbits, goats and other long-haired mammals were used for many applications.

For now, the focus of the textile mill would be wool. They would trade with the black market to obtain all of the Merino wool they could acquire. They would raise and shear the Southdown sheep and prepare it for weaving. They would expand their herds for this purpose and see into importing some of the Merino sheep. In reality the Merino Sheep would be monopolized until 1786 when King Ferdinand VI of Spain sent his cousin, the French King Louis XVI, several hundred fine Merino sheep.

The textile industry was not as it is known today. These early mills simply added the spinning of the wool into yarn. This yarn was then outsourced to households who would put the yarn on a hand loom to make linen and other cloth. It was a home-based business in this sense and a way for the colonists to earn some money and fill their cloth needs. There was much to learn on both fronts and Daniel found this to be a much larger task than he had envisioned. First there would be the acceptance of the fleeces after they were carded by the shepherds. Those would then be spun at the mill into yarn. It would then be distributed to a network of loom weavers to make a finished product. In this network would be many types of people from different backgrounds. Some would make excellent products and some not so good. These by products would have to be measured and paid for in cash. For this the paymaster would have to judge the quality and quantity of the cloth and come to an agreeable price that was fair to the weaver and the company. It would entail many small negotiations with many small producers and would be an endless circle of business. Even though this process was fraught with pitfalls Daniel was eager to learn the process. The more he knew about each part of the business the more successful he would be in his dealings and the management practices. He had an advantage over the people at the mill after spending his time among the herds and learning about the sheep and the carding process. This knowledge would now pay its worth in his understanding and performance here in this job. He could see the puzzle pieces fitting together and felt that Walter was very wise in setting this path for him to learn and run the business. He was happy and dove into his work.

The most common fibers used for hand spinning are sheep's wool, cotton, silk, alpaca, mohair (from angora goats), and angora (from angora rabbits). Most of the processing at the mill would be sheep's wool. The wool arrives after the carding process. That means it is cleaned of grease and lanolin and brushed to remove debris. This carded wool now goes through a process called roving. This combs the wool into single long strands known as pencil-rovings. These resemble yarn but are straight where yarn is twisted. The pencil-rovings are weak in strength. Twisting them makes them stronger. The mill spins the pencil-rovings making it into yarn. This process yields single fiber yarn. Most yarn has multiple fibers twisted together to add strength to it. The process is called plying. Single strands are now spun into stronger yarns. Finally, the yarn is dyed for color in the dying process and put on large spools or rolled into balls for market. This yarn is then sent to weavers to make cloth and other items. The process is similar for cotton threads and the same weaving process is completed to make linen goods and cotton cloth. The mill would work with some cotton.

Joshua's Work at the Saw Mill

Joshua would be working with the construction and launch of the Sawmill in the early days at his work. The Sawmill was a simple machine during this time. It was operated by a water wheel so it would have to be located near running water in a creek or river. It was essential that this be a water source that would continue to run year-round without stoppage. The saw would not work without the movement of the water on the waterwheel. The turning of the wheel would then generate movement on a wooden rod that attached to the saw itself. A drawing of this process is shown here.

Some of the mills operated in a covered building and others operated in the open. The early mills most likely operated in the open due to the constraints of financial resources.

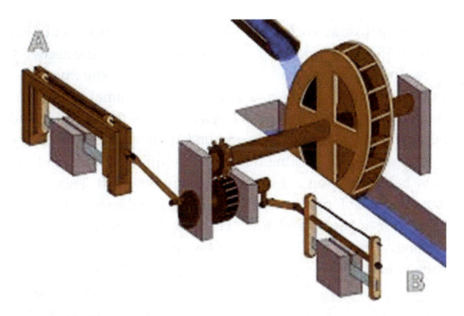

www.afrc.uamont.edu

www.pinelogging.org/Home/photos-1

The two years passed quickly. The boys studied and learned

their trade. Joshua spent many hours in the construction of the Sawmill and could operate, repair and build a mill if the necessity arose. They had a good site for the mill on the Mystic River. The water ran unhindered in cold weather with minimal icing at the site. The mill was now enclosed in a large building that allowed the operation to continue during bad weather. He learned the process and all of the fine details of the mill and was ready to move back to Boston to learn the shipbuilding craft. This would take somewhat longer and he would labor on the ships and their design for many years now. He was eager to continue his learning process. He would be indoctrinated into the management and ownership of the company with this final move in the company. This would be a full circle for Joshua. He began with wealth, felt poverty and hopelessness and now had returned to a more promising lifestyle. He was keenly aware though that it was not what he would have had in England. He quickly put it out of his thoughts. He had a lot of things to concentrate on now and would throw himself into his work and hope it would be enough.

Daniel had met his challenges also. He had helped to set up the herds of new sheep to increase their supply of wool. He had learned the weaving and had become and expert at spinning and adding plies to the yarn. He had developed his network of home workers and would soon develop a trade network with the wool markets both here and abroad. He had learned the dying and fluffing processes and was ready to return to Boston to work with Walter to learn his duties in the business. He would be a true businessman in his new role. He felt proud and independent finally. He was aware that his lot was better in the colonies than he could have hoped for in England. As the second son the title of "head of the family" and all of the inheritance would have gone to Joshua. He would live in Joshua's shadow for the rest of his life there. Here he would have his own business, property and independence not directly tied to the family or the family coat of arms. He was happy in the colonies but cautious. He knew that once before he had all that was familiar taken from him and knew it could happen again.

The Boys Return to Boston and Begin their New Business Positions

The year was 1660. Joshua was now seventeen years old. Daniel was fifteen years old. On their return Daniel continued his friendship with Mary Ball. She had given birth to her second child Martha Pond who was born April 13 1660. Little Mary was now three years old. She remembered Daniel and was always glad to see him. Like all children she had him wrapped around her little finger and would lead him to her table to play with her dolls and things. Daniel obliged while visiting with Mary. Robert, Mary's husband, was rarely home now. He was working on the fishing boats and it required much time at sea. It was a good living though and he hoped to save enough to have his own boat. He would bring home some of their catch from their treks and the family ate well compared to most. Mary had a garden and she worked in it regularly to raise many vegetables. She and the girls would trek into the forest and collect berries, fruits, herbs and medicinal plants. If she could she would bring home starts of the plants to grow on their property. She was a very good mother and a good woman. She still weaved at home to earn extra money for the family. Daniel was surprised by this and thought he could offer something better to her so she could make more money for her efforts.

Daniel had not been home six months when word came to him of a fishing vessel lost at sea in a bad storm. It carried Mary's husband Robert Pond. He was one of the missing and would not be heard from again. Mary was now a widow with two small children. Some records show a third daughter, Sarah, who married Desire Clap. Some records show only two daughters. Mary was in dire circumstances now. Daniel would help her with money at times and with the children. He enjoyed being around the girls. In his childhood there were no little girls around. He was learning how much different girls were from boys at this time. He was very busy at work so his time was limited as he focused on his duties.

Joshua had taken to shipbuilding like his father and uncle before him. He could see improvements to be made to the designs of the ships for strength, speed and safety and they were quickly incorporated into the ships under construction after discussion and approval. The need for ships by the colonies for defense and transportation increased as each new wave of immigrants arrived to the shores of Boston. In fact it was not just Boston that made up the customer base of the ship building company. Colonies up and down the eastern coast purchased the vessels. Another large purchaser was England and the King. Of course, like all other things in the colonies there was a sense of entitlement from that side of the water and they expected that they would purchase these ships at greatly discounted prices. Sam would have none of that and the prices were quoted the same for all. Joshua found this to be amusing and could only picture the faces of the Royals and bureaucrats in England when they received their quotes. With the Navigation Acts in force all legal shipping had to be done in English or Colonial flagged ships. All products were supposed to go to England with no other trading options. This did not take into account the ever-increasing effects of the black market. For the most part those sitting in England making these laws could not fathom that they would not be followed precisely as they were written. The idea that some would rebel and find their own markets seemed to pass them by. Sam and Joshua were just as happy either way. There was a huge market for new ships, fishing boats and packets. They had all of the work they could handle and waiting lists for more. They sold to the Colonies, England and the Black Marketers with the same gusto for each so long as they were not pulled into the politics of any of their customers. It kept them very busy and they continued to expand their business to meet demand. Demand was the one thing that made their price demands to England stand. There was no shortage of purchasers and any ship produced would be sold to someone. If they wanted ships they would have to pay the price. It did not set well with them and it made no friends of those in high positions in the English government.

Daniel's Continued Relationship with Mary Ball Pond

Mary's husband had been gone now for a year. He went missing in 1661 and Mary had finally given up hope of his return. She knew he had joined his God in heaven. Daniel noticed in his visits that he was not alone. There was another man now openly courting Mary. His name was Nicholas Allen. Daniel was feeling like he had a chance with Mary during this time. He could see himself married to her and helping to raise her children. He was now eighteen years old and firmly established in business. He had not openly courted or made his wishes known to Mary and for this he had only himself to blame. He did not have the proper guidance in these matters. He could find no comfortable way to broach the subject so he would leave frustrated and angry with himself. Now with another man in the mix he could feel the wrath of his errors. The procrastination of making his feelings known to Mary was having signs of personal disaster. He decided he would need to correct this situation soon and vowed to do just that. He would go on the Sabbath and address it this very week.

The Sabbath arrived and Daniel put on his best clothes for his trip. He took some flowers with him. As he arrived, he saw the girls in the yard. He played with them for a brief time before going to the door to announce himself. To his dismay Nicholas Allen was there ahead of him. He too was dressed in fancy clothes and from the looks of the vase on the table had arrived with flowers also. His clothes were much finer than Daniels. His flowers were much more colorful and grander than the bunch he had brought. Mary saw him and jumped to her feet. She was excited. She said she was glad he had come. She had the most wonderful news to tell him. Nicholas and Mary were to be married. They were married on 3 July, 1663. Daniel feigned happiness for Mary but his heart was breaking inside. He spent a short time there and when he found a break he excused himself and left for home. He gave his flowers to the girls in the yard. They quickly added them to their tea party. Daniel walked in silence back to the stables.

The boys were both resolved to be the best they could be at their given professions. After all; they had no one truly to care for or someone to care for them in these harsh conditions. Rather than worry with the complexities of the male and female interactions they threw themselves into their work with abandon and the years passed along. They became masters of their crafts. Walter had grown old and spent little time with the textile business. He had lost his wife and lived a life of solitude. He did visit however from time to time and made himself available to Daniel for questions and problems as they arose. He was a man of knowledge and contacts in the industry and there were none better. He had successfully introduced Daniel to his connections and allies in the business. He had schooled him in the finer points and knew that with few exceptions the business would be run as if he were still there. Daniel had proven himself and was now in charge.

Joshua was working side by side with Sam. Sam would never leave the business but Joshua was considered his equal on the docks at the Sawmill and at the camp. His word was the same as Sam's and his decisions were followed without question. It was five years since his return to Boston now. This fifth year after the return of the boys to Boston was an eventful one.

Mary was once again widowed. Nicholas Allen had died of unknown causes in the early spring of 1668. Daniel was 24 and well established in his business. Mary had once again turned to Daniel for consolation and guidance. Daniel was pleased to give it but it was different now. He had no expectations of his future with Mary beyond friendship and watching her daughters grow in to young ladies. The girls were now eleven and eight years old. He knew that she had passed him over twice for her own affections and did not want to ever feel that rejection from her again. It was safer to keep their relationship on a less intimate footing and he could not be hurt.

Joshua and Mary Sumner

Joshua found himself surprised by his own emotions at this time and place. He had been drawn into the Boston political circles. He did not wish to hold office or have dominion over his countrymen. He was however being asked to participate in the issues and volunteer his time, education and work on the causes and issues at the forefront of the colony. His name first appeared on a petition heard in the court in 1664. History has clouded the content of this petition in all manners except to know that by affixing his signature he had formed a record that came down through the family genealogy of this deed.

In his dabbling in the political affairs of this time he became entwined with the Sumner family. William Sumner left England and came to the colonies in 1636. With him came his wife the former Mary West. He was born in 1605 in Bichester, Oxfordshire, England. An interesting side bar is that in a later generation the surname West would be attached to my grandmother Clara and wife of Goff Chesney Hinshaw.

The family consisted of:
Elizabeth, born 1652 and was the oldest daughter and child
Mary, born in 1654
William, born in 1656
Hannah, born 1659
Sarah, born 1662

Experience, born 1664

Ebenezer, born 1666 (He would share an infamous adventure with Daniel Henshaw's only son.)

Clement, born 1671

Mercy, She was born 1675 and died at a young age.

William Sumner made the crossing in the same year as Richard Mather. It is not clear if they came on the same ship or at the same time. Sumner was active in the colony at an early date and would have been involved in establishing the government and ways of those who lived in it. It is clear that the earlier settlers had a large voice in the future. There were fewer of them to make the long term decisions which weighted their participation much heavier than those who would follow as the colony grew. He would have to speak his mind and deal with the intricacies of living with the Puritans and their ideas without crossing them. It was at a social gathering that chanced the attendance of the Sumner family and Joshua and Sam under the same roof. Joshua was used to these gatherings now as a business owner. They were for the most part dry of humor and long on wind. Except when an issue came to the front the conversation was political and religious blather. This gathering would be different. Joshua had spied a beautiful girl across the room and could not take his eyes off of her. This was unusual behavior for him and it was a bit bothersome. He was having trouble concentrating on the topics of conversation and his attention always wondered back to the girl. Sam had noticed and had a big smile on his face. He walked over to Joshua and struck up a conversation. Mostly he got affirmations and grunts from Joshua as his replies or he was totally ignored. This amused Sam even more. Finally, he said "Do you want to meet her?

Joshua broke his gaze and said "What?"

Sam replied "You aren't going to be worth a fiddle if you don't meet her now. You can't focus or do anything but stare at her. We need to put an end to this before she thinks you are touched! Come with me!"

Sam led Joshua through the room and to the girl. He struck up a conversation immediately with her. He said "It is Mary Sumner is it not?"

Mary replied "It is my dear sir!"

Sam said "I am Sam Wickford and this is my partner Joshua Henshaw. Joshua is an accomplished man for his age and has spent time in the forest and building saw mills. As of late he is building ships with me in our business. He is very good at his work but there is a problem. Something or someone has caught his attention and he cannot focus or seem to function until he can overcome this affliction."

Mary said "What can I do to help you Mr. Wickford?"

Sam said "You can make your acquaintance of Joshua so he can get back to his normal way of being! Joshua this is Mary Sumner and Mary this is Joshua Henshaw, my partner! I will seek out your father for some discussion and the two of you can get to know each other!"

With that Sam went in search of William Sumner and Joshua stood in front of Mary dumbfounded and embarrassed. Mary broke the silence and said "Well then Joshua I think we must resolve this affliction forthwith. I am Mary Elizabeth Sumner. I know of Sam and you through my acquaintances. Can we go and get refreshments and take a walk?"

Joshua stuttered a bit and replied "Y-yes Ma'am! That would be a fine idea"

This was how the courtship began. Joshua was able to pull himself together in a short time and felt more at ease with Mary. He had little experience in his role as a suitor and explained this to her. She understood and seemed genuinely happy that he had little experience. It went to prove that his intentions were sincere. Mary steered their attention to Sam and her father and took Joshua to meet him. It was necessary to follow the protocol if they wished to go for a walk unchaperoned. It was not hard to receive William's permission because Sam had already prepared the groundwork with Mary's father. He was pleased at himself and Mary's father was pleased that a man of Joshua's standing and wealth would have an interest in his second daughter. By custom the first daughter would have to be married before the second daughter could pursue her desires. It was premature to worry with this issue just yet. It would however be a long courtship as Mary's older sister, Elizabeth, was a sort of tom boy and not at all interested in submitting to the feminine wiles. It would take a special man to accept her, woo her and get her down the aisle! As their business expanded Sam and Joshua would be very busy at their work. Mary would be a guiding light to Joshua from this day forward. He would always seek to bask in her glow and do things to please her. He continued to have one issue that he could not shake however. The old demons continued to rage in him that drove his thoughts to England and the Ambrose family. He felt somehow incomplete as a man as long as the issue of the fraud stood. He kept this a secret to only himself for now.

Daniel and Mary Ball

Daniel was working a heavy schedule. In his time away from the mill he would visit with his friends or go to Mary Ball's house. He enjoyed the girl's immensely and they were very fond of Daniel in return. Mary would watch them interact and felt somehow at peace with it. For Daniel's part he carried his emotions internally and did not speak of them with any of his friends or Mary. He did not want to feel the hurt he had felt before when another suitor might show up at her door. None had come forward for now. Mary was not openly looking for a third husband. It was rumored that she was cursed and that any man that would have her would be condemned to a quick death after their wedding. It had happened twice already and this was the type of thing that those like Mather would pounce upon to scream their accusation of witchcraft or blasphemy. It was clear to their weak minds that she had done something to anger God! Mary knew she could count on Daniel for her needs and those of her girls. She was now thirty-three years old. Daniel was twenty-five. As the years passed the age difference grew narrower. Eighteen was a good age for a man. Daniel was well past that age now. He was considered a man and of marriageable stock. It was 1669. Mary's second husband had been gone now for four years. The relationship between Mary and Daniel had remained the same since their first encounter. Daniel held feelings for Mary but she was unaware of them. In fact she could never see past the age difference of when they first met and became friends. She was not opposed to Daniel in any way. It was just difficult to adjust her thinking from that of a brother to that of a lover where Daniel was concerned. A change had been taking place in her over time though. She hardly noticed it. As she watched Daniel with the girls she would marvel at what a wonderful father he would make. She saw him grow strong and into manhood and considered him a good catch for some woman. She knew he was a man of means with a solid future and holdings and felt happy for him after such a rocky start in the colonies. All of the things were in place except for her feelings on their current situation. She did not feel she deserved a man this good nor did she want to test the curse a third time. It was all for naught because Daniel had never broached the subject with her since he had known her. Little did she know he had intended to do just that the day she accepted the proposal from Nicholas. She did not know the heartbreak she had caused him. If she had it would have possibly been a different outcome at that time. It was the occasion of a wedding reception in Boston where Mary was approached by her friends. They asked if she ever had a notion to marry again. Mary replied "Even if I did no man would have me after my matrimonial history. Many believe I am cursed! I ask you what man would want to take that chance or even court me with those intents at my age with these issues hanging over my life."

They all laughed. Mary did not understand. Then her friend said to her "You silly woman. Daniel Henshaw would have you! He has always had feelings for you! Don't you see that! He has never said such to a soul but it is very clear in the way he looks at you and the attention he shows to you and the girls that this would be his most desirous wish! How can you not see that?"

Mary was stricken. It had never dawned on her that Daniel's behavior was more than a friendship. As she pondered the subject it became clearer and clearer that Daniel had been just the right man from the beginning and even with their age difference there were feelings that flowed in both directions. How could she have not seen it? She would look upon their relationship quite differently from this time forward. She would show him more attention and court him if she had to. She could now see the pain she had caused him but this wonderful man suffered it in silence and with no regrets just to be near her. Her friends reinforced her thinking with examples and gossip. By the time she returned to her home she was convinced that she did have an interest in entering the marriage arena one more time! Daniel still had no idea of what storms of emotion were about to inundate him. It was no longer up to him. Mary had made up her mind and it would come to pass no matter how long it took. Mary was sure that the girls would be very excited with this new turn!

The Courting of Daniel Henshaw

The girls were giddy as they made their preparations. They had cooked and baked all day and focused on Daniel's favorite foods. The house was cleaned and they were all dressed in their finest when Daniel arrived shortly before meal time. He immediately experienced the atmosphere and could not understand the change. He searched his mind to remember if it was a birthday, a holiday or some other remembrance that had slipped his mind. This yielded no results. He finally decided to accept it as a festive occasion for whatever its purpose. He was treated as the guest of honor and he seemed strangely out of place in this role. The girls played with him and teased him. The playing was normal but the teasing was something new. Mary herself had a different carriage to her this day. She was very attentive to Daniel and asked about his welfare and his work. Normal discussion between them did not focus on him alone. He answered each of the questions with great vigor and decided to just go along with the flow of the day and see where it was leading. After a time the girls quietly moved away from them and into their own play. It was like a bell had sounded to change the scene. Mary moved closer to Daniel. He liked this very much but was now on guard. She started the conversation slowly and reminisced about their history together. "Daniel, I remember when you first came to my father's house as a young man. We worked beside each other in those days. I thought you to be a wonderful young man."

Daniel said "Thank You Mary! My parents would have raised no other!"

She continued "As you grew you turned into a fine man. You have supported the girls and I through some very tough times and I have overlooked that you have grown and improved yourself constantly. I am sure that there are many young ladies that have noticed also!"

Daniel said "Not that I know of Mary. I have been to my tasks now for several years and I have had to focus my attention solely on those things as I learned them. Indeed, there were hardly any young ladies with the sheep herds or at the mill!"

Mary paused for a moment. It drew Daniel's attention to what she would say next. He waited impatiently. He felt that he was about to learn the reason for the festive atmosphere. Mary was a bit uneasy and nervous. This was not a characteristic that he often saw in her. She said "I do not wish for any of these ladies to be attracted to you Daniel. It is of a selfish motive I admit. I have realized that it is you that I have had feelings for over these years. These feelings are not as I thought. They had tricked me and turned them into an accepted normalcy so I have denied them to myself and to you. I do not wish to do that anymore and at the risk of rejection I want to declare my love to you!"

She blushed heavily. Daniel felt like he had been punched in the stomach and lost his wind. His heart was beating fast and he did not know how to respond. They sat and looked into the others eyes for a long time. Mary made the first move and their lips moved together in a long and meaningful kiss. He could leave no room for denying that it was not the kiss of a friend any longer. Daniel was reeling and did not know how to respond. He started to speak several times but nothing would come out of his mouth. His words failed him at this very important time. Mary was dumbfounded and thought that she had misread Daniel's emotions on the subject. She was embarrassed at her actions and began to cry. Daniel could not stand to see her cry and took her into his arms to comfort her. It was at this time that his mind cleared and the scene unfolded. Mary was declaring to him what he had wished to hear for many years now. He could not let another chance pass him by. He finally found the words. "Mary, do not cry! I was taken off guard and I am not experienced at these things. I have loved you since we worked the looms together in your father's home. I did not want to tell you then because of our age difference. Whenever the time seemed right to broach the subject there was a new man in your life that unseated me before I could strike up the courage to let my feelings be known. I tried to do this but on the last occasion you announced your betrothal to Nicholas. I was heartbroken and took a defensive stance on the subject. I cannot let this opportunity pass though. If you love me and I love you then nothing should stand in our way!"

Mary said "But it is said I am cursed and I do not want any harm to come to you!"

He replied "Curses are the stuff of Mather and his group. The fates that befell your two previous husbands were nothing more than happenstance. Being in the wrong place at the wrong time and a matter of bad health were the true cause of their passing not a silly curse. I would be proud to take the chance no matter what the reason!"

Mary cried once more. This time in happiness though. The girls ran from their hiding places and joined in the hugs and kisses. Their future had turned to one that they had seemingly always wanted. They too loved this man! There would be no rush to marriage. They would take their time and decide when the time was right.

Joshua and Mary Sumner

Joshua's relationship with Mary Sumner had continued and grown. From that first encounter they had seen each other often and made it known that they were courting. Mary had not been around many men like Joshua. He was not afraid of hard work and had risen from poverty. She did not know the full story of his life however. The part that was left behind in England had not been broached in these days of courtship. He knew that he would have to speak with her about it if things became more serious or marriage lay on the horizon. It was an issue that could affect them both and any children between them if he could not overcome his conceived duty to return to England and confront the Ambrose family. He had promised Daniel he would try to let it go but it was always there on the fringe of his thoughts. It ate at him like a cancer. He felt unfulfilled letting the evildoers enrich themselves in their deeds and at his families expense. For now, though it was too early in this relationship to worry about such things. He just wanted to revel in their happiness at the simple act of being together and enjoying each other.

Mary Sumner was of a family with standing in the community. Little did they know that in reality Joshua was from a royal bloodline but that information lay hidden from the common people amongst the fog of the Mather/Ambrose affair. Only his brother, Sam, Walter and Mather knew the truth. Mary did not care what others thought and the courtship continued. Mary's father was not disturbed with this talk either. He lived in a world of his senses. He could see, hear, touch and feel the quality of man that Joshua truly was. He knew that he would respect his daughter and provide her with security and a good home. He could present him with grandchildren which he enjoyed very much. The real issue was the marriage of her older sister. It was proper for her to marry first! Joshua, in his own way, saw this as a safety net for not having to expose his full story because it was not possible that the relationship would move forward as long as Mary's sister was unwed

The problem with Mary's sister was that she had no desire to marry or any prospects of a beau. It was impossible. In the colonies even a homely girl would have suitors because the ratio of men to women greatly favored the women in these things. A shortage of the fair sex opened many possibilities for each woman. Mary would simply have to get her sister interested, acquainted and betrothed to achieve her goal of marrying Joshua if it would be possible. At this point in time the formalities of a proposal and acceptance had not been contemplated but in Mary's mind they were on the path to just that and in a short time. Mary would have to be a good matchmaker to get her sister married and open the way to her own happiness. There must be a man that would interest Elizabeth and he must be found. To be clear, Elizabeth was a beauty on her own. She just chose to hide it under her tom-boy exterior and her competition to better any man she met.

Courtships and Complexities

The boys visited together as much as they could and as their work would permit. They both had good news to relay to each other about their relationship status. It struck them both that the women that they were committed to carried the same name of Mary. It was confusing to some people when conversations came to the topic. They were never sure which Mary they were talking about.

Daniel had the simplest path to matrimony. The only thing standing in his way was Mary's idea that there would be a reasonable time of mourning for Nicholas Allen. There was no time period specified for this activity and she did not want to show impropriety to his memory or to stir the ire of the community by remarrying too soon. Their friends did not see this as a problem but Mary seemed to be struggling with what this time period would be. At last she received a letter from Nicholas's sister. In it she made it clear that Nicholas would want to see her happy. This meant moving on in her life and the lives of the girls although they were not his biological children. In essence this letter released her from her perceived commitment and the period of mourning ceased. It still took some urging from her friends but finally they set a date to marry of August 12, 1670. This gave them another year to plan and to satisfy Mary that she had not dishonored her late husband. It worked well for everyone. Daniel went to Walter and Joshua. He asked about his land and was taken on a tour of available plots. He settled on one outside of town with a large stream running through it. It was just as he had pictured in his own mind. It was perfect. He asked Joshua to construct a dwelling on the site and a small milling operation using a water wheel and the stream. Sam and Joshua worked with Daniel to design the perfect dwelling that would make room for Mary and the girls. It needed to be large enough and sealed off well against the cold winters and marauding Indians and other unwelcome visitors. It was to be a wedding surprise for Mary. He hoped she would approve. He carefully planted questions about her dream house to her over this period and would incorporate them into the plans. He wanted it to be her vision also. As summer was upon them in 1669 the building began. Daniel knew that he could not take his bride and family to the stables and he also knew that the house that they now dwelled in was in poor condition and too small for additions to the family. They had wanted children of their own and this house would accommodate that possibility. It was very hard to keep the secret but Daniel and those working on the house kept it nonetheless.

Joshua began to feel the pangs of losing his patience. The planning and future nuptials of Daniel had him longing for his own. Both Mary and he had prayed on it and thought it was falling on God's deaf ears. They did not know what thing might tip the scales to find Elizabeth a suitable and willing husband. Elizabeth did not see the need for a husband and thought she could be perfectly happy and productive on her own. She did not like the pursuits of other women. She was more adventurous and felt inhibited by the role of a woman. She needed a man that would accept that and that she could share adventures with. She wanted him to see her as an equal and not a subservient wife. She reveled in upsetting the apple cart so to speak. She did things to stir controversy and to stir the gossip of the elder women of the community. She did not care what they thought but got some pleasure in whipping them into a frenzy of disapproval. It was what she lived for.

McCall and Elizabeth Sumner

By chance a man of the wilderness had come into Boston for a period. He wished to buy a new horse. His old one was lame and its time of usefulness had passed. His appearance stirred the gossips. They knew he was not a man of the church. They thought him to be Godless. He lived like the Indians and by his own hand. He hunted his food, trapped and sold pelts and lived off of his own wits. He rarely bathed because there was little time for that in the wilderness and bathing exposed him to his predators in a helpless moment. When he came to town he took a bath and got his hair trimmed. Elizabeth happened to be in town when he entered on his steed. She found him quite handsome and interesting. She wanted to know more about him. She found that approaching him directly would stir up the gossip so that is what she did forthwith. He was amused. She was bold and did not follow the accepted ways of these pseudo religious zealots. It was not true that he was a Godless man. Before his entry into the wilderness he had studied to be a man of the cloth. The behavior of the churches in the colonies drove him to the wilderness to live in his own faith and pursue his own God wherever he may find him. The thoughts of the Native American's on this front had also affected his beliefs greatly. He found that a hybrid of these beliefs fit his thinking on the subject much better than what he had been force fed from the church of the Puritans. He had been mostly alone and traded with the Indians, French and the various colonies for his needs and survival. He avoided the towns unless he had to resupply or had an emergency that required the contact. In this case his supplies had run out and he had an abundance of merchandise to sell or trade. Elizabeth confronted the man and spoke "I haven't seen you around town before. What is your name?"

He looked at her incredulously. Many people crossed to walk on the other side of the street when they spied his approach. He could not understand why this woman would confront him in such a way. He replied "Where I am from names are not important. The Indians just call me "Wild Man" but the white men call me McCall!"

She said "Can I call you McCall then?"

He said "You surely can if you have a notion to. I do not know why a lady like you would want to have any interest in the likes of me!"

She said "I find you interesting and not like the men in the town. I am not interested in the things that most women find exciting. I want more. I want adventure and travel. You have travelled in the wilderness and know many things that go on there and I am interested in knowing these things myself if not experience them!"

McCall said "It is a hard life Miss! A very hard life!"

She said "All the better! I can do anything a man can do and more!"

McCall said "Is that right! I don't know how that could be when you sit a horse side saddle!"

Elizabeth was taken aback! She replied "I don't ride side-saddle. I ride like you do and would wager I could beat you in a race. Get your horse and see!"

McCall pointed to his horse and said "My horse is lame. I came to town to resupply and get a replacement. Do you know of any?"

She said "I know all about horses and there would only be a few places that would have any good ones that would suit your needs and make a fair deal. I would be glad to introduce you to them so you can get a proper horse before I beat you in a fair race!"

McCall laughed and said "Lead on dear lady!"

Elizabeth and McCall were getting stares from those on the street. She did not care and reveled in the thought of the controversy. She knew her father might not particularly like it but he would accept it nonetheless. He knew what his daughter was about and that he could not and would not try to change her. They walked together up the road with his lame horse following behind. First, they went to the livery where the horse could be cared for properly. A doctor was called and it was determined that the horse would survive and return to be a useful animal but his days in the wilderness were over. With that information McCall and Elizabeth made their way to the docks. She found her quarry there. Mr. Richards owned a farm and dealt in good horse stock. He was her first thought when she knew McCall needed a good horse. She approached and made the introductions. She said "Good Day Mr. Richards. This is my friend McCall. His horse is lame and he must retire him from his duties in the wilderness. He will be looking for a new one and I told him you are a fair man with good stock. I would hope you could get him your best horse and your best price as a favor to me and my father!"

Mr. Richards looked at her and smiled "I have just the horse but it will cost!"

McCall said "As long as I feel it is a fair price, I have the funds to cover it. I have many pelts and things to sell or trade from my work!"

Mr. Richards said "I would like to see your pelts and things and maybe we can work a deal. I am quite a trader and deal in just about anything on the docks. Pelts are as good as money!"

They went to the farm that very day and found the horse. It was a good one and even better than McCall could have imagined. The horse was totally broke and ready for travel. A deal was struck and McCall got a very good deal with Elizabeth negotiating with Mr. Richards. He would be in town for a few weeks getting his supplies and selling his wares before returning to the wilderness. Elizabeth had set her mind to going with him when he left. He had no idea that this was what his future looked like at the newness of their acquaintance!

Elizabeth first approached her father about her idea later in the day after bidding McCall goodbye and arranging to meet up with him the next day to help him peddle his wares. She was an adept negotiator. What McCall had witnessed in her dealings with Mr. Richards meant that he could receive much more from his pelts than he could have hoped for through his own negotiations. It was a very good deal for him and he did not mind having some companionship from a female. His long times in solitude gave him cravings for just that. Elizabeth would educate him on the goings on in the colony and watching her negotiate he would learn to be a better salesman and get the most for his goods. He was happy to have made the acquaintance. She was different than any other woman he had ever met. He could also see the value that she had in handling his business with these traders

William Sumner was, to say the least, not ecstatic over the news from Elizabeth. He knew of McCall and knew him to be a fair man but did not truly know much about him. He had retreated to the wilderness when he grew weary of the Puritan demands. At times he wished he had the courage to do the same but he chose to work within the community to create change and he had a large family to support and raise to adulthood. Elizabeth was different indeed. She was headstrong and no civilized man would have her. He worried over her in the wilderness but knew she would go nonetheless. He knew she would go whether McCall accepted her proposal or not. She would simply follow him until he conceded defeat and accepted her as his partner. With this in mind he gave his blessing with the precept that he meet and talk with McCall before it was final. Elizabeth merrily agreed knowing that she would get what she wanted in one way or another.

Mary did not know how to take the news. It obviously had its benefits for her and her future but she worried about the rashness of her sister's decision and the quickness of it. McCall was a man of the wild. Would he treat her with respect? Could she take the life in the wilderness and survive there? How would she fare with the Indians and trappers? There were so many questions and concerns that ran through her mind that she felt guilty for her own good fortune. In the end she could only reconcile that Elizabeth would do what she would do and they truly had no say so in the matter. She did want to discuss it with her however!

Elizabeth was home late that night after guiding McCall carefully through the town and introducing him to the right people for his wares. She drove hard bargains and McCall realized profits beyond what he could have imagined. As Elizabeth crawled into her bed Mary was waiting for her. She said "Elizabeth! Are you awake? I wish a word with you!"

She replied "Yes Mary I am awake and if you are trying to bend my ear about my plans it will be for naught. I have decided!"

Mary said "I am not trying to talk you out of it. I just want to know that you have considered all of the ramifications of this life. Have you?

Elizabeth paused. She said "I have considered all that I can imagine now. I am sure there will be things I have not considered. Women aren't raised for this life for sure. I will learn. I will accept what I can and cannot do. I will have adventures though and that is what I truly crave. The life of a proper lady does not suit me and I cannot stay and rot away in it. You are different than I am. You embrace this life and you have found your future. I am still searching and I cannot do that from this stagnant place. I wish you all the happiness in your life. Please return the pledge to me sister!"

Mary smiled "I would have it no other way! Good night sister!"

Elizabeth said "Then good night to you too!" The lamp was damped and they were off to their own very different dreams.

Mary Sumner and Joshua

Indeed, Elizabeth had gotten her wishes. McCall saw the benefits of having her as his trading partner. He had not truly considered her coming with him into the wilderness but Elizabeth simply slipped into the role without him really noticing. On the day of his leaving she rode up to him with her gear stowed on her horse. She said "We never really had our proper race yet! I suppose then that I will just have to race you back to your wilderness!"

McCall said "We best be getting then! We don't want to be

traveling in the dark!" With that declaration they were off. They would see Elizabeth and McCall when they came in to town over the years. Joshua and Daniel would hear of her escapades through their Indian friends when their paths crossed. She was strong and forceful and would be fine in the wilderness. With her departure Mary would take her place as the eldest daughter and talk soon turned to her marriage to Joshua. Joshua still had some of his own inner searching to do. He had struggled with the idea of marriage for many years. He tried to reconcile his pull towards England against the fairness to a wife and family. In the end all he could do was illuminate his life to her and all of the things that went with it and see where that left him. He would do this right away because the pressure for marriage was building quickly now. Joshua decided that before things got to the point of no return, as likely they already were, he would tell Mary the whole story of his life and this strong pull he felt to return to England and right all the wrongs. He knew it could take a long time and might not be successful. He tried hard to forget about it but it was always there in the back of his mind. He had taken a slap in the face from Ambrose and that was the way a challenge was announced in this age.

Daniel was aware that his brother was troubled. He could only imagine his struggles. On this occasion Daniel's path had crossed with Mary in an unexpected encounter. They had pleasant greetings and some small talk. Daniel was not an impulsive sort but on this day at this time impulse took over. He could not bear to see his brother struggling with his new circumstance. He asked Mary if he could have a moment to discuss something of great importance and it began. They retired to a nearby park and sat on a peaceful bench away from others so they could have some semblance of privacy. As they found their seats Daniel felt a foreboding and wished he had not started the path he was on. He risked Joshua's ire and possibly that of Mary and her family. Joshua had always been there to help him and he felt it was time to return the favors he had received. He began "Mary I am glad that you and Joshua are close. I don't know if you are aware of our background. Not many are. But as you grow closer it is inevitable that the subject will come to the front. I must ask that you listen and swear to keep what you hear to yourself only. Joshua and I have been sworn to secrecy by the nature of the events themselves. I have seen Joshua struggle with this. He struggles with it much more than I do. He feels the weight of it falls squarely on his shoulders. I will relate to you our story if you agree to our confidentiality. Do you agree to this?"

Mary looked distressed but curiosity overcame her. She replied "Yes I will agree. I need to know!"

Daniel agreed and began the story as he knew it. When he had completed the tale, he looked at Mary. She was dumbfounded. Daniel knew that it would rock her perceptions of her own world and some of those in the community that she had grown to trust. He continued "It is then what it is. Joshua has struggled with his perceived responsibilities as the arms bearer in the family. He is drawn to return to England with the information he has and reclaim our heritage. I am afraid that will not be an easy proposition and the politics in force in England on this day would indeed complicate even a clear-cut case in the courts. My father and grandfather died fighting the Royalists and were known to be loyal to the Parliamentarian side of the conflict. As of now he has committed to staying here in the colonies but his heart is uncertain. His sense of justice has been tarnished. It would be difficult for him to let it go but I feel he must at the risk of his own life."

Mary sat in thought. Daniel said no more to allow her to develop her response. Finally, she spoke. She said "Daniel, I love your brother. I love him deeply although it is hard to show this to him. He is at an arms-length from me at all times and I have to find a way to get through that condition with him. I know he loves me but has a hard time showing it. Your story helps for me to understand him better. I will accept from him what he has to offer. If he must return to England, I will accept it on his terms. That is the depth of love I feel for him. It is sure to drive our lives in directions that could be difficult but when you accept a man as your husband you must also accept all that comes with him; the good and the bad. This I will do if he will have me."

Daniel was relieved. He was happy for Joshua and in awe of the love that Mary must feel. He finally said "That is the answer that I had hoped for. I am sure that Joshua will approach you soon with this. He is struggling with it now. Give him time and it will unfold. Please do not mention our meeting today. It is best that he feels he has settled his future and yours on his own accord!"

Mary said "You are a good brother and friend."

Daniel's heart was light. He was sure of the outcome but Joshua was still heavy hearted. He would meet with him and encourage the confrontation to settle the future as well as it could be settled at this time.

Joshua Bares his Soul

Joshua knew that the time would slip by him if he waited. He knew that delay was always an enemy but he did not want to force the subject onto Mary with the two extreme possibilities that would be the result. One of them good and one of them bad but it included any area that lay in between these polar opposites. In the end his conscience won out and he decided to address his past with Mary at the next available opportunity. To this end he invited her to share a picnic that next Sunday when he was sure she would be unencumbered and available. Even after baring his story to her it would not be over. They would have to decide who would be brought into their confidence that would also need to know if it was a positive outcome and of course if the worst were to happen Joshua would need some time to heal from his rebuff.

He prepared his presentation and practiced how he would deliver this revelation to Mary over and over. There was no one version that ever seemed like it would be correct. He discussed it with Daniel and Daniel told him to just broach the subject like any other and hope for the best. In the end this was what he settled on and what he would do. After all he had no guilt in what had happened to himself and his brother. The wrong doings had been at the hands of others. With Walter and Sam firmly in his corner it was reasonably certain that Mather's threats had been neutralized. There was danger that his agreement could be breached but he could not move forward without disclosure to those in his close circle that would need to know to understand his thoughts and actions.

The Sabbath grew near and Joshua was more nervous than he had ever known about the day. He had been through many pitfalls and none had seemed to affect him quite this profoundly. He met Mary on the church steps as had been their practice and he was awkward and distant. He was unaware that Mary already knew his secrets and would deal with them but Mary understood his behavior precisely because of that very secret that she carried. She would help him get through it with as little discomfort as possible. The church service was unbearably long and Joshua fidgeted in his seat showing his impatience. He wished to get this grizzly business with Mary over and done with and the delay made it unbearable. Finally, the service came to an end. Now there would be the social greetings and gossip outside the church for an extended period. Joshua knew that he would have to tolerate this so he did not offend his close friends and neighbors and this he did. After this time he found himself aloft in the wagon with Mary at his side heading for their time of disclosure and bonding. He hoped for the best but was prepared for the worst. They rode in silence for much of the way and Mary tried to produce some discussion beginning with the weather and moving to the gossip she had heard at the church.

Joshua had picked a nice area of his newly acquired property along the creek. He was careful not to reveal his plans for this place just yet and the location of this picnic would be away from what he considered the prime building site for their possible future home.

The day had sprung eternal. It was one of those days that made a man happy to be alive no matter what circumstance that he found himself in. This was a day that was God's gift to ease suffering, provide respite and elevate the spirits of those of mortal blood. Joshua was grateful. He knew this day was another pivotal point in his life. There had been so many but this was high as a priority and one under his control. He eased into it now like sitting in a good and comfortable saddle on a seasoned mount. His tale became less stressed and flowed easier. He had yet to broach the subject but knew the time would present itself and he was comfortable in its outcome no matter how it fell.

The food was spread and eaten and a feeling of comfort and warmth spread over them both as they lay back in the grass and felt the sun's warm rays bath their bodies in its love. Mary spoke of her family and pleasant memories from her childhood. She progressed to the current times and like it was scripted onward to the future. This was just the opening that Joshua needed to broach the subject that he wished to discuss with Mary and he wasted no time. He said "I enjoy hearing of your childhood and family. I have memories myself but not of the happy nature that you describe. I have been guarded with the history of my brother and I but it is not for the reason that you would expect. I have done this under threat and misery. I would like to share it with you now if that would be acceptable to you. I feel that we are moving forward in our lives and our time together and I will not allow you to enter it in a fog. We came to the colonies after being abducted by our caretaker and relative with the help of others that you may know. My father and grandfather perished in the storming of Liverpool in the Civil War. My grandmother and mother died of the plague a few years later. We came under the care of Peter Ambrose who quickly took control of our assets and through fraud and deception took our heritage and assets to his own needs. We were drugged and put aboard a ship to come to New England and the care of the Reverend Mather as his accomplice. I must ask that you keep my confidence on this subject and that we discuss later anyone that needs to know and will further learn the story as our future develops. Some will have a need to know and others will not. This is a sudden confession and I know you will have many questions or concerns and I am here to answer those before I come to my purpose of asking you here today."

Mary paused as if to drink it all in. She started "Joshua, what you describe is none of your own doing. It is at the hands of greedy and dishonest individuals and you have nothing to explain or apologize for to me. I accept you as the good man that you have proved to be!"

Joshua was taken by surprise. He expected much more. After a brief time for both to absorb the revelations Joshua started once again. "I was the first-born son of my family. It was I that was to carry the arms and defend the family against all challenges. With the death of my father and grandfather I was cast into this role at an early age. In my time the family has been stripped of its holdings and disgraced. It falls to me to lead the family name and reconcile these things in the future. I feel anger. I feel loyalty and I feel a need to avenge my responsibilities of my position. I feel the pull to return to England on a future time and unseat those that are unrightfully sitting in my father's seat. I fight this urge at Daniel's urging but it is very strong and I cannot say I will overcome it. I know you expect marriage and I would much want the same with you but I cannot entertain this without full disclosure to you of all things that lie within my soul and my heart. I hope you can understand this and come to a decision with all of the facts at your disposal. I will understand if it is too much for your spirit to accept or that it is not what you would see your future would hold."

Mary began to cry. She said "You silly man. I will take you for better or worse and I will accept whatever your heart tells you. Our time together would not be honest without this issue at its forefront and in the open. I would hope that you would successfully fight these demons that lie within you but if you feel the need at some future time to reconcile your destiny, I will accept this without comment or regret knowing that it is something that you must do to complete your own life's cycle and destiny. Now, come and hold me close and we will venture forward into what our future will hold for us." She reached and pulled him to her bosom and a long and passionate time ensued between them. Their souls were now as one and there were only the formalities to complete to live with whatever their life together would bring to them. Mary understood that no man controlled fate or those things that God would put in their path. She knew that they could only deal with them as they came. There would be good and bad and this was not anything that did not occur in any path of love. They would stand as one in all things and go forward. She knew Joshua was a good man and would provide for her and their future family not withstanding his desires and the pull of his destiny.

Joshua felt that a weight had lifted from him. He would share his news with Daniel and then Sam and Walter. The circle of knowledge would be expanded with this marriage. At the least Mary's parents would be brought into the circle. Discretion was paramount still but even with it there was truly little chance that Mather would rise-up to the challenge against them now. There were others in Sam and Walter's confidence on the matter and the boys did not know which friends this included. They could deduce some of those that could be trusted but there were others that Sam and Walter had contacted and worked with in Liverpool and most likely other parts of England. Either way it was of little consequence if Mather was exposed. Even in his brand of religion the guilty could expect to reap what they had sown. Joshua would move forward however and keep the agreement to the best of his ability.

Disclosure

There was a sort of meeting called by Joshua with those close to him to announce his newly formed plans. Mary would be present and in that way they would know she was to be trusted in this band of those enlightened in the agreement. They would meet at the pub in the private room upstairs. There would be privacy there and all things could be openly discussed. The following evening would adjourn the meeting. There would be happiness he believed for the most part. He did not want to dwell on the other for long but it would need to be addressed. Joshua met with the proprietor and reserved the room and set the menu. There would be drink to toast the union and food to celebrate. They would stay after and discuss the business end of the union.

Joshua met with Daniel in the early morning. He could not hide his happiness and disclosed the substance of the evening to his brother immediately. He would need his alliance and help in planning and passing the word to those who would attend. Daniel was happy for Joshua. There was no hint that he was aware of Daniel's meeting with Mary earlier in the week and that was the way he wanted it. He knew the intricacies that must exist in this relationship with all of the secrecy and the importance of those involved. Sam suspected the substance of the meeting and handled the invitation to Walter.

The evening was upon them before they knew it. The guests arrived punctually and drinks were served. There were spatters of small talk and some nervous fidgeting so Joshua adjourned to the main announcement at the earliest time. Mary moved to the head of the table and they both stood and tapped their spoon on the crystal of their glasses to get the other's attention. Hand in hand they announced their upcoming nuptials to the congratulations of the others. Mary's parents were in attendance.

As the congratulations were passed Sam made his way to Joshua and asked the pertinent questions. Walter had discussed this possibility with him early in the morning when the invitation was extended. Sam asked when they could talk and Joshua replied that there would be time that evening and he would like to include Mary's parents in that meeting since they would now be party to its outcome. This was quickly agreed and dinner was served.

After all had filled their bellies after dinner drinks were served. They all retired to a private room. The atmosphere became serious as the women were invited to join into the conversation. This was usually a men only domain. As they entered the room Joshua and Daniel stood together in the front and addressed those in attendance. Sam and Walter sat to their sides and Mary joined Joshua. Joshua began "Most of you know the substance of this meeting. First of all it is a joyous occasion celebrating the joining of two people into matrimony. In that it is surely a joyous thing. I have asked my brother to join me as there is other business that needs to be addressed to enable this joining to go forward. For those of you who are new to this group I would need your agreement that nothing said in this room is to be repeated outside of this group and your discretion is of upmost importance. Do I have your agreement?" Sam looked to each of those outside of those who already knew the story that was to be told and received an affirmative nod from each. He continued "My brother and I were brought here after the death of our parents at a young age. The circumstances of our relocation were under less than honest conditions. Mary and I have discussed this and have come to agreement. There must be understanding about what the future holds to move forward into matrimony. I will now relate the history of Daniel and myself to you all. I will hold nothing from you so you understand our history, legacy, motivations and how this could affect the future, present and our past." With that he launched into the story of their young lives and the things that had transpired since their arrival to the colonies. Many sat in the chairs dumbstruck. Some were in disbelief at the betrayal of those that they had trusted. Others were simply trying to wrap their thoughts around the vicious acts that these adults had visited on two young and innocent children. Joshua continued "Telling the story is only part of what I have come to discuss with you all. I was the oldest son. As the oldest I was at the head of the family at the time of our abduction. I feel the need to set things right in England and to reclaim my family properties and legacy. I was the holder of the family Arms. I have discussed this with Daniel and Mary and I have pledged to fight the demons that rage inside of me on a daily basis that call for my return to England and set things right. To do less seems to disrespect my mother, father, grandparents and family. The other side of the argument is that I can make a new life here and forget the past. This I have promised to try to do. If the draw to my past would become too strong I must be free to see it through. I pray that I will have the strength to stay the course here. It is an issue that remains to be resolved. It is now in the open and Mary and I have agreed that I must do what my heart demands whether it be now, 10 years from now or never. I must keep my options open on this issue to make my own decision when that time may come. For now, we will put it aside and celebrate the upcoming events. Let the planning for a wedding begin!" With that Mary, her mother and the other women in attendance excused themselves and retired to the adjacent room to begin planning for the wedding of Joshua Henshaw and Mary Sumner.

Sam then stood and said "Our business here is not finished. Walter and I have a presentation of sorts for Joshua and Daniel." Walter picked up a large tube that sat by his chair and pulled out a scroll and held it. Sam continued "A few years ago the colonies appointed a heraldry commission to honor family arms and to award them to deserving men. Joshua-Daniel your arms are not lost and reside still in England. They are still honored and part of the history of that country. However, you are now here and our presentation to you now will be your American Arms. Walter, will you do the honors?" Walter unrolled the scroll and the boys were in awe.

To Joshua and Daniel Henshaw

You are awarded your American Coat of Arms described as such: Argent a chevron between three heronshaws [i.e., herons] Sable.

1. Henshaw, Joshua (in Dorchester, Mass., 1653)

2. Henshaw, Daniel (in Dorchester, Mass., 1653)

Sons of William Henshaw of Toxteth Park, Lancashire England

Sam once again spoke "You are now both the owners of the family arms. Joshua you will continue to represent your family here. Daniel you will carry the arms here that you could not carry in England by King's law. It is good for the both of you." The boys were overcome. They shook hands and hugged each other in brotherhood. They would now stand together and it should be no other way.

Sam and Walter had seen the battle going on inside of Joshua They hoped that in this way they could quell the draw that was pulling him back to England to re-acquire what was lost. The path he would follow if he returned was wrought with danger and setbacks at every turn and might still end in failure. They did not wish to see their friend; business partner and proxy son go through this turmoil. Maybe now he would be satisfied without completing this mission.

And so it was. Joshua and Mary Elizabeth Sumner were married in the spring of 1670. (No date of the marriage was found just the year. It was normal for the time to marry in the spring months)

The wedding day was exceptional. It was one of those spring days that displayed the new blooms of flowers and the birth of the young from the long winter hibernations. The birds were singing their own songs of hope. Those closest to Joshua and Mary were all in attendance as were so many others that had not made the list but wished to celebrate the day in honor of the couple. Joshua never saw or understood his popularity in the community and therefore could not understand the interest and commitment of those who came to honor them. He assumed that it was the Sumner pedigree that drew all of these onlookers and friends. It was not as grand a wedding as was planned for his parents before the tragedy struck of Sir Thomas's death. By colonial standards it was quite an event. Thus began their lives together. Children would not be far behind. It was a wish of both Mary and Joshua. It is likely that grandparents would be another supporter of bringing grandchildren into their lives.

So, on a pleasant day in May in the year of our Lord 1670 with flowers in bloom and the new birth of spring Joshua and Mary Elizabeth Sumner were wed. It was a wonderful wedding. This alone was perfect but there were surprises. The day before their vows Paul and his band of Indian hunters arrived in town. Joshua and Daniel were pleased to see him and his friends. Their friendship had endured all of the hostilities between the tribes and the settlers. Even with the escalation in raids that had been occurring as of late it did not affect their vows to friendship and mutual support. They had a feast that night and Paul was told of Joshua's marriage on the following day. Paul was distraught as it was the tradition of his people to provide gifts on such occasions. Paul and his band were just beginning their hunt after selling off their lode. Paul as usual had a very meaningful plan.

As morning rose the Indians had disappeared. Joshua, with Mary's blessing, had invited them to the wedding as their honored guests. Many of those in attendance were looking forward to interacting with them. Many of the women and children had little interaction with the Native Americans except to hear the horror stories of the marauding bands and the evil that they visited upon those unfortunate enough to be in their path. This would be good for all involved. As morning drew near Paul appeared. He asked Joshua to accompany him to their camp. Upon arriving there, the Indians had hunted and acquired a young deer. Paul said "Joshua, it is our tradition that you present this deer to the feast. But first we must cut out the choicest steak that you will present to your wife's parents. Let me explain our tradition to you.

Paul spoke "Long ago, before the white man came to our shores, when a brave came to thoughts of joining, he consulted with his mother and father about the matter. After a period of courting and wooing the parents of both would arrange everything for the marriage. Since your parents were not available, I will act on your behalf as much as possible at this late time in the marriage ritual

Presents were then given. The groom would go far into the forest to find suitable game. He took his best hunting bow because of the special occasion. He would bring down his game. This was usually a young deer or young bear. He would tie the front and hind feet together with a line and then put it on his back to begin his journey to his village. Because there was no time we acquired the deer for you. Now you must carry it back to your village and dress it and roast it. When it is finished you will take the choicest steak to Mary's parents as your betrothal gift. If it is accepted you are then lawfully engaged by the laws of our gods. Once this is accomplished your bride will take some ears of corn and grind it into scones of white-cornbread and present it to your family. Since your family is not here, she will present it to Sam and Walter as your proxy. This bread is to be made before sunrise on a certain day before the wedding. It is luck that made this day align with your marriage. We have had our squaws prepare the bread for Mary. It is tradition that this bread is to be taken by her uncle or grandfather to your parents. Since I do not know who these men are I will stand in that place for the tradition to continue. In very rare occasions the Mother or Father would deliver the bread. It is then up to the families to prepare the celebration with much feasting and celebration including members of both clans or tribes and intimate friends. This has already been done you have told me. On the wedding day the guests were seated in a circular formation around the couple. A ceremonial fire was lit and there was dancing around the fire. The wedding dance is performed here. The tribal prophet or sachem would step into the circle with the Ceremonial Pipe and perform this ritual.

He will take a puff or two then hold the pipe upward to the sky for a brief moment; then slowly and gracefully, he will move it toward the Earth and hold it there for a little while. Then, with a sweeping gesture he will move it toward the North, and to the East, and to the South, and quickly toward the place where the sun set; the West. After a few moments of meditation, he will then hand it over to the chief who, silently and very slowly, will take a few puffs from the Pipe. Then, holding the bowl end of the pipe toward his body, he will hand it to the next man to his right, and he in turn will take a puff or two and pass it on. And thus the Ceremonial Pipe will travel around the entire inner circle of leading men. Everyone will handle it carefully and reverently as they take their few puffs from it. To the Lenni Lenape the ceremonial pipe is sacred. It is evidence that the joined man (the wayward one) is attached to the Great Mystery. The pipe is returned to the Priest Sachem He will again hold it upward with outstretched arm, before him and he closes his eyes as he stands in silent meditation for a little while before placing it upon an altar stone beside the fire.

This will end the ceremony and you will be married by the white man in your ceremony and by the Indian in ours. It will be a very good omen for your family and your future. It is by luck or the will of the Gods that our Sachem travels with our band and I will act as the Chief in this ceremony if you will have us."

Joshua was overcome with feelings for this man. He had seen fit to include him in his own tradition and it was the best present that he could give. Daniel was eager to tell Paul of his upcoming wedding and asked that he return to perform the ritual for his own marriage to which Paul readily agreed. Of course, they would have to work out the time that Paul and his band would return to the area so they could participate in the festivities.

This relationship with Paul was a great thing but there were events going on in the colonies that would strain the relationship and place both the boys and Paul and his band in great danger and fear in the near future.

Joshua's Wedding

The wedding day was already in its full glory for Joshua with his early morning meeting with Paul and Daniel. Mary was a whirlwind of activity preparing meals, cleaning and getting in her wedding attire. By all measures she was a beautiful bride. Mary had her own surprise that morning. They had been unable to communicate to Elizabeth and McCall. She had given up hope that they would be in attendance but on that morning they had appeared to trade their pelts and were immediately caught up in the fray of the big day. Elizabeth was not into the girly things of life but she suddenly had a keen interest in the goings on and the bridal traditions. Mary suspected that she was longing for a wedding to McCall. Mary brought her up to date on all that had happened and the plans for the day. She was excited about the Indian ceremony that would be immediately following the vows. This was a different person than the one that had taken to the wilderness. Elizabeth said "I don't go by my Christian name anymore. I just go by Lizzy. McCall and I were married a while back by the Indians but it don't seem to count like your wedding does. Maybe someday McCall will take to a Christian ceremony. I doubt he would do it here though because of his views of the local Christians and their bigotry and greed. With him being ordained and all I expect that he would want to marry that way to avoid living in what some would call a sinful way. We see it as being married in the biblical way. We will see if anything like that could happen. McCall was bathing and cleaning up for the festivities. He was a dichotomy. On one hand he had abandoned all things civilized and on the other he was the epic ordained minister. He was in the process of adjusting and adapting his own beliefs to his own personal faith and then to reconcile it to the ways of the wilderness and the new world. He had several different avenues of thought on the subject. This he seemed to do easily though. He was an enlightened man of the time on these issues. He could reconcile and make room for all people's faith and beliefs while keeping his own brand of Christianity to himself. Of course, he discussed it with Lizzy but there were very few others that he had the opportunity to speak to on the subject with their relative isolation for months at a time. He had spoken to some of the tribes about this subject and they had educated him on their beliefs and culture. Some of these Indians had converted and some had not. He also learned of the growing unrest in the Indian villages over the incursions of the English and other settlers onto their ancestral and tribal lands. He tried as he could to explain the white man to the Indians but there was hatred and impatience from both sides. He could see trouble coming and this was indeed an issue that would come to no good without some cooperative and binding agreements between the two. He held little hope that the pompous leaders of the colonists would do either or keep their agreements once made. Thus the clock was ticking until the day that the tempers would boil over and hostilities would begin.

In spite of all of the tensions the festivities could not have been a happier time and were enjoyed by all. Its cross-cultural element made it an event that would be long remembered. As the evening wore down Joshua and Mary took to their wagon to spend the wedding night together and enjoy each other intimately for their first time. Joshua loaded their gifts and things into the wagon and off they went to much shouting and cheering. He steered the wagon out of town and Mary was giving a worried look. She said "Joshua, we are leaving town. Where are we to stay on this very special night? There are no accommodations this way." Joshua smiled and replied "It is not your worry my wife. There are accommodations in this direction that you know little of as yet!" Mary spoke up "I have lived here all my life and there is nothing of that manner in this direction! We must turn around. I do not want our wedding night fouled! Please Joshua!" Joshua grinned and said "If we do not find accommodations to your liking in the next mile we will turn back." They rode on for a time and Joshua turned the buggy onto a lane. Mary was dumbstruck. She had been this way many times in her life and no lane had existed here. In fact she was this way no more than a few weeks prior and this lane did not exist and was covered in brush. She inquired "Where has this beautiful lane come from. I have never noticed it before?" Joshua said "It has appeared from hard labors over the last year and a half and guided by my inquiries and your responses." They came to a stop in front of a sizeable log cabin. It was unique for the area and time but Joshua had learned the methods from those at the logging camps and put them to use for a good home. Mary asked "What is this place Joshua and who is it that lives here?" Joshua grinned and he said "Well Mary, we live here. It is my wedding gift to you and our future generations. Shall we get busy making that generation now!" Mary was shocked but after a few minutes she was grinning ear to ear. She grabbed Joshua and kissed him passionately. They entered the house for the first time and were quick to the bed. They made love there all night until they were completely exhausted and fell off to a deep sleep. It was not until the following morning that Joshua gave her a tour of their new home, outbuildings and property. He had incorporated each of her wishes into their new home. He got out his notebook and showed her each one he had written down from their discussions leading up to this moment. She was elated and impressed with the depth of his undertaking and realized what deep love he must have for her through this time. She was a very fortunate girl indeed!

Daniel was not to be forgotten though. He did not want to upstage Joshua's marriage so he bowed to their plans and made his own around them with Mary's approval. After all, two weddings would be two festive days for the community instead of a single day. In these days a festive event would be much wanted by their friends and acquaintances. The pall of the religious zealots brought so much darkness to everyday life. So Daniel's marriage to Mary was also set into motion. Mary was still at odds with the appearance of being married too soon after the death of her second husband and the additional time made sense to her time line and social acceptance of the event even though many in the community and her deceased husband's family believed that time had passed months prior. In any event Daniel would now raise Mary's children by Robert and this would make them all very happy in their new lives.

Joshua Henshawe
Thomas Henshall, c1631
William Henshawe, c1608-1644
Kendrick ?
Joshua Henshawe, B: 1643
Evan Houghton
Katherine Houghton 1615-1651
Ellen Parker ?

M: Elizabeth Sumner ?
Joshua Henshaw, 1672-1747
William Henshaw, 1672-?
Elizabeth Henshaw, 1675-1675
Thankful Henshaw, 1677-1716
John Henshaw, 1679-c1736
Samuel Henshaw, 1682-1761
Elizabeth Henshaw, 1684-1732
Katherine Henshaw, 1687-1773
Daniel Henshaw, 1689-?
Mindwell Henshaw, 1693-?

Shortly thereafter Daniel and Mary Ball were wed in that same year.

(There is no record of what year Daniel and Mary wed but it can be extrapolated through her previous marriages and the birthdates of her daughters that this date represents a likely time frame)

Daniel Henshawe

Thomas Henshall, ?-c1631

William Henshawe, c1608-1644

Kendrick

B: 1644 Evan Houghton, D: 1732

Katherine Houghton 1615-1651

Ellen Parker

M: Mary (Bull or Ball) Allen

Daniel Henshawe,

When Robert Pond died, Mary secondly married on Jul 3 1663 to Nicholas Allen or Ellen, who also later died.

Daniel Henshawe married Mary (Bull) Allen(Mary Bull)(Mary Ball). Mary, daughter of ?? Bull or Ball"of Bury St. Edmund in Co. Suffolk, and widow of 1) Robert Pond and 2) Nicholas Allen of Dorchester in New England". She was born about 1636.

Mary had first married Robert Pond, by whom she had children:

Mary Pond, born Jul 14 1657.
Martha Pond, born Apr 13 1660.

It was at first concluded that the brothers should marry in a dual ceremony but there were family, religious and community considerations that played into the two marrying separately. Both would have their own special days with their new wives and new lives.

Daniel's Wedding

Daniel had received word of Paul's return. The wedding plans were made and on hold for just this minute. He ran to Mary and told her it was time to get things ready and they would be wed this following Saturday upon Paul's return. The invitations were put out and the preparations made. This time Paul took Daniel hunting to get his own deer. Mary was taken by the Indian women to make her bread. The presentation of the choice steak and bread were made and accepted. The festivities would begin. It was a wedding much like Joshua and Mary's celebration. It followed the same script and all were looking forward to each thing in it. The exception was that Mary would not be surprised on this night with her new home. She suspected what was in the works with Joshua's wedding and Mary's talk of the home. She went to Daniel and inquired if they were to have a new home too. Daniel was evasive but Mary cut to the truth. She said that she would appreciate working with him in building their home and being a part of it from the beginning. Daniel grinned. He would have thought nothing less from Mary and readily agreed. On their wedding night the girls stayed with Mary's parents. The trip to the house was quick and their love making began immediately. There was no need for a tour of the house for both of their hands and minds were into it. After this night they would officially move to the home with their girls and begin their new life from there. Both Joshua and Daniel's homes had areas for Paul and his band to camp during their visits. These areas were open to all peaceful Indians or others who moved through the area in their hunts or travels. The one stipulation was that they had to exist in peace while there even if two different tribes or groups were present at the same time. It never failed them.

Happier Times

Both boys felt that they had come around in a full circle. They were not restored to the level of their family's wealth before their troubles but they were now in the elite of the colonies and active in its life, government, social and political circles. They had found the love of their lives and had begun the journey forward with their new lives. For this moment they felt renewed and happy.

Joshua and Mary were living in a virtual utopia. A mill had been built on the property and Joshua oversaw its operations and collected the profits from the sales of its outputs. He worked on the docks with Sam also. At home Mary was insatiable. She had become a wonderful lover and threw herself into passion at any available opportunity. Daniel, Walter and Sam would tease him over it when he would show up disheveled and lacking sleep. They would all laugh at his condition but it was all in good spirit. Mary had a more serious idea of it beyond its enjoyment and pleasure. She sought to bring children into the marriage and begin their family. Joshua had misgivings with each visit from the vengeance demons. It was not surprising however when nature took it course and Mary announced her pregnancy in late spring of 1671. Strangely Joshua found happiness in this along with his trepidation. Children were very much wanted but he now had to face the real possibility that he might later desert them to his quest. He put these thoughts aside for now and embraced his upcoming family responsibilities and knew that a solution would be revealed to him through his faith. On a cold winters day in early 1672 Joshua Henshaw II was born into this world. It was Mary that chose the name knowing that heritage and tradition was of upmost importance to Joshua and the Arms bearer of this family would carry forward the tradition of having a Joshua Henshaw in each generation. At least it would be the way for now. Joshua pondered this for a while. Mary did not understand his reluctance. Finally, Joshua told her "I understand your thoughts and I feel this is right. It is an old thought that arises to darken the mood however. At the time we were in England Ambrose had a son. He was born after my birth and closer to Daniel's birth. Ambrose knew that I had been born Joshua. With his future plans in hand he also named his son Joshua. I do not know if it was to cause confusion or to be a snub at my father and mother. In any event this was my dark mood and I will get over that. To have my son carry my name forward and hold the family arms will be an honor and I will cherish it!" Mary was silent as she drank it all in. She felt sympathy for the pain that Joshua must feel over the things done to him and his brother. It brought fear to her because it was clear that these things had not left his mind and seemed to still reside at the forefront of his thoughts. Even a happy time such as the birth of his first-born son was dampened by these dark circumstances that he could not put aside this many years after their occurrence.

They had hardly set the routine of having the new baby in the house before Mary had another announcement. She was again pregnant. Apparently with the return of her passions nature had once again taken its course. By the end of 1672 William was born into the world on another cold day in New England. Both boys were healthy and were happy babies. With two babes to care for the passions slowed for now and there was a time of adjustment in duties, schedules and their home life. Babies will do this.

Joshua was a wonderful father. He spent his off time with the boys playing and assisting in their care. Mary was very appreciative of this as two young children were quite demanding of her time and attention. She received much needed breaks to address her other household duties without interruption. Joshua was happy to assist in these duties. He considered being a father as hardly work at all. He kept their attention and the boys loved and respected their father. They were devoted to him and wanted his attention at all times. They were daddy's boys.

Daniel had a much different circumstance in his marriage. There were children from the first day of marriage. He did not mind because he had long ago established a parental relationship with Mary's daughters and they loved him like a father. Daniel had been this figure to them through the death of their natural father and their stepfather. He was the only stable male figure in their lives since the beginning. The girl's love for him was apparent when they assisted their mother in scheming to bring Daniel to matrimony. The talk of further children had not arisen although Daniel felt a yearning for fatherhood and a son. Since he too was now a bearer of the American Arms he wished for a male heir to pass them to upon his passing. Life continued at a brisk pace establishing his ready-made family and developing his business interests. Daniel had a textile mill built on the property to process wool and spin yarn. Like Joshua this was his business solely and separate from his business with Walter. Their business was the consumer of most goods processed at this home mill however. Daniel's mill was staffed by his friends Tommy, Benny and Isaiah. In this endeavor he had kept his promise to them to include them in his good fortunes. With them working in the mill he knew that they would do good work, be loyal and be close at hand as his good friends. They too would share in the profits of this mill. It was an outcome that none of them could have hoped for without their introduction to Daniel those many years ago.

King Philip's War

In the early years of the colonies, Massasoit, Squanto and others helped the colonists with the introduction to farming and without this assistance they could not have survived the first winters. The English continued to land on the shores in ever increasing numbers. Towns were established on ground once the dominion of the tribes. Windsor, Connecticut (est. 1633), Hartford, Connecticut (est. 1636), Springfield, Massachusetts (est.

1636), and Northampton, Massachusetts (est. 1654), on the Connecticut River and towns such as Providence, Rhode Island, on Narragansett Bay (est. 1636) continued to encroach on traditional Native American territories. Tribal elders were still reeling from the deaths caused by White man's diseases brought by the fishing boats prior to the Plymouth landing in 1620. No tribe was untouched by the massive amount of death brought on by smallpox, spotted fever, typhoid and measles and other infectious diseases carried by European fishermen. No good could be found in the minds of the Indians to allow the spiraling influx of these foreigners to the land. They took what they wanted, killed off their families and kinsmen, fouled the hunting grounds and demanded that they abandon their own culture to adopt the ways of the Christians and colonists. They had annihilated the Pequot Tribe when they had risen against them and there was no misconception that this would be the goal of the colonists if more hostility arose. Algonquin tribal leaders such as Massasoit, Sassacus, Uncas, Ninigret and some colonial leaders negotiated a shaky peace for several decades. For this first half century Massasoit of the Wampanoag tribe kept peace with the colonists so he could trade with them and have them as allies against their traditional foes the Pequot, Narragansett, and the Mohegan tribes. The trade- off was that he had to allow the incursions of more and more arrivals onto Indian lands and deep into the Indian territories. Of course, the settlers sought out the prime land on which they would homestead leaving the Indians with the less desirable areas. Pressure was building as they do when cultures, dreams and livelihoods clash. Land sales were forced on the tribes with little understanding of English land ownership rights or the contracts and deeds that they were signing. With the death of Governor William Bradford in 1657 and Massasoit in 1660 the peacemakers passed on to their rewards. Massasoit's son, Wamsutta, became the new Sachem and continued his father's traditions of peace. Both Wamsutta and Metacom appeared in Plymouth Grand Court and adopted their Christian names. Wamsutta became Alexander after Alexander the Great and Metacom became Philip after the Macedonian prince of that name. Both were raised in the beliefs of their father. These included an atmosphere of keeping peace and a spirit of brotherhood with the newly arriving colonists. Even after all of the bad outcomes that had come to the shores with them. These had cost the Native Americans dearly. There was as spirit of forgiveness and conciliation to the ebbing flow of the colonial arrivals. It was clear what the outcome would be in the not-so-distant future. There were many events that would lead to inevitable outcomes but one in particular was the colonists allowing their livestock to roam onto the Indian lands and trample their corn and crops. These crops were the mainstay of the Indian diet and without them many could starve during the winter months. There were many complaints from the Indians to government officials but generally they listened politely and ignored the problem. These decisions were regularly decided in the colonist's favor. There was increased competition for the use of the natural resources in the area including game, water and good land. Again the Indians were outmanned and out-armed and their demands were ignored to favor the white settlers. Many Indians were then forced to sell their lands to the colonists just to survive as compromise seemed one sided and the use of force had proven to be ineffective and disastrous to the tribes and their families. In 1662 colonial forces took Wamsutta at gunpoint to Plymouth under their custodial control. He was taken in front of the court and confronted about rumors of an Indian uprising. Wamsutta pledged his friendship to the colonists that had been the tradition of his father. He was released after this pledge. Shortly after he was taken he became ill and died during his journey back to his home. The Indians were angered by these pompous and greedy colonial leaders. Many believed that he was poisoned in their care.

With the passing of Wamsutta his brother Metacom came to power. In his heart he had anger at the treatment and ultimate death of his brother and the betrayal of the Indian overtures to a peaceful existence with the colonist for almost a half century. The Indian's had given no sign that their pledges to peace were faltering. One thing was clear at the beginning. The colonists would continue to usurp Indian lands. The pattern would repeat itself throughout history. First the settlers would move into Indian lands and establish permanent housing, settlements and their own government of the area. They would then take more and more of the surrounding land for their own use. This land would be the choicest of the parcels with access to the fertile grounds and water supplies. They would establish friendly trade and cultural exchanges. These were usually heavily weighted on the side of the settlers because of Indian customs, ignorance of colonial laws and commerce. They were easy to take advantage of in all of these matters and advantage would be taken. Eventually and usually too late in the process the Indians realized the frauds and swindles being perpetrated on them and would have two choices. Bow to the desires of these people and give up their ways of life, cultures and beliefs or to fight. Metacom decided to fight. This too was disastrous. The Indians always found themselves outnumbered and outmatched. Colonial weapons were much better than the crude Indian weapons. The bow and arrow were much less deadly than the ball and musket. Technology of the time was greatly against them.

The beginning of the hostilities started as most wars. A small event occurred and it escalated out of control. This specific event was the murder of John Sassamon. Sassamon was what was called a "praying Indian". He had converted to Christianity and taken his Christian name of John. Sassamon was a graduate of Harvard and a translator. He also acted as advisor to Metacom (King Philip). Metacom through Sassamon passed a message to the colonial government at the beginning of his reign:

[Philip promised] that he would not sell no land in Seven Years time for that he would have no English trouble him. "
-John Sassamon on behalf of King Philip, 1663

Through his position Sassamon also became an informer to the colonists and warned the Governor that King Philip had spoken of raiding the outlying towns in the colonial settlements. Metacom was called to Boston to answer these charges which he denied. With no other proof he was told that if these threats should come to pass or further rumors were heard that the colony would be on a defensive stance. Relationships with the tribes could become violent. The colonial government demanded that the Wampanoag surrender their weapons which they did with some exceptions. He was forced to sign a new treaty promising peace in 1671. The colonial authorities forced a promise from Metacom to pay an annual tribute of 100 pounds sterling to the colonial government. Because not all Indians would surrender their muskets the colonials declared that Metacom had not totally complied with his agreement and required that he sign yet another treaty with even more concessions. This one subjected the Indians to act under the laws of Plymouth and the King. With that he was dismissed from the meeting. Metacom did not like being told what to do or that he could not speak his mind as leader of his tribe. It should be noted that at this time there were 80,000 settlers in the colonies and only 10,000 Indians that survived after the severe loss of life from disease and hostilities. Many of the surviving Indians were older men, women or children. Many of the men and braves had perished to the diseases or hostilities with their ancestral enemies or the colonists. Some had been taken captive and sent into slavery by both their natural enemies and the colonists. The colonists would sell them to the West Indies or back into England. The Indian's lots in this service were widely varied but nonetheless took the freedom from a freedom proud individual. It also removed able bodied warriors from the area and further diminished the ability of the tribes to stand for themselves and their rights. It could not have been well accepted by any of the Indians from any tribe that had to suffer this indignity not to mention the anger that the Indians must have felt at the loss of family members, friends and the displacement from their ancestral homes. The incursion of the settlers brought them closer and closer to the Indian villages. Philip later demanded that those in charge of the colonies were not the highest authority and demanded that the English King, Charles II, come to the colonies to negotiate the treaties. He stated "I shall treat only with my brother King Charles II of England. When he comes, I am ready!"

Shortly thereafter Metacom was betrayed by Sassamon in Boston. Sassamon was found dead. Over the next few days three of King Philip's warriors were arrested, given a trial and summarily executed for the murder. Tensions rose. Within the Indian nations the system of alliances and enemies drew their lines. The Wampanoag Indians joined with the Nipmucks, Pocumtucks, and Narragansetts. The Mohegan, Pequot, Massachusetts, and Nauset Indians sided with the English.

The warring began when some Wampanoag braves killed cattle grazing near their tribal homes near Bristol, Rhode Island. The English farmer killed an Indian to exact his own revenge for the killing of his livestock. This set into motion the hostilities that would last the next fourteen months and decimate the colonies and the Indian Nation.

The earliest of the Indian alliances came when the Nipmunks joined the Wampanoags. They attacked the settlement at Brookfield situated deeply in Nipmunk territory. Word came of troop movement through the area led by Captain's Hutchinson and Wheeler. The Indians set their ambush and when the time was right brought their attack to the colonists in a deadly manner. Eight soldiers lost their lives in the ambush and the rest of the force retreated to the Brookfield garrison. The Indian forces did not call off the attack and followed the soldiers to their stronghold. The Brookfield garrison was a wooden structure. The remainder of the soldiers and the surviving settlers had sought shelter there. The Indians brought their attack by sending a flaming cart to the side of the garrison. The flames engulfed the wall and the waiting game began. The flames spread and would soon breach the wall. The Indians would follow this breach and annihilate the garrison. Those inside realized the inevitable outcome and used the remainder of their drinking water in an attempt to douse the flames. They could only slow the burn and soon it would spread and grow. Their choices were limited. They could stay and burn to their deaths or flee and be set upon by the angry Indian attackers. Neither would end well for them.

In a near Biblical intevention these settlers and soldiers were saved. A sudden storm blew up and heavy sheets of rain fell subduing and eventually extinguishing the flames before they could breach the walls. Reinforcements arrived shortly thereafter and their rescue was no longer in doubt. The attack had reduced the village to ashes however and it was abandoned for many years thereafter.

The Indians turned their attentions to the settlements along the Connecticut River Valley. This was an important area to the colonies because of its farming. It was known as the breadbasket of New England. The Indians knew that the colonists were spread out in this area and large concentrations of the settlers were few. They could also restock their own food stores with the booty from these raids. This was in contrast to an attack on Boston or one of the other more densely populated and better defended areas that could be disastrous to their forces. The strategy was to attack targets where they had an advantage in numbers. It was the same strategy that they had faced when fighting the Colonials in force. In the fall of 1675 the Pocumtucks (residing in along the northern part of the river), Squakheags (residing in present day Northfield) and the Norwottocks (greater Hadley) joined the Indian forces.

They first attacked the town of Deerfield (Pemawachuatuck "at the twisted mountain"). The English retreated and abandoned the town to regroup. Large amounts of grain were left behind. As an afterthought the command knew the grain was needed to resupply the garrisons at Hadley, Northampton and Hatfield. They dispatched a Captain by the name of Lathrop to lead the recovery mission. The trip back to Deerfield went well. No sign of Indians were to be had. They entered the settlement unmolested, loaded their wagons and began the return trip. The day was hot and the soldiers were tired from their labors. The lack of contact made them complacent and they laid their muskets in their wagons and continued unarmed. They stopped and picked grapes to enjoy on their journey and help their thirst. At the point where their path crossed a brook, large trees felled by the Indians, blocked their way. As the English bunched together on the trail, the Indians sprang their trap. Within minutes seventy-one soldiers were killed. The soldiers were reinforced shortly but it was too late for them to be saved. Captain Moseley's force brought an attack to the Indians but could not maneuver to gain an advantage. The battle was lost before it began and the Indian force continued to hold the advantage. Moseley did not break off and pressed his battle but the Indians showed no respect to their enemy. They shouted out "Come Moseley, come! You seek Indians, you want Indians? Here is Indians enough for you!" Mosely could not gain the advantage and the battles and exchanges continued through the rest of the day until the darkness fell on the battle hours later. Moseley did not want to risk his men further to a force superior to his own that knew the terrain and countryside and could operate in the darkness to their advantage and liking. He withdrew from the field. All that was left was to return to the field at daylight and bury the dead who lay where they fell. There were some unpredictable outcomes to this action. The colonies were in panic. The utter defeat of their forces with such ease did not promote a feeling of security. The outlying settlements were vulnerable and the forces needed to defend them were slim. Most colonists, even though they outnumbered the Indians 8:1 at this time were engaged in their normal business and personal lives. Many were attached to local militias but none had anticipated being called to duty on short notice but the call came nonetheless by Governor Josiah Winslow who unlike his predecessor had no intentions of appeasing the Indians or keeping the peace.

Daniel was away in the wilderness with the herds for this period. The Indian raids had not left Walter and his interests untouched. The friendly Indians supported them and even helped them if they were near. It was the raiding Indians that made life with the herds dangerous and they were losing livestock at an alarming rate. Wildlife was scarce now in the area as more and more settlers poured in to it. The Indians were at war and they could not return to their lands for farming or housing. To do so would make them a stationary target for attack by the colonial forces. They had to continue to move and cloak their homes and families from harm. Thus, food sources were scarce and their future stores would be depleted by missing the planting season for crops. It was their one weakness in their campaign at this point of the battle. Daniel would be here for some time it seemed. Joshua was called to arms and answered. He would muster in to the active militia to defend the colonists, settlers and his business interests. He was troubled however because he knew the spirit of the Indians and that they could be their friends instead of enemies. Each could help the other as long as there was a spirit of cooperation, care and mutual respect. Sam's treatment of the Indians at the logging camps was a prime example of how this could and would work. He was sad that it had come to war. War in his life had always ended in disaster. He also knew of the Pequot Wars and how this tribe had been wiped out by those in charge of the colonial forces. He expected that this would end in much the same way. He prayed to his God that it would not. He had grown to hate war and the grisly outcomes left on those who survived from both sides.

There was more. As Joshua was pulling his supplies together to leave Mary was crying. Joshua tried to comfort her but there was no success. He asked if there was anything he could do to help her. Her response was "Joshua, I am with child once again. The boys are young and I will be under a heavy load with you gone. Please return safely and with great speed. I will need you home soon. I know you must defend our home but I have trepidation nonetheless." With a kiss Joshua told her he loved her and would return soon and healthy. With that he left to join the militia. As the door closed Mary fell to her knees and prayed to God for his safe return and a healthy child. She also asked his help in seeing her and her boys through this time. The Puritan viewpoint of these initial defeats at the hands for the Indians was that God was punishing them for a lack of strict discipline in the strict religious codes of the Puritans. It was a way to strengthen their hold on the demands made to those of their flock. They would use any event or idea to exact power and satisfy their greed to collect more and more from those under their influence for their own use. The Indian matter allowed both goals to be realized at once. This time was used to take care of matters that would have normally been scrutinized by those that were now off to war. The target was now on the back of the weak and they were quickly made out to be the cause of the bad outcomes in the field. The first target was the Quakers. The persecution by the Puritans was stepped up and they were under the constant threat of attacks, death or being driven from their homes. The second group targeted by the Puritans was the Christian Indians who remained neutral during this time. Many were arrested and imprisoned and many more were simply hanged. It was expedient to take care of these problems while they were not under the public eye and they could blame these innocent

Indians for God's punishment on the battlefield. They could direct the fault towards them even though they had no fault or part in it. These Indians had complied with all of the demands of the government and Puritans and wished only to live in harmony in the community and in peace. Those who would defend them were away and those that remained acted as one mind. No one could speak out against the abuses since they were being waved under the patriotic and religious banner to supposedly reconcile with God for their lack of compliance. Bolstered by their successes the Indians continued their raids. The settlements at Hatfield, Northampton and Springfield were raided and thirty houses were burned. Prince Philip's band added another ally. The Agawam tribe had joined in these attacks. In the beginning they remained friendly to the colonists as had been their history. It was again the colonists who made them enemies from their own actions. The settlers had taken their children hostage in an effort to guard against this friendly tribe attacking them. The tribe had no such plans to attack or act against them in any manner. In fact they could have been helpful to the settlers. With their children stolen from their homes and held in captivity they rose up against the settlers. They felt a degree of vengeance as they watched the settlement at Springfield burn. They longed for the return of their children but could not be assured that they would ever see them again. Joshua was unaware of all of these occurrences. As his group entered the field they were frustrated at every turn. The attacks came from nowhere and were carried out quickly with the Indians melting back to the forests before they could arrive to engage them. Joshua was in awe of their tactics and ability to strike and disappear. There were small engagements from time to time but the Indians wanted no parts of head to head battle when they were greatly outnumbered. They also knew little of European battle tactics and fought gorilla style which dumbfounded the command of the English. Respite from hostilities would only come when the weather turned for the New England winter. The attacks became less frequent and eventually stopped to wait out the cold months. The Indians moved into a camp at the foot of Mount Wachusett closer to Boston which they saw as the ultimate goal to drive the English from the continent. It was not misdirected thinking. The Indians usually camped at Turner Falls and left some remnant there when they moved. From their new location they were within easy distance of many small towns and villages in the east that could tighten the perimeter around Boston itself. They were strangling Boston's interior supplies from its settlements and disrupting the livelihoods and crops of those in its borders. Both sides suffered in this manner. Algonquins grew much of their own food. The need to stay mobile and not stay too long in one place all but eliminated their ability to grow crops and supply their needs. They would need to hunt and forage for food. Now they would also battle hunger and disease created from malnourishment and dehydration. They did control the entire center of Massachusetts as winter set in. Joshua returned home for the winter months. He needed to involve himself in the business and address his responsibilities that the war had forced him to abandon during this time if inactivity. Mostly he needed to be home to help Mary with the boys and her pregnancy. Upon his return he was shocked to see Mary in full pregnancy with a largely protruding belly. He did not think to ask how far along she was but now knew she was several months pregnant before telling him of it. She could deliver at any time from what he could see. He asked her about it. Mary said "I did not want to add anything to your burden with work and the Indian issues. I was handling it well and when the time came you would have known through nature's own accounting to my body and we would discuss it then. I wanted you to know though before you left."

Joshua replied "I would want to share all that we have together even these things. We are the same now. We are of one mind, one body and one spirit and in that we will share the good and the bad together if that is acceptable to you!"

Mary replied "It is more than I could have hoped for!" Over the next several days Joshua busied himself with the boys and visited the docks to see what critical work he needed to address before he was called back to his military duties. There was much to do. Sam was elated to see him. They spent hours going over new plans for amendments to construction on ships they were building. Joshua had a natural mind for it and could picture the structures and their improvements to performance, speed or safety. The boys played merrily in Joshua's quarters on the docks while the two men recounted his time away, his work and future. They returned home at dinner time. As they entered their home the food was boiling over on the fire. Joshua rushed to the pot and removed it from the fireplace with the iron. He placed it in its holder and called out for Mary. She did not answer. He searched the house with the boys calling out to her. He went to the back of the house to the barn and found Mary lying unconscious on the hay. Her dress was heavily stained in blood near her abdomen. He knew that she was in danger. He had no one to send for help so he loaded her and the boys on the wagon and set off for town and help. They traveled at a high rate of speed into town and there were several near mishaps. Joshua knew time was not his friend however and kept whipping the team to keep their speed up. The boys were hanging on but greatly enjoying themselves with the bouncing and speed involved. Joshua came into town yelling for help as he pulled up to the doctor's office. The doctor resided in the upstairs of his office and wearily answered his calls. Once he saw Mary he knew it would be a long and possibly sad night. He sent Joshua to retrieve his nurse and the mid-wife who would assist him. Joshua left on the run and with panic in his heart. He could not imagine his life without Mary in it now. The mortality rate of women giving birth was not good in this world and even worse in the colonies. In the early morning hours Mary gave birth to Elizabeth

Henshaw. She would be the third child and only daughter to date. The doctor was not smiling however. The situation was dire. He called Joshua out of the room and said "The baby is in great distress. Her lungs had a hard time acquiring her first breath and her breathing is shallow. Her heartbeat is not strong. She might not make it long unless we see some changes and God works his magic. I am telling you this to prepare you for the worst. I do not believe that baby will survive long and if she does there will be many handicaps that she will have to overcome. I will pray for her and your wife and family. For now, Mary is stable but greatly weakened and exhausted. I have given her something to make her sleep and rest. It is best for her. We will watch the baby's progress and keep you apprised. You will need to get your rest also. It will be a long ordeal over the next few days. Joshua took some pillows and lay on the floor by Mary's bedside. The Sumners had fetched the boys and took them to their home to care for them while the issue was in doubt. Joshua greatly appreciated their help and Mary would also when she was aware. Joshua awoke to a pair of eyes watching him. The baby was awake but her breathing was fitful and labored. He got up and went to her and held her until morning light. She bonded with him and their eyes met. The spark of life was simply a flicker. She touched his face with her small hands and cooed her love to him. He felt the love of a father and he responded to her touch by touching her face and gently rubbing her back. She liked this and was content. Her face would contort from time to time as pain racked her small body but she was a Henshaw and would accept what was dealt to her and throw it right back at the world. She would not be defeated. As morning broke Mary awoke for a short time. Joshua updated her on the baby and the boys. It put her at peace for now. The pain came and the doctor dosed her with medication for it and once again sent her to unconsciousness. Joshua continued his time with his daughter. He knew she could not speak yet somehow they communicated.

It was the bond of a father and daughter. Through her eyes she let him know that her time was coming soon to rejoin their God in heaven. She would spend a few more hours here on Earth with him though and this would be her lifetime as short as it may be. Joshua would waste none of it. He would not sleep or eat until his daughter was at peace. The day went on. Mary stirred occasionally and the Sumners visited as did Walter, Sam and Daniel's Mary. They could not pull him away from his trancelike attention to his daughter however and drifted in and out of their consciousness. Joshua introduced Elizabeth to each of them and her to them. It would be her only chance to meet these important people in their lives. Miraculously she lived through yet another night. She did not want to let go of Joshua but both knew it had to happen. As morning light broke the horizon and the sunbeams spread their path across the floor Elizabeth lost her light. She parted this Earth and Joshua thought that she simply followed the sunbeams to heaven as they were God's invitation to join him in a better place for eternity. He kissed her and let her go on in peace. He would miss her greatly but had reconciled her life, death and eternal place in heaven to himself. He knew she was a special child and had bonded with him in a way she had with no other. He would see her when the time came and live with her in their faith and memory until that time. He was at peace. With the passing of Elizabeth he finally found his sleep at the foot of Mary's bed. It was hard to draw the line where consciousness ended and sleep began. The lines were blurred. Joshua felt her presence in his thoughts. In this state she could finally communicate to him. She told him that she was at peace and not to worry. She showed him those that she would now dwell with in this afterlife. Joshua was startled to be face to face with his mother and father. Behind them stood others and he could not recognize except his grandmother Haughton. William and Katherine spread open their arms and Elizabeth went to them. Joshua could no longer feel her weight in his own arms even though he knew that he held her when he fell off to sleep. For a moment he felt envious that Elizabeth would be with all of those lost to him in his world. A bright light cast a soft glow behind them. The light emitted a feeling of warmth and a feeling of deep love. Joshua knew the feeling but it had been taken from him all those years ago but here he was now experiencing it. He did not wish to wake. He knew that he would lose his connection to Elizabeth when this happened and he was not ready to let her go. He looked into his father's eyes and saw a look of sadness. He pointed off into the horizon to the east and said simply "Go!" With that their bodies and faces began to fade into the light and soon they were gone. Joshua searched and did not want it to end but to stay would mean to die and a sudden realization hit him. He was not allowed to stay with them-at least not yet. He had things to accomplish in his life that he had not completed. It was clear to him that he was being sent back into the real world to accomplish his destiny he just did not know what that looked like yet. He strongly suspected that he did know what he must do but did not want to confront it. He had enough to confront right now to face Elizabeth's death and to see Mary and his family through it. He also knew deep down what his destiny was about. He could fight it no longer. He knew without doubt that he was returning to England. He simply had to plan. The details of it to be fair to his family, wife, brother and himself had yet to develop. He was in no hurry. He knew when he was called again to wake that he would lose all of this and he would see her no more. The time with his parents and ancestors too would be lost. But wake he did. He checked on Mary and she was still in her drug induced sleep. She would soon have to reduce this medication and move on in her life as she healed. The physical healing would be only one part of the process. It was the mental healing that Joshua could not fathom. He hoped he could impart his time with Elizabeth, his dream and his surety that she was in a better place surrounded by those we all loved and trusted. He would do his best. Over the next minutes the room became clear as his mental fog lifted. He made out faces of those who loved Elizabeth in real life and those that they could call true friends. The doctor took Elizabeth from his arms and said "Joshua, she is gone!" Joshua simply replied "I know! Is Mary aware?" The doctor said "No, not yet." As Joshua arose from his sleep his friends came in close to touch him and offer their condolences and help in getting through these troubling times. Mary came awake with a start. She looked to Joshua and he shook his head to acknowledge what she already seemed to know. Tears began to flow. They came slowly at first but a torrent in a few moments. It was good. She needed to grieve and this was the beginning of healing. Later on when they were alone he would relate his experiences of the night. He would not bring up the exchange with his father or his decision about the future. It was best to work towards that in his way. Of course, he would have to bring it to Mary, Daniel and those important to him when the time neared. For now, he was needed here. Mary and the boys would need him. Spring would soon begin and it was a dichotomy to Joshua. All of the sadness and triumph that he had just experienced with the ascension of his daughter to those who had gone before her compared to the renewal of spring flowers and the songs of the birds. This upcoming promise of spring was dampened with the sure knowledge that the Indians would soon launch hostilities that had lay dormant over the cold months. The Colonists could claim no such respite. The Narragansett tribe was a powerful tribe that lived in peace with Roger Williams in Rhode Island. The colonists had no reason to believe that this would change except for their paranoia and desires to rid the territories of the Indians once and for all. Over the winter this paranoia only grew and by December the colonists could contain themselves no more. They knew where the Narragansett's made their winter camp. They mustered their men and moved on them in what would come to be known as "The Great Swamp Massacre" An Indian informer was at the forefront of this action. He betrayed his own people to the colonists with the location of their camp. General Winslow was dispatched with Benjamin Church. Church had a reputation as an "Indian fighter". Winslow and Church commanded one thousand men from Massachusetts, Plymouth and Connecticut colonies. The thousand-strong force marched to the south of Rhode Island and entered the Narragansett territory violating their boundaries. The Indians had made a safe camp. It was located in a swamp making the approach perilous and even more so in the dead of New England winter. They had further surrounded it by a palisade to add to its security and increase the difficulty of a frontal approach. The soldiers arrived unnoticed by the Indians which in itself was a fete. It is likely that the severity of the weather at the time was the cause of this stealth. The Indians were huddled up for warmth and simply trying to survive a New England blizzard. It was this blizzard that was used to the attackers advantage. With heavy snow fall and whistling winds the force made its approach. There were no sentries that could be seen. There was water separating the soldiers from their intended target and a plan had to be hatched to overcome this barricade. They simply dropped a large tree that fell across the water to the other side creating a sort of bridge and continued their crossing of the water hazard and on to their attack. The noise had now alerted the Indians who ran to their defensive positions. The breach of the palisade was very near and they had lost most of their defensive advantage by the depth of the breach before they could respond. Many soldiers fell during the initial defense of the camp but after several attacks the walls were stormed. Benjamin Church found the body of Captain Gardner on his approach. They had been good friends so he took time to inspect the body for signs of life. He found none. He described what he saw in his own words that he wrote down for posterity.

"...blood ran down his cheek, (and I) lifted up his cap, and called him by name. He looked up in (my) face, but spoke not a word, being *mortally shot through the head. And, observing his wound, found the ball entered his head on the side that was next the upland where the English entered the swamp. Upon which, having ordered some care to be taken of the Captain, (I) dispatched information to the General that the best and forwardest of his army that hazarded their lives to enter the fort, upon the muzzle of the enemy's guns, were shot in their backs and killed by them that lay behind."*

Some of the advance waves of the attack had been killed by musket fired by their own soldiers and friends from behind. This would make the assault much more deadly. The soldiers pressed the battle. They systematically penetrated the camp entering and executing those in each teepee or shelter. They would set the teepees afire and burn them to the ground. Any survivors would perish in the flames. The death tolls were staggering. As the battle ended the surviving Narragansett warriors retreated into the forests and entered the war in support of King Philip. Their winter camp lay in smoldering ruins. Among the ruins were the bodies of over five hundred Narragansett Indians. Most of the dead were women and children. Any found alive were taken captive or killed depending on their health or severity of their wounds. Those taken would be sold into slavery mostly in the West Indies. The surviving Narragansett's were to be fierce in their attacks. They events in the swamp incited an irrepressible anger and rage from the loss of their loved one's in this unprovoked attack on their peaceful camp. It was clear for all to see that the Indian Nation could not put any credibility in agreements made by the colonials or their leaders. They have deadly results. These dealings amongst the Indians were considered an act of honor by those in charge of the colonies. Their word was binding and the Indians would keep their agreements. These new inhabitants could not be trusted and the politics of the new world were being learned by the Indians with deadly results. One thing for sure was that this action had made a bitter enemy where none had existed before. There would be no quarter or shelter to those under their retaliatory assaults in the future. The Bible called it "an eye for an eye" but the Natives saw it as survival and fighting their enemies on the same footing as the enemy fought them. These drastic atrocities were begun at the hands of the colonists through the Pequot Wars and now King Philip's War. Newly reinforced and anger burning in their eyes the allied tribes resumed their attacks. As King Philip spread out from his makeshift winter camp worry followed. He was very close to Boston and the attacks came fast and furious and with a new level of violence that mirrored the attack in the swamp. Medfield, Groton, Sudbury, Plymouth, Rehoboth, Providence and Marlboro were attacked and burned. Joshua was called back into service and had to leave immediately to keep the Indians from mounting an attack on Boston and Dorchester. He was torn because he knew Mary and the boys needed him to help with the healing process on the loss of their daughter and sister. On the other hand if the Indians could reach the area there could be more loss of life in the family. He could do something about the latter situation. The other one was in God's hands and he would let his faith govern his thoughts on that. He hoped that Mary could reach down deep into her faith to find her way through this terrible loss. He knew she was strong and would impart her strength and healing into their boys. For now they would stay with Mary's parents so they were not isolated outside of town and for their emotional support. Joshua had not witnessed the atrocities of "The Great Swamp". He was appalled to hear others brag of the depraved deeds that they claimed at their own hands however. Some of his closest acquaintances seemed to be involved on some primal level. Joshua vowed that he would not be a part of these things even in the heat of battle and under orders. For the most part the militia found themselves chasing ghosts. The Indians could strike like lightning and finish their grizzly business then fade back into the forest before a military response could be mounted. The leaders and troops were frustrated and wanted to engage in battle. At night Joshua kept to himself and his own thoughts. He sincerely hoped that he would not see Paul or his warriors lined up on the other side of the dispute. In his mind he knew that they would avoid entering the conflict on either side if possible. In this Joshua could take solace. They were camped near Lancaster on this night. Little did they know that King Philip and his warriors were camped very near to their picket fires. As the campfires were burning out and breakfast was cooking the next morning word came to them that Philip's forces had been seen in the area. With nothing more to go on the troop finished the meal and broke camp. Scouts were sent out to find Philip but there was little to do until a contact was made. There was a garrison at Lancaster. It in itself was little more than a fortified house. The house stood at the foot of a hill and gave the Indian attackers full advantage of the higher ground behind it. The settlers fled to the garrison and quartered themselves inside. The house was the home of Mary Rowlandson, her husband and family. In addition to being their home it did double duty as the garrison. The Indians knew the layout through reconnoitering the area prior to their attack. Mrs. Rowlandson wrote down her account of the attack

> *"At length they came and beset our own house (which served as the garrison) and quickly it was the dolefullest day that ever mine eyes saw. The house stood upon the edge of a hill. Some of the Indians got behind the hill, others into the barn, and others behind anything that would shelter them, from all which places they shot against the house, so that the bullets seemed to fly like hail. Some in our house were fighting for their lives, others wallowing in their blood, the house on fire over our heads, and the bloody heathen ready to knock us on the head if we stirred out. Now might we hear mothers and children crying out for themselves and one another, 'Lord what shall we do?'"*

In the end many lie dead. Rowlandson herself was taken captive. During her captivity she was moved from place to place during the final six weeks of the cold weather of that year. The conditions of her captivity brought her near death but she persevered. Her captivity and the captivity of others caused a problem now for King Philip. They were not provisioned for war even at the beginning. Losing the ability to plant and harvest their crops further depleted their food supplies. The levels were critical. They found that their supply of muskets and powder was just as bad. They had their traditional weapons but they were no match for the muskets that would be brought against them. With the war continuing they had no resource to replenish their ranks. Those killed or injured were counted as one less to take to battle. The colonists however had a continuous supply of reinforcements and more settlers arrived regularly and would be brought into the fight as needed. They were well supplied with provisions, powder and muskets through the arriving ships. It would be a war of attrition if things did not change. The decision was made to ransom the captives. This would provide money and food that was much needed and it would remove extra mouths to feed from the fires. It also signaled the colonists of the strategy to use against them knowing the condition of their people and supplies. Rowlandson was soon returned to her home. That is to say what was left of the burned out structure. The release or escape of these captives had other benefits to the colonists. It was a young boy who would provide the information leading to the next Indian massacre. He had been held at an Indian camp on the northern part of the Connecticut River. From there he had escaped. As he returned to the colonial ranks he was able to direct the militia to the exact location of the camp where he had been held.

Captain Turner and Captain Holyoke mustered their troops for an immediate engagement. They moved in on the site of the camp in the darkness of the night. At dawn they launched their surprise attack. The Indians were taken completely by surprise and could not mount a defense in time to counter the charge. Most of the casualties lay at the opening to their wigwams where they identified the threat and tried to escape. Those that did escape the initial attack tried to swim the Connecticut River but this was spring and the waters were swift and turbulent. They escaped the range of the muskets only to be drowned and swept over the falls near the camp. Other warriors from nearby groups gathered and mounted a counter attack. Captain Turner was killed but the main body of the attackers made their way back to the safety of the garrison at Hadley. The attack had achieved its goals by this time and the war camp of the Wampanoags and Nipmunks ceased to exist. The Indian alliance could not be sustained and the remaining Indians were in disarray. Most fled north but some continued to fight although the outcome was predictable at this point. Joshua was appalled at the level of violence and primal instinct unleashed by those people he thought to be civilized. They were washed up in a wave of mob violence that escalated with each death. They slew women, children, old people and warriors with the same gusto for each. Joshua did not understand the logic of vanquishing a foe that was no threat to them such as the elderly, women and children. Many of the Indians had been friendly once and would return to this eventually. There had been many deaths on both sides and the homes of both settlers and Indians had been destroyed. In addition to the death in battle many died from exposure, disease and malnutrition because of the collateral damages to the others homes, crops and supply chains. Could no one see that there could be no winners in a conflict such as this? Joshua again turned to his God for understanding but none came.

Philip made his escape with a handful of warriors. He made his way to the tribal seat near Swansea at Mount Hope where the hostilities had begun months ago. Benjamin Church was in pursuit. With his complement of friendly Indians he scouted

King Philip for the next months. Philip and his band raided isolated farms as a survival measure to secure food and supplies for his people. It was inevitable that he would be found. Philip had made overtures to the Mohawks to join their cause. He was rebuffed and his power began to fade. In August of 1676 Church came upon the band and captured Philip's wife and son. They were immediately sent off to slavery in the West Indies and never heard of again. Philip was found near his seat at the same time. An Indian riding with Church silenced him and ended the conflict with a single shot. He was shot straight through his heart. It was a shot that in essence stopped the heart of the Indian nations. Joshua was present and had a flood of emotions. He knew this would end the conflict so that was a good thing. He could not help but feel sadness though for Philip and his family and all of the other Indians that had been slaughtered during this unnecessary conflict. It was a total annihilation of the culture and it would never recover. Of course, there was the sadness for those lost on the other side of the battle. They too had suffered greatly and the loss of life was huge. Over 600 militia lay dead and some 50 settlements and been totally destroyed, burned or damaged. Recovery would be made but it would take months and even years in some cases. The monetary losses to the struggling settlements were overwhelming. Yet the horrors were not finished. Church ordered the head of Philip to be cut off and placed on a spike for viewing. The remainder of his body was quartered and the pieces hung in the trees. Several others had their bodies desecrated in similar manner. Joshua was shocked at the need for vengeance and the grizzly and inhumane manner of it even after the issue was settled. Philip's head would be sold and it would be displayed for many decades in public places. Joshua felt this sadness most. His respect for those he fought with and lived with would never recover. He had seen the ugly side of humanity and intolerance of other cultures, ways of life and religions. It was yet another dark part of life that he had to reconcile with his experiences, beliefs and faith. He turned away and started his journey back home alone. He did not want to be around those that would act in such a manner. His solace would provide him time to reconcile his own part in these hostilities and to try to find forgiveness for both sides of the quarrel and those that acted out of their own faith in their atrocities and celebration of this bloody business. It was sure that he would have a different outlook on many things after this experience. Like many things we experience in life it molds and changes outlooks and the person that emerges from it has changed, weathered, and forever diminished in spirit from these experiences. Like all the other things in his life though he would log it as another experience and learn from it as much as he could. Joshua took his time making his way home. He had to come to terms with what he had seen and what he had done. He had not participated in the atrocities but he had played a part in them nonetheless. He could not submerge deep enough into his faith to come to terms with this breach of humanity. His relationships with the men in his unit and the community as a whole had to be rethought. In fact in his life to date he had seen nothing but the dark side of life save the few years that he lived with his mother and grandmother after the death of his father and grandfather. He had seen greed, murder, fraud, theft and a complete abandonment of the basic premise of a Christian life. He could only do what he could with what was under his control to set the wrongs right. He longed to be back in their ancestral home where he could at least somewhat control the things within his power. He thought of Paul and his small band and hoped for their survival. The current atmosphere in the colonies was not conducive to peaceful existence with any of the Indians including the friendly ones like Paul. This was driven home by the massacre in the swamp and in general the history of the colonies going back to the Pequot War where the behavior was the same. It was clear that those in command wished to see the Native Americans completely eliminated from their world either voluntarily or by death. With the exchange of attacks many would prefer the death of all of those who they had and were warring with now. There were few people who were not touched by the death of an acquaintance, family member or friend in the conflict. Many had lost their homes, crops and personal property greatly complicating their lives and ability to adapt and survive in an already hostile environment even without the Indian issues. He wandered for a week trying to reconcile his thoughts before returning to Mary and his boys. He had another surprise upon his return.

Mary was overjoyed to see him. She had no news of his whereabouts or if he had survived the hostilities. Communication was not good in the colonies and it was further hindered during the chaos of war where so many settlements and homes were burned and their occupants massacred. Paul had visited her secretly in the night to confirm her well-being and to tell her what to do if their area came under attack. He was concerned for her and the boys during this time. He had slipped back into the forest before he could be discovered but had told Mary he would be near and watching. He would come to her defense if the need arose. Thankfully it did not. The night before Joshua left to rejoin the militia Mary had instigated a passionate night. Partly because she did not know what the outcome would be for Joshua and the real threat that he would not survive. Another part of her actions were because she needed to overcome her own emotions from the loss of her baby. Joshua was a very willing participant and likely for the same reasons. While he was away Mary had begun to show the familiar signs of pregnancy and after a few months her suspicions came to fruition. Her belly grew and she knew another baby was growing insider her. She was scared and did not know if this baby would be healthy or die. She wondered if there was something wrong with her that would not allow her to give birth to a daughter since her two sons had come through the birth ordeal healthy. She knew there was as much a chance of having a boy as a girl but as a mother generally knows she was sure that this was a girl coming to them. Joshua did not have to talk with Mary to know she was with child. He had been away many months and her appearance told that story. She rushed to him and held him and the tears came. They were tears of happiness on his return at first and then they were tears of fear for the pregnancy and her misgivings. Later that night she would voice these to Joshua but now she just wanted to hold on to him so he could not leave her again. The boys would wake in the morning and take up his time so the night was their time that she could have him alone.

As the arrival of the baby neared her fear escalated. The boys would pick up on the tensions and become upset. They would ask their father about it and want assurances the new brother or sister would be well. Joshua could only steer them down the path of faith even though it was a hard concept for children this young to grasp. He battled his own doubts of his own faith during this time after the war. This was not the Puritan faith but the faith that came from life's experiences and the teachings of his father and mother and the church he had come to trust. He no longer attended the services brought on by the Reverend Mather and sought out a more spiritual level to address his God. He generally did this at home or when he was alone. His faith, lacking a church home, came on a one to one relationship in prayer and worship with God. He too had fears for the new baby. He knew that he had to be the rock that all could lean on but it was difficult with his own doubts. He had trouble sleeping and was exhausted. He returned home from the docks one afternoon to an empty house. Mary had left word that she was going to spend some time at her parent's house and more so as the delivery would come closer. The Sumners were closer to the doctor and midwife and the response times when needed would be much shorter from there. She wished to take all precautions and up the probability that this baby would be healthy and survive. Joshua fell into a fitful sleep that night from his exhaustion.

He heard a small voice. He felt a rush of warmth and love. A bright light came to him and he saw on a small chair the image of Elizabeth. She said to him "I am excited that a new baby will be there soon. You should not worry. She will be healthy. I know this. There will be many reasons to be thankful with this child. She will be the first daughter for Mary and I will be her guardian. Turn to your faith and all will be well. I must go now. Those I am with are calling me back." Joshua did not want her to go but he felt inside that Elizabeth had no choice in the matter nor did he have a choice. He awoke and felt rested and a sense of comfort. His fear of the outcome had ceased and he felt the happiness that comes with a new baby for the first time. He prayed on his knees for a while but knew all would be right on this matter. He still had his issues with humanity and the evils that frothed from its turbulent waters. This one issue though was resolved in his mind and he would be stronger for Mary and his boys for it.

The pregnancy progressed with little complication. Mary watched each minute detail and even the smallest of deviations or pains would send her spiraling into panic. Sam knew that Joshua needed to be home as much as possible at this time and sensed that he had other issues that bore heavily on his conscience from his experiences in the Indian War. In time they would discuss these but Sam knew he was not ready yet. The best he could do was to support him and Mary in the birth of this child and he would do this by allowing Joshua liberal time with his family.

Mary's time was nearing and the family drew close and tightened their circle around her. It was a tense time but knowing the support and love that surrounded them helped immensely. Mary for her part understood Joshua well. She knew he fretted about his work and she urged him constantly to go to the docks. He was distracted but knew this might be the best for them all. It would relieve his stress some and ease the tensions surrounding the pregnancy itself. He started slowly and spent some time there and after a while he was putting in full shifts with the promise that word would be sent immediately to him if there were any issues to be dealt with.

It was a Saturday. Joshua had gone off to work but he had mixed feelings of leaving that day. Something was nagging at him and he could not get a handle on it. He arrived on the docks and threw himself into his duties. Before long there was a commotion and Daniel appeared. With a nod from him Joshua knew he was needed at home. They jumped two fast horses and rode quickly on the path to the Sumner's house where Mary and the boys were staying. The horses fell into a rhythm on the ride and this was almost hypnotizing. Joshua's mind opened up and he was in deep thought with the beat of each hoof landing on the hard ground. Suddenly she was there in his mind. Elizabeth was smiling. She raised her hands to the heavens and then cradled them like a mother holding a baby. In fact, she was holding a baby girl in her arms on second look. She was happy and the baby was cooing and kicking. Elizabeth looked up to him and said "it is my time to be thankful. It is my time to play with my new sister before I send her to you! Be happy she will be healthy and a joy to you!" With that her vision disappeared. Daniel was calling to him and finally he snapped his attention to his brother.

Daniel said "Are you all right? I have been talking to you but you have been somewhere else!"

Joshua replied "I am fine brother! All is fine and I am to be the father of a healthy girl!"

Daniel looked at him funny but decided not to pursue it. It was not uncommon for fathers to be a bit touched in the head around this time. He knew whatever Joshua had found had changed him and calmed his demeanor. He was thankful that he had found this peace and in a way it had given him some of his own under these conditions. He felt too that all would be fine in the end.

They arrived home in a sweat. The horses were lathered and snorting from their workout. The brothers rushed into the house and were stopped by the doctor upon their approach to the room where Mary lay. He said "At this point all seems to be on schedule and fine. I see no complications."

Joshua said "Doctor, I know we will be fine and I will be the father of a wonderful little girl!"

The doctor said "Well, I cannot tell you if it will be a boy or a girl but all other things are aligning just right by all appearances for now".

Mary screamed. A contraction wracked her body and the doctor said they were coming closer and closer together meaning the baby would arrive soon. The midwife stood watch for now and helped her through her pain. A sense of calm was radiating through Joshua and he entered the room to be with Mary. He took her hand and told her that everything would be fine and soon they would have a daughter. Mary seemed to transform with the touch of his hand. Her panic subsided and calm prevailed. The subsequent contractions caused little pain and came and went smoothly. Those in the room saw this as some kind of miracle but it seemed that Mary understood the confidence in Joshua and now felt it herself. She knew it would be fine. She set to the work of delivering the baby. It was not fast work.

Mary was in labor for a few more hours but it went smoothly. Shortly after midnight the candles in the house flickered in unison and a cry was heard above all of the first breath in this new world. The baby was indeed a girl and they reveled in her beauty and health. They were blessed. Joshua could only think of Elizabeth when he looked into the baby's eyes and there was a sort of wink that came to him as he watched her like she shared their secret. The tension and stress was over and happier times had arrived for the present.

Mary said "With all of the issues I have not thought of a name for her!"

Joshua said "I have had dreams and I have listened to others talk about the ordeal. One word continued to come forth. That word was "thankful" Let her name be Thankful for I am sure that we are all indeed thankful to have a daughter who is healthy and beautiful. We are all thankful that we were able to have another child and our second daughter. I am sure Elizabeth is looking on us now and is happy!"

So the child was named Thankful and would be a special child in all of their lives. Joshua believed that a little part of Elizabeth resided in Thankful and it was a comforting and happy thought to him.

The boys both had found their own peace in Massachusetts for now. Joshua had started his family and for now his business and family was enough. In his mind he had committed with the birth of his children to stay and see them through until they could fend for themselves. To them were born John, Samuel, Elizabeth, Katherine, Daniel and Mindwell. These children came between 1678 and 1693. They all brought their own personalities, likes, dislikes, talents, temperaments and individualism that makes up a family and makes each individual and family unit unique. Both Mary and Joshua were happy during these years. For now, the quest for the family lands and property in England would stay on hold for a while longer. Together with Sam they spent many hours discussing the ships and making improvements. Any subject that had to do with England or the events that shaped it were avoided. Sam feared that bringing any history of the English to light would only rekindle the fire in Joshua to return. He would do all he could to keep him on track in the colonies. Like Daniel he believed that only bad things could come from his return and taking up his mission. The longing to be in his true home were still strong.

Daniel's Progress

Daniel was his own man during these years. The girls grew

and grew. They had not thought of furthering their family but in the back of his mind he wished to have a son. With the coat of arms he needed an heir to pass it on to when he could no longer bear it himself. It was with surprise that Mary came to him in 1677 to announce her pregnancy. Daniel at first could not grasp it and thought it to be unreal. It took some convincing but eventually it sunk in that he too would be a father. The matter of a son or daughter was still in doubt but his elation would accept either equally. He rushed off to tell Walter and Joshua about his good fortune and that they would be an uncle and surrogate grandfather once again. Daniel was very happy. He had contemplated the birth of a blood relative for many years. The girls were his children and it never occurred to him that they were less than his daughters. They were thrilled with the prospect of a new baby in the household. Mary was thrilled but guarded. She knew having a baby at her age was perilous for her and the baby. She would be in her early 40s at this time. She would not put a lid on the unbridled happiness and took the teasing about her age in stride. She silently prayed that all would be fine in the outcome of her pregnancy and that a healthy and happy baby would be the result. She did not share her concerns with Daniel and bore them solely within herself. It was still fresh in her mind of the death of Joshua and Mary's baby. Of course, there was the doctor, friends and others that could see the difficulties of this pregnancy and she asked them all to keep these confidential in their nature and not discuss them in public or outside of their own communications. They all agreed and understood. They would stand by her side and help with what they could. There was an official announcement of course. Daniel gathered all of his men friends at the pub and put out the news to them. They all celebrated his good fortune and there was drinking and lively discussion of the baby for this period. There were other gatherings that mirrored this one but with much less drinking and boisterousness. It was a happy time for all except

Mary who was worried. She toiled and her belly grew over the next months and as her time neared she met with the doctor. He was anxious about the babies positioning in the birth canal and discussed it with Mary.

She knew of such things and labor and delivery would certainly be a hard time under these circumstances. The baby however remained strong and healthy. She had reconciled herself to a difficult and painful delivery and knew if anything was to go awry it would be at that moment. She prayed more fervently in silence.

The days passed quickly except for Mary. They were at a crawl for her. Her weight and immobility made every small task more difficult. Her nerves weighed on her and every kick of the baby sent her into a panic until she was sure it was just a normal process of pregnancy. Daniel was unaware of her worry but was there for her every minute he could be there. She was pleased that there seemed to be no complications. The girls pitched in to make things easier for her.

The big day finally arrived. Daniel came home after taking break from his work. He knew that it was time as he climbed the stairs to the front porch. The house was a beehive of activity and the girls were in the sitting room in a state of excitement. They, more than anyone, seemed to revel in the idea of having a new baby to play with and help grow. They ran to Daniel as he entered the house and brought him up to date. The doctor had arrived with his nurse and the midwife had been there when her water broke. The doctor saw Daniel and motioned him into the hallway outside of Mary's room. He said "Things are going well with one complication. The baby is breach meaning that it is positioned to come out rear first which could cause some complications. We will attempt to turn it before it delivers. We do this quite often so I do not contemplate any issues

with this!" Daniel was worried but decided to trust his faith and the doctor's skill in the matter. There wasn't anything he could do about it anyway. He went to the room and greeted Mary and kissed her hand. She smiled at him until another contraction started. Daniel left to join the girls as the space in the room was limited and with the three attending her he was in the way. The doctor said that he would update him if anything transpired. He waited with the girls and they heard a frightful amount of screams and painful wails. After what seemed like an eternity the cry of a babe split the air. It was a strong cry and announced the birth of the new baby. The girls were first to run to the room with Daniel close behind. The baby was now swaddled in blankets but was crying and protesting being rudely introduced to the new world in such a way. In the blankets Daniel could not tell if he had a daughter or a son but the doctor saw the confusion and said "May I present your new son and brother to you all!" and held him so all could see. The girls squealed with glee and Daniel stared in awe. Mary looked worn out but was wearing a big smile. All of her worries were over and both mother and baby were fine. It was the son that Daniel had prayed for to carry on his Coat of Arms and he could not have been happier. Soon the word spread and well-wishers and friends began to arrive. It was not an official introduction party but it was very close. Daniel looked up to see Joshua and his Mary standing in the doorway and they both embraced like brothers should in these times of good fortune. The crowd was led out of the room and the baby was fed and put in his bed for the night. Mary also needed her rest but it was a happy night with wonderful dreams to be had by all.

Time went forward and Joshua's family grew. More and more England and its King interfered with life in the colonies. Constant warring with the French and others kept life on uncertain terms for the colonists. England required much from them in their efforts. They demanded supplies, men for battle, ever increasing taxes and trade restrictions from even the poorest of the area. They pushed on the people and those that were not wealthy held on by a string. With the Massachusetts Bay Colony abolished paranoia had set in and pushed by the Puritan Clergy and the Puritan way of life they manifested great fear among the citizenry. It was the churches only way of maintaining control with their legal authority gone and their history of persecuting anyone that did not believe in the way they had set forth. Other beliefs were not tolerated and punished severely including death sentences. Fear and doubt kept them in line. Their days of church control were waning and those who had enjoyed the fruits of this control were not yet willing to give it up. Going forward this would manifest into a very dark time and it wasn't too far into the future.

After the grotesque behavior of his friends and neighbors in the battlefield Joshua was in full debate in his private times of the things he had seen and done. This carried over into the fault logic. Each man had made his choices and some had simply acted under orders but with a mob mentality to do things that they would not consider doing away from battle. Joshua was ashamed of his own actions and blamed himself and each individual who had raised a hand against the helpless. But deep down he knew that the British officers were trained in just this type of controlling behavior and in their way conditioned these unquestioning responses to orders and grisly behaviors. They knew how to work their troops into a fury and to mobilize them to hate, kill, massacre and torture without reprieve to the vanquished. His father and grandfather had fallen in a battle that meant nothing other than the King wished vengeance on a citizenry that had not opposed him or taken arms to fight him. Yet he attacked and counterattacked until they were defeated and dead or maimed beyond help. Over time it became clear to him who was at fault to lesser and greater degrees but the main subject of blame rested on the Kings shoulders once again. Joshua hated the royals and the ones that laid siege to his own family until they had taken everything from them. It was during this realization that he knew he could wait no longer. He must return to England and do his very best to recover what rightly belonged to him and his brother and give justice to his ancestors. He had arrangements to make but he would leave very soon. It was the fall of 1687 and he wished to depart when the weather turned in the spring of 1688.

That night he decided that he could not put off talking to Elizabeth. When the children were in bed he would address the issue with her and his decision. Until then he could now relax some having the decision made and his mind at peace with it.

They had a good dinner. He had brought out steaks and other good things to be prepared for dinner. He joined the family in the preparations and they sat down to what would usually be reserved for a holiday meal. The children enjoyed it greatly but even they knew something momentous was about to happen. Joshua did not discuss it with the children that night. He wanted to get it out in the open and have a discussion with Elizabeth so they could together broach the final decision with the children.

As the children finished their lessons and retired to sleep Elizabeth approached him before he could begin. She started the conversation "So it is! It is decided I take it? I know you too well. When this originally came to my attention you told me that you would try your best to put the past aside but I knew that this was not a matter of if but of when you could wait no longer"

Joshua face flushed. He was embarrassed. If she could read his thoughts this easily he guessed that at least the older children had too. He asked "Are you angry with me?"

She said "I love you and will support your decision. It won't be easy but we made our deal many years ago and I will not go back on my word."

Joshua felt a feeling of guilt but he had considered that in his thought processes in coming to this conclusion. He said "I love you too! I wouldn't blame you for being angry! I have thought and thought on the matter but I just cannot get beyond this. If I am successful it will be a good thing for our family, our future and you!"

She said "I know your intentions are good for us. I am worried about your safety and the damage it will do to your mind if you are not successful."

Joshua thought a moment and said "Let us hope then that I will be successful. In my mind though I must try, win or lose, or I cannot be at peace any longer! I will prepare papers so that you and the children are taken care of and will live well in my absence. I will try to be home as much as possible but some absences will be long. I am not sure of what I will encounter but I surmise that they will not capitulate without a fight! The Stanley family is influential in England. Ambrose is despicable and a wild card as to how far he will go to maintain his life and my property in his control. I will be careful and enlist allies as I find them. The older children under your direction can help with the businesses and household. You almost run the businesses now anyway. You are much more intelligent than me in those aspects of our life."

"So then it is settled. We will speak with Daniel and make arrangements for his help. That is if you haven't swayed him to join you" Elizabeth chimed in! They both laughed.

Joshua said "Last I talked to him about this matter he had said that he wished to join me but I know he will stay behind on this effort. He is settled in this land and was very young when we came here. He was born after my father's death and doesn't remember the time and deeds of the time as well as I do! He does not share those deep feeling for betrayal that I feel because he was so young. It was hammered into me as to my duties to the family as the first son and arms bearer. Daniel also must think that under English law only the eldest inherits property and he would have nothing to gain but I swore that would not be the case and I will stand by that if I can reacquire our lands. I would hope you all would join me in England and make that our home if it is possible."

Elizabeth replied "We will see! There is much to do before

that time comes and many questions as to the outcome of your efforts yet to be decided!"

After a long quiet pause they both fell into a fitful sleep.

The spring of 1688 would begin Joshua's quest to its original starting point and Joshua would mount the best offense that he could to make the wrongs there right. Daniel declined the offer to join him but gave his support. Joshua pledged once again that if their lands were restored that he would share in them equally if he wished that. Through the winter of 1687 and 1688 many things were accomplished. Papers were gathered, travel arrangements made, financial arrangements and duties to the family and its business laid out with Elizabeth in charge with the counsel of Daniel and the emotional stress of the situation. He would at long last make his return!

ABOUT BOOK ONE

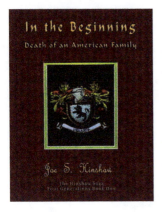

Book one is a chronical of the Hinshaw/Henshaw family and includes genealogic information and the early stories of the family. The family were rich land owners and prominent in the Liverpool area. Sir Thomas was knighted and held the family arms. Thomas's oldest son William married Katherine Houghton who was the sole heir to the Houghton family lands and legacy. The book includes the many dramas that they suffered at the hands of greedy family members, the King and others. It ends with a total betrayal by the same people.

ABOUT BOOK THREE

Book Three is the story of Joshua Hinshaw's return to England to set his world straight. It turns into an epic battle to right those things that wronged his family and heritage when he and his brother were taken from their homes to the colonies by unscrupulous family members and acknowledged founding fathers of the Massachusetts colony. His struggles are mighty and end with a measure of victory that is ultimately snatched away one more time.

CPSIA information can be obtained
at www.ICGtesting.com
Printed in the USA
BVHW051357150721
612048BV00006B/546